THEY CALL ME MS.

A Vic Carella Mystery

by

Terry Adcock

ISBN: 978-1-7376251-0-0

CHAPTER ONE

The sign on the door of my Georgetown office read: "Vic Carella, Investigator and Finder of Lost Objects." As proprietor of this firm and its sole employee, I had just given myself permission to knock off early for the day after delivering the goods to my client's attorney on a nasty divorce case. It was tricky, but I managed to track down the missing assets the lying little jerk—I mean, my client's husband—had stolen, and now, she and the kids could remain in the family home while her attorney strategized on a settlement. I believe the satisfactory results justified a few celebratory adult beverages, don't you?

I dragged a chair over to the corner to water the hanging ivy geraniums before leaving for the weekend. The springy seat wobbled underfoot as I overextended to raise the water bottle above the rim of the basket.

Preoccupied as I was, I did not hear the door to the outer office open and close, and I nearly fell off the chair when a gruff voice behind me said, "Nice. Very nice."

I turned to find Charlie Chaplin's doppelganger leering at my legs, except this reincarnated version was heavier around the bottom with thinning hair.

"Young lady, come down from there and inform Mr. Carella he has a client waiting," said the last dinosaur roaming the earth. He stood in the middle of the room and took in the office décor with a critical eye.

Well, *excuuuse* me! Why I didn't kick the guy out of my office on the spot is a total mystery, even to me. My instincts told me he was a nuisance, itching to unload his problems on someone and lining me up as the designated recipient.

Lucky me!

"Is *Mister* Carella expecting you?" I asked, wondering whether I had missed a voice message when I checked the machine this morning.

"Does it matter? Tell him Mitch Goldberg is here," he said, like that settled the issue. He brushed his sleeve as if to remove a spot of lint. He wore a natty pin-striped suit, and the handkerchief that spilled from his breast pocket resembled an artful floral arrangement.

"And may I ask the nature of your visit?" I continued with maddening politeness.

"I need his help, dammit! Why else would I be here? I heard Carella has a reputation for discretion, which is good because he's going to need it. Someone stole my yacht, and I want it back!"

"Hold it. Hold it." I held up my hands to stem the torrent of words.

Okay, I understood that owning a yacht was kind of a big deal, not that I would know anything about it. And I imagined losing one was an even bigger deal. Even so, boys and their expensive toys did not impress me.

"Who has time to play with boats anyway? A grown man like you should be out there working the mean streets and making a decent living like everyone else."

He drew himself up to his full but diminutive height and said, "I *do* make a decent living, young lady. How do you think I can afford a yacht? Now, will you kindly find Mr. Carella?"

As I carefully stepped down from the chair, I noted Goldberg didn't miss a second of my impromptu floor show. I approached with my hand outstretched and said, "Vic Carella. So *very* pleased to meet you."

"You—? But . . . you're a woman," he said. Surprise registered on his boorish face.

"Thank you for noticing, Mr. Goldberg. And you're a Neanderthal. Now take a seat."

Goldberg started for the door, hesitated, and then turned back as I punched up the cushions on my old leather wingback.

"Sit," I commanded. After two tours of duty with the military police, one learns to take charge and short-circuit problems pronto. Besides, I was in a rush to get started on a well-deserved, liquid-refreshed weekend. I felt like a school kid held past the bell as I thirsted for my afternoon recess.

I settled in behind my desk and said, "Shall we start again? You mentioned something about a missing yak?"

"Yacht," he corrected me. My needling clearly annoyed him, but I could see he wanted to get something off his chest. I waited him out, and at last, he said, "The night before last, I hosted a party aboard my yacht, but yesterday morning when I went back to tidy up, she was gone."

Goldberg reached inside his coat pocket and handed over a picture of the missing vessel. I gave it the once-over. I didn't know squat about boats, but I had to admit it was an impressive-looking rig. I glanced at my watch, hoping this would not take long. I gave him my standard spiel on services and expenses, thinking he might change his mind and go elsewhere. Goldberg didn't blink for a full ten seconds, and then gave me a brief nod.

Trapped in a web of my own making, what else could I do except smile at my new client?

"It's like this, Ms. Carella—"

"You can drop that 'Ms.' stuff right now. It's just Vic."

"Of course," he said and killed the better part of an hour describing how his friends had arranged a little birthday party for him.

Oh, did I mention they held it onboard his brand-new *yacht?* Goldberg certainly did, only about a hundred times.

From Goldberg's description, it was quite the gala affair, complete with captain and crew hired for the occasion, while Goldberg and twenty of his closest friends enjoyed a carefree night of sailing and drinking without the worry of mundane things such as navigation or tricky docking maneuvers.

Goldberg recounted in great detail how his golfing and sailing pals who were along for the ride enjoyed playing pranks on the other guests. Who knew that a toilet bowl covered in transparent wrap could be so much fun? Apparently, stuff goes everywhere but down.

"How do you know your pals didn't move your boat just for a joke?"

"They may have. It's something they would do, but they all denied it."

I felt sure Goldberg's pals were playing one of their infamous pranks and having a big laugh at his expense right about now. Still, I would follow up on this possibility anyway for my client's peace of mind. I hit him up for a hefty retainer and jotted down some information about his closest associates.

As the saying goes, who needs enemies with friends like his?

Goldberg rose to leave and then sank back down in the deep cushions. Something else was visibly troubling him, so I gave him time to sort it out. All the bluster had deserted him, and he was no longer the force of nature he'd been when he first arrived.

He fumbled around for a minute and then blurted out, "I haven't been totally forthcoming with you, Miss Carella…uh, I mean Vic. There are a couple things I neglected to mention."

Oh, really? This could be illuminating. What could this little man possibly have gotten into? Several obnoxious thoughts paraded through my mind, which I promptly dismissed. I didn't want those images stuck in my head for the rest of the day.

"Don't worry. Whatever we discuss is entirely confidential."

"Good." He licked his lips before continuing. "I've gotten into something way over my head with those guys," he said, indicating the list of names he had given me.

"I'll bet your friends are into some kind of smuggling racket. Am I correct?"

Fast yachts. Fast times. Little men wanting to be bigger men. It would have been obvious to a blind man. You guessed it too, right?

At least he had the grace to look contrite. Now it made sense why he came to me and didn't file a report with his insurance company or the Coast Guard.

Oh, the shame of it all. Mitch Goldberg was a bad boy and afraid of getting caught.

"What kind of contraband are you dealing? If it's drugs, you can walk out that door right now because I won't get involved with any crazy drug dealers."

"No, it's nothing like that. Mostly, we picked up people from one location and dropped them off at another, and occasionally, we delivered a few crates of guns."

Was that all? Was that even illegal anymore? A little human trafficking . . . a little gunrunning. Goldberg made it sound almost trivial.

"Are you out of your tiny mind? How did you let yourself get talked into something like that?"

"In the beginning, it was easy money," he explained. "We cruised down to Florida and back every couple weeks. It was just one big party after another with a little business thrown in on the side. You know how it is."

"Actually, I don't. Your friends have you over a barrel, and now they want more?"

"Oh, it's gone way beyond that." He shook his head. "I just want to get my yacht back and fade away. I've tried, but I can't locate it anywhere." He kept wringing his hands.

Hell, he made me nervous just watching him.

His breathing quickened and sweat beaded on his forehead. "I may have tipped my hand when I confronted them. They said if I went to the police, they would kill me."

"They used those exact words? They made specific threats?"

"No, not specifically, but the message was clear enough. I believed them. That's why I came to you. Well, not you in particular. I mean, I expected to find *Victor Carella*…"

"Mr. Goldberg, may I suggest when you find yourself in a hole, it's best to quit digging. So tell me, do you want me to find your yacht or not?"

"You're damn right I do. My yacht's disappeared, and I want it back."

"Why not hire some muscle? There are plenty of repo men about."

"It may come to that, but for now, I want a low-key approach." He inched forward to the edge of his seat. "Forget your standard rates. Just locate my boat, and I'll double your usual fee. And if you make it happen within the next forty-eight hours, I'll even throw in a bonus."

He retrieved the check he'd just given me and tore it up, then wrote out another and handed it to me. I glanced at the growing string of zeroes. Things were getting serious, and he certainly had my attention, but with these new revelations, I wasn't sure I wanted to get involved.

"If you've been smuggling guns and people for some time now, how do you know the police aren't already aware of your little racket?"

Goldberg closed his eyes and groaned as if in pain. "I suspect you're right. However, we're talking about a seven-figure boat here, and I'm not taking a loss on it. If they leave me no other choice, I'll go to the Feds with everything I know. And I know plenty."

"Is that a wise move? Why antagonize everyone until you have explored your options?"

"You sound like my attorney. He said the same thing. I'm not playing nice while someone rips off my boat. I want to see some positive results. Are you in or out?"

His generous check appealed to the mercenary in me, but I wasn't sure I could keep Goldberg's involvement from reaching the big ears of the law, assuming they didn't already know. On the other hand, if Goldberg spilled the beans on his own, it would be a moot point.

While I pondered his predicament, I drummed my nails on the desktop; the sound was like the *rat-tat-tat* of a machine gun on full auto. Goldberg sat there with sagging shoulders and a hangdog look on his face, like he was all done in. The emotional effort of confessing his sins together with the potential heavy financial loss had taken its toll on him.

It was a challenge that pulled at me, and with a reputation as the ace "finder of lost objects," how could I refuse?

"Okay, I'm in," I said at last. "Right now, I want you to go home and get some rest. You look like you need it. I'll take it from here." The relief on his face was immediate and piteous. He reached across the desk and pumped my hand with a bit too much enthusiasm.

"Thank you! Call me immediately when you have some news. I'll let my attorney know it's all in hand at the moment. He advised me not to contact the police because the situation would likely resolve itself, but now we'll see some action!" He hurried from my office like a recalcitrant schoolboy escaping the principal's office.

After Goldberg's hasty departure, I leaned back in my chair and propped my feet up in an unladylike manner while I considered his situation.

It took a lot of brass to steal a man's boat right out from under his nose, so I did not doubt the lengths to which his so-called friends might go if crossed, assuming they were the ones who stole Goldberg's yacht in the first place.

My commonsense side nagged me to return his retainer and forget the whole business; this was not my field of expertise. I tend to take on cases I'm reasonably certain I can resolve; for me, failure is not an option. It's taken quite a few years, but after experiencing my share of setbacks during my teens and early military days, I've pretty much overcome any fear of failure I may have harbored back then. Doing the job correctly and accurately was all that mattered. And I wasn't about to backslide just because Goldberg waltzed in promising a big payday. Besides, I already had my doubts about Goldberg and his associates.

On the other hand, I've never been one to take sound advice, not even from myself.

Although I had anticipated a weekend full of delightful diversions, and in spite of the nagging doubts, Goldberg's problem intrigued me, so I decided to start right away.

Alas, work is my virtue, and I'm its slave.

Before I tracked down his guest list in earnest, and despite the threats to Goldberg, I thought it best to notify the Coast Guard to be on the lookout for the missing *Bella Michella*, a sixty-foot Hatteras motor yacht that had slipped her cleat hitch.

My next call was to Pete Beckham. Pete was my oldest friend and a political junky on staff with the *Washington Statesman*. He was an absolute ferret whenever I needed background on anyone in the Washington Metro area. I guess that comes from being a top-notch investigative journalist.

Pete and I were old comrades-in-arms. We met while stationed together in Wurzburg, Germany. Pete was a member of the division's communications group responsible for all information and press releases concerning military affairs in that district.

We frequently ran into each other at the local *gasthaus*, or tavern as you might call it. We got discharged from service at about the same time, and since I was at loose ends, Pete suggested my background as an MP would prove more lucrative if I moved to DC. Pete's never steered me wrong. When he came on the line, I started right in.

"I need some fast info on a guy named Mitch Goldberg. Ever heard of him?"

"Is that Michael Q. Goldberg?"

"Yeah, I'm looking at the name on his check now. Why? Is he some kind of VIP?" I asked as I recalled the ridiculous caricature who presented himself at my office.

"Listen, I'm tied up in meetings the rest of the afternoon, but come over now, and I'll have something for you by the time you get here."

I left the office and cabbed over to Fourteenth Street near Thomas Circle. I entered the lobby of the *Statesman* to the sound of catcalls and whistles from the familiar faces at the security desk. I flashed a "get bent" smile in their direction and clacked my way across the marble expanse to the Information Center, the sound of my Gucci heels reverberating in the four-story atrium lobby. I handed the receptionist my card and asked for Pete.

"Good afternoon, Ms. Carella," he said, reading my business card. He was new, young, and fresh looking.

"Ms.? Next, you'll be calling me Mizz Fuzzy Britches. It's just Vic. And get Pete down here ASAP, buster. I haven't got all day."

I smiled and batted my eyes at him to soften the tone, but he wasn't buying it. In the background, I heard the security guards snicker as the receptionist's ears turned red. Perhaps I should brush up on my people skills.

"I'll see if Mr. Beckham is available," he said and turned his back on me as he spoke into the phone.

As I waited, I reflected that in eight years of practice, this was the most unusual commission I'd ever accepted. Errant spouses and hidden community assets were my specialty. Then again, I'd grown accustomed to a certain lifestyle, plus I'd just wrapped up my latest case. And although I was reluctant to take the job, I liked the steady cash flow. Besides, it would make a welcome change of pace from my normal routine. As the saying goes, any port in a storm.

Hey, now that's funny. I'll bet old Goldberg would drink to that!

"Hello, gorgeous. You're looking too good." Pete was the only person who could get away with a line like that with me. That's because I knew he reserved his ulterior motives for his divine Melanie.

"What did you find out?"

"I thought I recognized that name. Your boy, Mitch Goldberg, is in big demand as an investment counselor to the rich and famous. He's made quite a name for himself. Unfortunately, he's also under federal investigation for possible money laundering. What's this all about?"

The money-laundering angle troubled me. Funny how that had not earned an honorable mention when Goldberg described the smuggling operation; the two went together like ice cream and cake. I'd bet Goldberg was up to his eyeballs in that as well, the little rat. I wondered what other important tidbits he neglected to tell me.

"The plot thickens, but I'll take it up with my client when I see him. Here's the deal. Goldberg thinks his business associates boosted his shiny new yacht, but he's deathly afraid of them. Can you give me the rundown on these guys as well?"

Pete gave me a quizzical look and wriggled his fingers as I handed over Goldberg's guest list. His eyes lit up as he scanned the names.

"Marvin Bocci, assistant to the assistant to the mayor."

"'Assistant to the assistant?' For crying out loud. Is everyone a niche specialist these days?"

"What the hell have you gotten into? Marvin Bocci…he's the mayor's dirty trickster. And Andre Adema . . ." Pete ticked off each name in turn. "He imports produce from Mexico. He's another guy known to work the shady side of the street. I don't like this, Vic. What gives?"

I'd seen that look of consternation on Pete's face before, usually when I was about to get into something way over my head that could land me in trouble.

I pushed on like I hadn't heard him. "Anyone else?"

If I had a telephone directory handy, I could have gotten the scoop on half the population in the city. I marveled at the depth and breadth of his connections. Pete knew everyone worth knowing—and some not worth knowing, if you know what I mean.

"Yeah, Boots Johnson," he said, tapping the list. "Don't let the name fool you. This guy's a dangerous piece of work too. You need to slow down and listen to me, girl." He waved the list of names under my nose. "Any one of these guys will eat your lunch for breakfast. Whatever it is you're thinking of doing, don't!"

"Do I tell you how to jimmy information out of a crooked politician? What's the story on Johnson? Is he some kind of assassin?" The open foyer amplified my voice, and several people looked in our direction. Pete took my arm and steered me away from the reception desk.

In a quiet voice, he said, "I came across Johnson's name last year while researching how easy it was to buy weapons on the black market. As I heard it, there was a dustup between several federal agencies over the 'unexpected retirement' of a couple of Columbian arms dealers, and Johnson was somehow involved. It's possible he's the one the Feds are really interested in, and they're using your client as bait."

"So he's a shooter?"

"Nah, he's a negotiator, more of a backroom boy. But rumor has it that when Johnson doesn't get his way, the opposition disappears."

"Great, I'll start with this Johnson guy. Know where I can find him?"

"Go easy, will you?" Pete gave me a wary eye. "Try the Grill. You'll appreciate this; Johnson's been cultivating several international contacts. By the way, how did you get mixed up with Goldberg in the first place?"

"Picked me out of the phone book for all I know. Who cares? He showed up crying about losing his toy boat, and I promised to find it."

"I would have thought his own people would do that for him. Don't those big boats have GPS or something?"

"It's more complicated than that. Just get the information and call me." I left Pete standing by the elevator, studying Goldberg's list of assorted guests.

If the Feds had Goldberg on a watch list, that could make things more difficult. Several questions came to mind, but for the moment, I didn't dwell on them. Three blocks over, I pushed through the revolving doors of my favorite watering hole for a beer, some conversation, and to test my luck.

The Old Market Grill had what the food critics liked to call a sedate ambiance with its dark-paneled walls and an outsized antique mirror behind the well-burnished oak bar.

The late-lunch crowd was in full swing, so I knew getting a table was out of the question. I headed for the bar where I saw Sally, the usual midday bartender, pouring drinks as fast as the servers could plop down a ticket. She saw me and gave me a quick smile.

We were best friends, but I hoped she didn't think the only time I ever stopped in was to pump her for information. That wasn't true . . . okay, except for today. The fact was I hadn't been around in over a week. We'd become close friends ever since I came to DC. It happens like that sometimes when two personalities click. I liked to think our friendship worked on several levels: she was a bartender and I liked to drink beer; and although she wasn't a detective like me, she was just as curious about people as I was which is code that we both were downright nosy. Like I said, we clicked.

If I worked for one of the three-letter federal security agencies around town, I would classify the things Sally heard from her side of the bar as "vital to the nation's interests."

The open secret in this town is that people privy to sensitive information liked to brag. There's an inherent need to feel important even among the high-dollar lobbyists and consultants that congregate in DC. There is a powerful allure, like a siren's call, to being the one-in-the-know.

Sally leaned forward to place a tallboy in front of me. She had smooth dark skin, a flirtatious laugh, and big, beautiful eyes that melted hearts all over town.

"Hello, stranger. It's been a while. What can I do you for?" she said as she wiped the bar with a towel.

"For starters, thanks for not busting my chops. Believe it or not, I'm hunting for a stolen yacht, but there could be a money-laundering angle as well. Anything come to mind?"

"Federal, state, or local?" she asked with a straight face. It was a sad commentary on our times, but too often true.

"I'd have to go with private. Ever heard the name Boots Johnson?"

Sally turned her head to look down the length of the bar where a group of men stood drinking their lunch. "I hear there are some new players in town looking to fund a small militia."

"Are you kidding me? Sounds like a bad joke—'A guerilla walks into a bar…'"

Sally shrugged. "You're the one who's asking."

"Okay, okay. So, which one is my cowboy?"

"Um, I'd strongly advise against it," she said, again glancing sideways down the bar. "But if you're hell-bent, Johnson's the one in the cashmere. He's been hanging around the past few weeks collecting new friends."

I followed her gaze and easily picked out the one she mentioned. The guy had "player" written all over him. I judged him to be in his mid-thirties. With his dark gray suit, overstarched shirt, and wavy hair combed straight back, he exuded the look of the stereotypical Washington lobbyist. His silk tie was shades of pastel purple and pink. Cowboy, indeed, although he was wearing the obligatory Western boots in tooled black leather.

Don't you find some things are so predictable they don't bear mentioning?

He caught me looking at him and flashed a perfect smile in my direction. I'll bet he closed a lot of deals with that smile. Hell, I wouldn't mind taking a peek at whatever he was selling. He came over and sat on the barstool next to me. I'm a sucker for the shy type.

"Can I get you another drink?"

"No, thanks. I just stopped in for a quick one, but I'm still on the clock. You know how bosses can be," I said, playing the office mouse routine.

"Boots Johnson," he said.

When I shook his big, warm hand, I noticed the manicure. But of course!

"Boots? That's an unusual name. Vic Carella."

"As in Victoria?"

"Yes, but I prefer just Vic."

"Do you work around here?"

"Actually, I'm all over DC. I'm with a courier service," I said, giving him my standard off-putting cover story. "We hand-deliver packages and important documents between offices, you know, for local clients who can't wait for overnight service."

Out of the corner of my eye, I caught him giving me the once-over. We talked for a while, trying to get beyond the standard drivel of who-what-and-where, but I won't lie to you. I was working him hard—cooing in all the right places, lots of fluttering lashes and big-eyed wonder at the lines he handed me.

I had his number though. He wasn't even getting into the ballpark, much less running the bases—which he clearly had in mind—no matter how many times he tried to step up to the plate. Hey, can you tell I like baseball? Go Nats!

We sparred with each other a bit more trying to size each other up, and then I let him talk me into meeting him for drinks the following evening. I left the Grill and headed home to my two-bedroom apartment in the Grosvenor Building over on Forty-Second Street that I shared with my watch-cat, Marlowe. He greeted me at the door as he did every night. I reached down and gave him a couple of good, hard rubs, and his back arched with pleasure.

He was a handsome Snowshoe, a cross between a Siamese and American shorthair. The four white paws were a dead giveaway, and he had a white blaze down his nose. He twitched his Hercule Poirot half moustache at me and trilled a welcome in that melodic purr of his.

I popped open a fresh can of tuna and placed the dish next to his water bowl. Some nights the darn cat ate healthier than I did. He had a strong sense of smell and could navigate room to room and around furniture so well you'd never know he was blind.

I pulled an ice-cold Corona from the fridge and sat down at my kitchen desk to check emails, hoping Pete had dug up something on the list of names. I wasn't disappointed.

Pete sent me a short bio on each of the lug nuts with Goldberg the night his precious yacht went missing, including Boots Johnson. For a guy who supposedly worked in the shadows, Johnson was pretty well-known in certain circles. His name popped up on quite a few law enforcement databases.

I was scanning Pete's descriptions, looking for anything odd that stuck out, when I noticed a pattern forming. Goldberg's friends were all successful small business owners, each with cash-intensive and low-profile but highly profitable enterprises, in which splurging on conspicuous luxuries, like yachts, would raise little concern.

Goldberg said his friends enjoyed playing jokes. No wonder they could laugh it up with such confident abandon; they could well afford it.

The thought occurred to me again that Goldberg's buddies shifted his yacht to another marina for safekeeping to rein him in and teach him a lesson. Was this, as I originally thought, nothing more than a prank, and Goldberg had taken the bait all the way? If that were true, he was going to be in for a good ribbing, but I still needed to make the effort. I hoped his sense of humor held out when he got my final invoice.

If it wasn't a practical joke, then who among Goldberg's acquaintances had it in for him? How close were these guys? Did they go way back together, or was Goldberg trying to run with the big boys? Who might be jealous, or who got screwed on a deal? These questions and more ran through my mind as I read each summary to see if someone stood out as a likely suspect. No one did, but I wasn't worried; it was early yet.

What gave me pause for concern was the nefarious smuggling operation Goldberg had described. Regardless of whether he got pranked by his friends, Goldberg still painted a dark picture that was hard to ignore. If caught, the entire crew would take the full federal rap, not to mention the scrutiny they'd get from a plethora of international agencies who might want a piece of Goldberg and his merry band of pirates as well.

I closed the email thread and searched the internet for local marinas. I had not expected the sheer number in the immediate Potomac River area, much less those along the Chesapeake Bay and nearby Virginia coastline. I knew that no matter how persuasive I was, there was little chance I'd get any useful information over the phone about someone's private boat.

There went my weekend. It looked like I'd be chasing down Goldberg's elusive yacht.

Chapter Two

The next morning, I was up early to plot out a route that would intersect with the greatest number of marinas I could hit in one day. While online, I did some fast research on boats and boating so I could hold a reasonable conversation with the nautical experts I'd likely run into during my investigation. Like any specialized subject, it was impossible to absorb all the information in one sitting, but I got a sense of the important things to look for.

Of course, Marlowe let me know what he thought about having his morning routine disrupted. He planted himself across my map and refused to move until he got his morning rubdown.

I started to change into my running outfit but decided to postpone my usual morning run; I was impatient to get on the road. Before setting out, I went through what I called my street routine, where I reviewed my personal preparedness. Luckily, accessories for concealed carry have come a long way in recent years, which is good because I'm always well equipped.

A physical inspection ensured I had my Glock 26 secured in the concealed pouch built into my purse along with a spare magazine. I kept the mags loaded with 135-grain jacketed hollow points—my man-stoppers.

As an afterthought, the tiny flat-sided Kel-Tec .32 disappeared into my jeans pocket as well. Sometimes a nonlethal solution could chill out a situation fast, and for that reason, I kept the little pocket-rocket loaded with blanks just in case I needed an effective distraction. The loud bang combined with the threat of immediate death could tame even the most dim-witted grunt intent on grievous bodily harm. But, at a minimum, I never left home without my primary piece; it made me feel confident and secure.

Before hitting the road, I printed a list of marinas from an internet directory, starting with the Chesapeake Boat and Anchor—surprise, surprise!—a bayside marina owned by one of Goldberg's so-called friends.

Exiting the Beltway, I picked up the John Hanson Highway toward Annapolis. I turned down several back streets until I located the small marina. As I rolled into the parking lot, I saw an incredibly huge man crossing the boatyard.

From Pete's description, this had to be Boris "the Bear" Zharkov. His arms stuck out like two stout limbs protruding from a wide oak tree. The big man didn't need a forklift to move boats around the yard, because he looked capable of doing so by hand. If this was Goldberg's golfing buddy, I'd like to watch this monster crush a few golf balls on the driving range.

"Mr. Zharkov," I called out and flashed my business card as I approached him. I stood with my arm extended, but he just looked at the bit of pasteboard in my hand.

"Vic Carella. An acquaintance of yours, Mitch Goldberg, hired me to locate his missing yacht. And I thought to myself, what a coincidence, you knowing Mitch and owning a marina too." I glanced around, taking in the boatyard. "Any chance you've got his boat stashed someplace around here just to give him a hard time?"

Zharkov gave me a deadpan stare. I could almost hear the rusty wheels going round within that simian-like brain. I got it; he was going to be a hard case.

"Is this what you do for a living? Search for missing boats?" he scoffed.

"No, not usually, but it's what I'm doing today. Mr. Goldberg is rather anxious to recover his property. Do you have any information that might help me locate it?"

"I don't know nothing about Mitch's damn boat," he said at last. "Anything else?"

"You were at the party the night before it went missing, is that correct?"

"Yeah, so what?"

"Mitch mentioned several people at the party like to play jokes. Is that the case here, Mr. Zharkov? You swiped his yacht for a joke?" I said, hoping to keep things light.

"Why did Mitch call you? He's weak; he should pick up the phone and call me himself if he wants to ask questions about his stupid boat!" Boris said, waving his arms in the air.

Whoa! The crazy Russian was already wound up pretty tight, but why? It was only natural Goldberg should go after his megabuck yacht, right? I mean, who wouldn't?

"So, you have an idea where it is?"

"I didn't say that, but Mitch shouldn't bring in outsiders to check on his friends."

Yeah, right. Friends who threaten to kill you, but we'll ignore that for the moment.

"There's nothing complicated here," I said, hoping to placate him. "Mitch asked me to take a quiet look around and locate his yacht with a minimum of fuss. You might appreciate him not mentioning any of this to the police. If you ask me, I believe he wants to keep things low-key to avoid more embarrassment."

"Go ask Marvin Bocci or the other guys. I don't know nothing about it." Boris left me standing there as he headed toward a ramshackle trailer that I assumed he used as his office.

"Personally, I think it's one of the greatest gags I've ever heard of, that is, if you really took it," I shouted as he retreated, but he didn't break stride.

"Mind if I look around and check out the boats?"

The Bear kept walking as he waved his hand in the air dismissively. I took this as his assent and went on a quick tour of the marina.

In neat, tight rows, I counted roughly twenty boats propped up on stilts, presumably scheduled for mainte-nance. I watched as two yardmen applied blue paint to a couple of hulls, while another outfitted a sleek racer with a new prop. The speedboat looked lean and fast and had a paint scheme that was an explosion of color. Waterside, a couple of dozen boats were tied up in individual berths rocking gently against rubber fenders to keep from scrap-ing against the dock.

I took out the picture of Goldberg's yacht he had left with me. The *Bella Michella* was in profile, and I could make out the registration number on the bow. Again, boats are not my thing, but it was easy to see that all the boats at the Boat and Anchor were in the twenty-to forty-foot range. A few were bigger, but none matched

Goldberg's sixty-foot masterpiece. Zharkov's marina did not run to a separate indoor storage facility, so there were no out-of-the-way places to conceal Goldberg's yacht.

I still had a slew of questions I wanted to ask, but I did not see the Bear prowling about. I glanced toward the trailer and could make out Zharkov's massive outline behind the shaded window as he watched me. I left for my next destination.

As the day wore on, I soon realized this was not a one-person job; there was too much geography to cover to conduct a thorough search. I didn't know how someone could make a sixty-foot yacht disappear, but for all I knew, it was already on its way to the Caribbean or South America, where every third-world thug would love to get their hands on a bargain-priced yacht. Still, I would have to cast my net wider if I was going to get a line on the damn thing.

I loved talking nautical.

It was late afternoon, and the frustration at having no luck got the better of me. None of the marinas where I made inquiries had ever heard of the *Bella Michella*.

I eased into a small marina in Riva to wrap up my afternoon. It was an out-of-the-way place tucked far up the South River and looked unlikely, but then so had every other marina I'd visited that afternoon.

The neon sign in the window of the dockside restaurant proclaimed it was open. It had been a long day, and I was tired and hungry. I went inside for a quick bite to eat.

From the dilapidated interior, I could see why they called it the Dirty Whaler. The last coat of paint to grace these walls must have been at the grand opening, but it sure had character.

The menu consisted mainly of crab-with-whatever. I ordered a Corona and the Maryland crab cake sandwich. I hoped for the best and expected something less, but when the meal came, I was pleased; it was all lump crab meat with no filler.

"My compliments to the chef," I said between mouthfuls. "This is great."

Several locals seated nearby nodded their agreement, and then turned their gaze back to the television mounted over the back of the bar where a couple of college teams pounded each other on the gridiron.

The bartender looked pleased as he came closer. "We get that a lot. Best crab cakes on the Chesapeake Bay," he boasted. "Mike Carver," he said and stuck his hand out.

"Vic Carella." I returned his forceful grip.

"Are you from around here?"

"Just passing through. Say, maybe you could help me. I'm trying to locate a boat, the *Bella Michella*. Ever heard of it?" I laid Goldberg's picture on the bar.

Mike studied it for a moment, and then shook his head. He automatically replaced my empty Corona with another. "Haven't seen her before, but that don't mean nothing. Lots of boats come and go that don't stop here for fuel or supplies. What do you want with her?"

"She went missing recently. I'm helping a friend locate it."

"That's a shame. Sorry, I can't be more helpful. Have you tried some other marinas? There are lots more up and down the Bay."

"Tell me about it! Nah, I'm giving it up as a poor job. Hey, at least I tried," I said and saluted him with my beer. He smiled and moved down the bar to serve his thirsty regulars.

When I got ready to leave, I looked around for Mike Carver to settle the tab. He was on the phone at the other end of the bar, so I left money on the counter and included a sizable tip to show my appreciation for the excellent lunch.

I doubled back along Riva Road and merged onto Route 50, heading west toward town. I got into the center lane, put it on seventy, and cruised on autopilot for a while. I enjoyed long, leisurely drives because they helped me to relax and think.

Something about that conversation at the Dirty Whaler nagged at me. It took a while, but finally, I worked it out: no details. There was no mention of details whatsoever.

The way I figured it, when you're talking boats, most people want to put them into perspective, like whether it's the size of a Boston Whaler or something bigger, say, a Viking or an Ocean Yacht. Or its length; boaters appreciate footage—the bigger, the better. But Mike Carver didn't ask about any of those things.

Oh sure, he worked at a dockside bar where boats regularly come and go, so maybe there was nothing to it. I mean, people work in libraries, but it doesn't mean they've read every book.

Nevertheless, it bothered me in a way I couldn't explain except to say I didn't believe him. Behind that friendly façade, I felt he was holding something back, and that made me curiouser and curiouser as Alice might say, but I'd find out what old Mike had to say for himself another day.

Right now, all I needed was a hot bath, some soft music, and a glass of Pinot Grigio to get me in the mood for my "date" with the hunky Boots Johnson.

# # #

The Old Market Grill was fast becoming my second home, I thought as I scanned the bar. I didn't see the six-foot stud anywhere, not that I worried about being stood up because that's happened before. Okay, more than a few times, so don't remind me.

I told myself he was only one of several suspects I had to cross off the list, but that did nothing to diminish the surge of pleasure I felt when he came through the door. With his olive complexion and piercing dark blue eyes, he was an attractive man. He certainly captured my attention.

He gave me the once-over that took in the bell curve of my golden hair, LBD, pearls, and heels. I must have passed muster, because I noticed the slight grin.

"Been waiting long?" he asked, but we both knew better.

Polite talk, I like that.

The hostess showed us to a table by the window, where the crowded Washington nightlife passed by without end. We were on our second round of drinks and enjoying some pleasant conversation when Boots asked, "What's your game, Miss Carella?"

His tone was friendly enough, even solicitous, but my internal antenna began to quiver. I played it cool.

"I don't know what you mean. I'm just out for a quiet evening. And you?"

"Having any luck locating Mitch Goldberg's yacht?"

With an ambiguous shrug, I said, "How do you know about that?" I was now on full alert.

"It's my business to know things. You're a private investigator, am I right?"

"You've obviously figured that out already, so what's your point?" I wasn't sure where this was going, but I was at a severe disadvantage, and we both knew it.

"It occurred to me that I might be able to assist you." His tone of voice was all innocence. "I'm acquainted with Goldberg through Boris, of course. I heard he had misplaced his latest acquisition, but with my extensive contacts, perhaps I could help you locate it."

He was smooth as glass and never suggested the least little reproof for the white lies I told him the day before. He must have read my mind, because he said, "The pickup job yesterday, well done. Very professional. So, how about my offer?"

"You know I can't discuss my client's business with you. This is strictly a search and recovery job. I'll give it a little time and see what turns up."

Even though I'd have loved to tap into additional resources, I wasn't buying the Helpful Harry routine. What was he after?

He sipped his drink while his eyes fixated on me the entire time. I felt uncomfortable until he turned on that high-wattage smile of his and laughed it off as a joke. The guy saw and knew too much, and he made me nervous. I never felt—what was the word I wanted—intimidated? Nevertheless, he had an effect on me.

"What are your particular interests, if you don't mind me asking?" I could see he was working out a plausible story to spin for me, but he wasn't giving away anything for free, that was for sure.

"You might say, you and I are in the same line of business, relatively speaking."

"Oh, really? How so?"

"You match people with things they've lost. I match people with things they need. In our own way, we satisfy the desires of our respective clients, wouldn't you agree?"

"I see what you're getting at. But it would take a long walk around the block to make that connection. What are you working on now?"

People don't easily part with the truth. They play the angles, figure out the leverage points, or simply flat out lie. And then sometimes they surprise you.

"I'm helping some folks south of the border with a problem. Which border is immaterial, but suffice to say they're in a dispute with their government."

Wasn't this the nature of Washington, DC, all over? Here was actionable information freely divulged over drinks, and probably profitable information, too, if whispered in the right ears. That is, if I were so inclined. So far, Boots's admission tied in with what Goldberg told me. To what degree remained to be seen.

"I'm not judging, but whatever it is you do, it's not strictly legal, is it?" When Boots did not respond, and the silence dragged on, I felt compelled to follow up. "Perhaps I shouldn't ask."

"I appreciate your discretion."

"How did you get mixed up with my client and his friends?"

"That, too, would be telling. Let's talk about something else. What do you do for fun on weekends?"

Really? Next, he'd want to know my favorite color. The brief exchange of information ended all too soon. I wanted to know how he fit into this little melodrama concerning Goldberg, but he stonewalled me at every turn. He couldn't remain enigmatic forever. I had my methods.

Boots took a sip of his drink and then said, "My offer stands should you ever require help." He opened the menu and gave it his full attention.

I wondered what was behind the sudden offer of assistance. I mean, what was in it for him? We ordered steaks and salad. While we waited for the meal to arrive, our conversation continued along the lines of the banal, except for a few instances where Boots probed without results. I couldn't shake the notion there was trouble close at hand beyond that of a missing yacht. I sympathized with Goldberg about getting in over his head. I felt like I was wading into turbulent waters with no clue how deep it could go.

We finished our meal over inconsequential small talk. Even though I needed more background on Boots and his current activities, I dared not ask now that I knew he was running the same drill on me. Did his dealings have anything to do with Goldberg losing his yacht? Did their respective ventures overlap, or worse, run into some sort of conflict? It was easy to imagine Goldberg coming out on the short end where the reticent Boots Johnson was concerned.

Boots touched his napkin to the corners of his mouth and laid it beside his plate. He said, "How about joining me for drinks tomorrow afternoon in Annapolis? Mitch and his friends will be there; you might learn something. Or is that interfering in your work?"

I didn't answer right away as I considered the ramifications. "Is this where you tell me Mitch Goldberg and his pals are a swell bunch of guys? That is, in case I couldn't figure that out for myself?"

He waved a hand as if to dismiss such a suggestion. "Not at all. I wouldn't turn my back on any of them, but that doesn't stop me from doing business with them."

It was only natural he was curious how much I already knew, and I could see he was determined to find out as much as possible.

"It would save time tracking down each of his friends individually. Why not get a closer look before you take them on? That is, you *were* planning on talking with everyone at Mitch's birthday party, right? I was at that party, and I can tell you they can get a bit rough. But, they're good for a few drinks, and who knows, you might enjoy yourself."

Fun guys, huh? That was rich considering Goldberg's description of their recent boating trips and his desperate plea for help.

"Boris already knows I'm working for Mitch Goldberg. He might not take too kindly to a gate-crasher."

"Then I'll tell him you're with me, and he'll just have to deal with it. What do you say?"

I said I'd think about it and let him know. He turned on that charming smile of his and presented his business card. He said I could call anytime, with special emphasis on the *any* part.

When we parted outside the restaurant, Boots shook my hand and said he hoped to see me in Annapolis. He turned and sauntered down the sidewalk with his hands jammed in his pockets, whistling a tuneless melody.

I had expected him to lean in for a goodnight kiss and was half certain I would have pulled back. Not out of some pretense of virtue, you understand, but just on principle. After all, I had Mr. Boots Johnson pegged as a smooth operator.

When the gorgeous hunk didn't even try, I felt . . . well, damn, I stood there feeling a little cheated, if you must know.

I arrived back at my apartment to find Marlowe waiting by the door as always—bless his heart. It felt good to be home, safe once again as I bolted the door on the world. I went over the evening's events in my mind and came away disgusted with myself.

This was not me. I was always the one who was cool under fire, always on her game. Then why did I suddenly feel like a young twit at her first Teen Club dance? This guy . . . If I wasn't careful, this guy could get under my skin. And I'd been warned off him—twice!

Try to maintain a little decorum, I chided myself.

CHAPTER THREE

The next day, I arrived at the Annapolis City Dock at half past noon. The pubs were crowded, and the sidewalks overflowed with people wandering in and out of quaint little shops as everyone enjoyed an afternoon stroll along the waterfront.

The warm October day brought out scores of boaters who paraded their pride and joys up and down the Spa Creek Canal known as "Ego Alley." All day long, boats entered the mouth of the narrow waterway, and at the head of the turnaround basin, they executed a graceful about-face under the careful scrutiny of throngs of onlookers before returning to the open waters of the Chesapeake Bay.

Boots Johnson waved to me from one of the dockside bars. The raucous group at his table was already three sheets to the wind—or, for the less nautical among us, all were well on their way to alcohol-induced oblivion. Don't worry; you'll get the hang of it.

Boots took me by the hand and led me around as we cruised through the bar. There were too many people weaving in and out of tight little groups to be certain who belonged with whom. It was like a nineteen-sixties Woodstock concert, where everyone appeared to belong with everyone else. You're familiar with Woodstock, right? Mega field party, big-name bands, rock-and-roll history? Never mind.

We snagged a couple of drinks from one of several servers dedicated to serving the private party; the flow of drinks remained unabated throughout the afternoon. Crossing Market Space along the canal, we leaned against the pylons where we could do a little people-watching inconspicuously.

Boots indicated a seductive young woman. "The petite blond is Sabrina Farkas. She belongs to Boris, but I don't understand the attraction; he's such a coarse brute." The deep, even tan she sported attested to many idle hours in the sun.

"Are you jealous?"

Boots merely grunted. "The loudmouth in the print dress is Katya Sevvin, queen of the two-for-one specials at her husband's pizza joints. That is, two for her, one for you."

"Now that's just tacky, but I see what you mean." The woman was as short and round as her husband— who Boots identified as Anatoly Sevvin—was tall and slim. It's said opposites attract. Now, why is that?

"See the lard-ass troll sitting in the back in the Hawaiian shirt? That's Marvin Bocci; he works for the mayor."

I picked out another heavyweight who had been pounding one drink after another since I arrived. The big man's florid features marked him as someone well on his way to a massive organ failure of some kind. Were all of Goldberg's friends made in his own well-fed image?

"So that's the 'assistant to the assistant' as I heard it."

"Yeah, and he's completely unencumbered by any impediments like morals or scruples."

"Who are the others?" I referred to the gaggle of people milling about the party.

"There are a couple more you should meet, but the rest are just freeloaders whenever the liquor's flowing; no one worth knowing."

"Are they always in party mode?"

"They haven't missed a single weekend as long as I've known them. My liver gave up and deserted me a month ago."

"As troglodytes go, they look like one big, happy family. What's your interest in this bunch of rag tags? What's in it for you?"

"Let's leave my business interests out of it, okay?" Boots was stone-faced as he watched another powerboat approach the turnaround basin.

"It's just that…"

There it was again, that impenetrable iron curtain shutting down even the most offhand inquiry. I had to find a way around his façade that alternated between friendly and downright hostile.

It occurred to me that Boots, the cool operator, didn't fit in with Goldberg's crowd. He was as different as, say, Boris and his trophy babe.

"I haven't seen Mitch today. Doesn't he enjoy hanging with his buds?"

Boots didn't answer right away as he continued to observe the sleek racing boat. The boat's three massive outboard motors growled deeply as it made the tight turn.

"I haven't laid eyes on Mitch since the night of his party. Got any leads?"

"Nope. I've been racking up expenses with no tangible results, but I'm confident things will pan out. Besides, I've got statistics on my side; yachts like Mitch's rarely get stolen. They're conspicuous and too easy to trace. I'm pretty sure one of these guys is in on the joke, or maybe all of them."

Boots turned to me with a serious look on his face. "You might want to expand your search farther south. Try Crisfield."

What was this? Boots Johnson didn't volunteer information as far as I could tell; this was totally out of character for him.

"What's in Crisfield?"

"A friend spotted a yacht down south. The description fit the one belonging to Mitch."

"How sure is your friend?"

"Very."

It wouldn't hurt to check it out, although I worried about being played. Since I didn't have a better lead at the moment, I'd give it a shot.

Boots said, "We should mingle a bit so you can justify that whacking fee you're charging your client."

We rejoined the party in full swing. Boots drifted off to talk with some others. All I can say is they must spend quite a bit of coin on a regular basis for the management to tolerate the obnoxious behavior of Boris and his entourage. The commotion clearly annoyed several customers, who deserted the bar altogether.

In a rich baritone, Boris began singing a tune native to his beloved Russia that sounded vaguely familiar to my ears, and soon Anatoly Sevvin joined in. They entertained the captive audience at the bar with a bravura performance that could be heard clear across the harbor.

Two police officers on patrol along the waterfront popped in for a look around. The Russians quieted down and picked up their drinks. It didn't pay to draw attention from the police, not when you are already "listing to port" as they say. Are you starting to catch on now?

Marvin Bocci slouched forward with his chin resting on his chest, and near the bar, I spotted Anatoly Sevvin talking to a couple of men who I assumed were Andre Adema and Oscar Sabo, two more of Goldberg's inner circle. I sidled up to them to find out what they knew about the missing yacht, but as I approached, they separated and went in opposite directions to avoid talking to me.

"You're new around here." I turned to find the kewpie-doll, Sabrina, holding on to the edge of the bar as if it might drift away. She struggled to focus her glassy eyes. "Say, aren't you with Boots Johnson?"

"Sort of. Hi, I'm Vic." I smiled and held out my hand. She seemed hesitant to let go of the bar, but finally transferred her grip to my steadying hand.

"Sabrina." With a shake of her head, streaked blonde curls whipped across her overpainted pixie face.

Up close, I noticed her former beauty was fading, and a cruel thought occurred to me: if all I had to look forward to was going home with Boris the Bear, I, too, would remain well and truly drunk.

"Are you coming to Florida with us?" Realizing she still held my hand, Sabrina let go and grabbed the bar again as if it were the Rock of Gibraltar.

"No one invited me. When do you leave?"

Oh, goody, the boys are off on another adventure in illegal trafficking.

"In a couple days, I think. I only found out at the last minute. Are you and Boots traveling together? That's real cozy. He's nice." I detected a hint of envy mixed with remorse.

"Are you okay?" I couldn't tell if she wanted to talk or was about to toss her cookies.

She glanced quickly over her shoulder. Her mood changed, and her voice took on a petulant quality. "I don't enjoy going away. It's not fun anymore, and I feel sorry for the girls."

"What do you mean? What girls? Is someone in trouble?" I wanted her to open up, but over the years, I'd learned you can push a drunk only so far and so fast.

"I don't really know you, but you seem all right," she said, trying to hold herself erect and failing miserably. "You should get away before it's too late."

"Too late for what?" The sudden appearance of Boris startled both of us. Sabrina clammed up, but she was slow turning away. Boris jerked her around to face him, twisting her arm as he pulled her close.

"What were you saying just now?"

"Nothing, hon. Just that if Vic is coming with us, I didn't want her to be late, that's all. Some new company would be nice, you know?"

"She's not coming."

The sharp crack could be heard over the noise of the crowd at the bar. The backhand whipped Sabrina's head around; only Boris's tight grip kept her from ending up on the floor.

"I told you to keep your mouth shut. You're too stupid for new company."

All activity ceased, and conversations stopped in midsentence as everyone watched the scene unfold. Sabrina lowered her head and cried in shame. Boris glared at me, daring me to say something, anything. His hands twitched like he wanted to tune me up as well.

I mumbled something about not being able to get away on short notice. The unprovoked and public display of violence robbed the sunny afternoon of all enjoyment.

Boots Johnson stepped between us to crowd Boris and force him back. In a strong, quiet tone, he said, "Is there a problem here, Boris?" His hands hung loose at his sides, and he leaned forward on the balls of his feet, like a boxer anticipating his opponent's next move.

The two men glared at each other until the moment passed. Boris nodded in my direction and said, "Your girlfriend, she's not coming with us. I wasn't planning on any new people."

"Vic knows it's polite to wait until she's asked. She would never impose on our little soiree."

"Huh?"

"You made your point, Boris; she's not coming. Now, can we all calm down?"

Boris gave a noncommittal shrug of his broad, round shoulders and rejoined Anatoly and the others. Sabrina sat alone at the bar; she did not appear nearly as inebriated as she had moments before. The sound of tinkling glasses and guarded conversations slowly returned as nervous patrons tried in vain to recapture the mood of their lazy afternoon.

Boots turned to face me, but I held up a hand before he could speak. I'd had enough for one afternoon. Boots said to call him as I retreated through the crowd. The

Bear stood near the exit, and I had to pass by uncomfortably close to get out the door. His brutal features were immobile, like stone, and his eyes were mere slits as he gave me the hard stare.

Poor, poor Sabrina. I'd hate to be in her shoes tonight.

The drive home was uneventful, and I sent up thankful prayers for that. For the second time in as many days, I found myself on Route 50. The long stretch between Riva Road and Davidsonville was a particular favorite for motorcyclists with their Japanese crotch-rockets. It was not uncommon to see daring young bikers maintain wheel-stands for well over a half mile and farther. I estimated the two speedsters who shot past me were doing well over one-twenty. I looked down to see that I was doing seventy, but in comparison, it felt like a stroll in the park.

I settled in for the cruise home and reflected on the events of the afternoon. Only yesterday, Boots inferred Goldberg's friends were a fun bunch. Not that I would agree. Goldberg had succumbed to the lure of easy money, but I couldn't detect anything easy where Boris and his crowd were concerned, unless it involved an endless supply of booze. I suspected whatever Goldberg did for them, he earned every penny—the hard way.

That reminded me. I needed to call Goldberg to report in. It bothered me that he hadn't mentioned the pending Florida cruise; here again, he withheld vital information. What else was he holding back? The inconsistencies were starting to add up.

And what had Sabrina been talking about? She appeared genuinely concerned when she mentioned some girls. Who were they, and what did they have to do with anything? The next time I saw Goldberg, I'd make him cough up the whole story, even if I had to squeeze it out of him.

The sun had slipped behind the trees by the time I arrived home. There was a spot on the street in front of my apartment building, and I got a chance to practice my parallel parking. My building has an underground lot, but I took the open space anyway. Without looking, I stepped out of the SUV and broke my own standing rule to always be aware of my surroundings.

And damn near died for it.

From a gap in the hedgerow that lined the opposite side of the street, a dark figure rushed toward me before I could react. Something heavy, like a tire iron or a blackjack, slammed into my ribs, knocking the wind out of me so that I couldn't call out for help. I fell against the door and slid to the ground. The thug standing over me wore a balaclava to cover his face, and he was dressed head to toe in black.

I reached for my purse to retrieve my gun, but the thug kicked it out of my hands. I held up my arm to ward off what I felt sure would be the final crushing blow. As my last act of defiance, it was pretty damn weak.

"Police! Put your hands up *now!*" The shout sent my assailant scrambling into the woods. I heard running feet as someone crashed into the brush in pursuit.

I wasn't sure what was happening and jerked away as a pair of hands reached toward me. A voice full of concern said, "Take it easy, Miss. I'm a police officer."

The plainclothes officer was good-looking in a rough way. He had close-cropped hair, and hard lines creased his face. It was a kind face that had known brutality but still showed compassion. He helped me to my feet. After I regained my balance, we determined there was no other damage apart from the severe bruising to my ribs; thankfully nothing appeared to be broken. Nevertheless, each deep inhale was excruciating. As a comedian once said, this was going to leave a mark, but I can assure you it was no laughing matter to me.

The police officer's partner soon rejoined us after losing sight of my attacker in the darkening woods. From the way his jacket stretched across his shoulders, he was built like an offensive lineman. They waited patiently while I composed myself and continued to probe for further injuries before escorting me to my apartment building.

Don't get me wrong; I was grateful they arrived when they did, but what were the police doing here? My curiosity must have been evident on my face because the helpful one held up his ID and gold shield for my inspection.

"Lieutenant Alan Scanlin, Metro Police. And this is Sergeant McAllister." McAllister produced his badge as well but remained silent and watchful. DC's finest were at my service.

"I don't know where you came from, but your timing is impeccable. Thank you."

"I know you're hurting right now, Miss, but if you don't mind, we need to ask you a few questions."

"In reference to?"

"Mitch Goldberg. Is he a client of yours?"

Their timely arrival was no coincidence. The scent of bad news hung in the air as I looked from one to the other.

"Let's take this inside, gentlemen, where we can talk in private."

McAllister punched the button for the elevator. While we waited, they were discrete and refrained from filling the void with needless conversation. Once inside my apartment, I offered coffee, tea, or something stronger, but they declined.

Scanlin started in. "What can you tell us about your relationship to Mitch Goldberg?"

"Before I do, can you tell me what this is about?"

McAllister spoke for the first time. "Just answer the question, ma'am." His tone was clipped, as if he had used up all that polite patience he exuded while outside.

"He's a new client, but I'm sure you're aware of that already. What's going on?"

"What were you working on for him?" Scanlin looked around my living room and made himself at home on my couch.

McAllister remained in position near the door in case I made a break for it, bruised ribs and all. They worked great together, these two. Central casting right out of the 1940s could have sent them over.

"You said 'were,' as in past tense. What's happened?"

With a nod from Scanlin, McAllister gave it to me straight. "Late last night, Mitch Goldberg was found dead onboard his yacht. Someone broke his neck."

I felt like I had the wind knocked out of me all over again. The news of my late client left me speechless. I hadn't seen this coming. I mean, how could I? The case was too new to anticipate such a drastic turn of events.

When I finally found my voice, I said, "Tell me, did you find his yacht near Crisfield?"

Scanlin bolted to his feet. He wasn't the only one with big news.

"What do you know about that?"

"I picked up a lead that I planned to follow up on tomorrow. Any idea who tipped off Goldberg about his boat? It vanished a couple days ago, and he hired me to find it, but it looks like he beat me to the punch." I went into my kitchenette to find some aspirin.

Scanlin didn't look too happy that I threw cold water on his case. I rejoined them in the living room.

"Do you know who killed him? Was there a struggle?"

Finally, my follow-up questions broke through to him. Scanlin stopped pacing and wiped a hand across his face. "You know, I think I'll have that drink after all if the offer's still good?"

I poured each of us a stiff shot of Kentucky bourbon. The stoic McAllister deigned to join in as well. I washed down four pain killers in one gulp. Scanlin, on the other hand, enjoyed the warm glow as he sipped his bourbon in the style of a true Southern gentleman.

After a few minutes, Scanlin said, "I hate to admit it, but we don't know a lot. The Coast Guard found the boat and notified the local sheriff. When they searched the body, they found your card in his pocket and contacted our department. I'm curious why the deceased needed an investigator. What's the tie-in?"

"As I said, Goldberg's yacht went missing, and he wanted it found on the q.t. I figured his friends swiped it to get a rise out of him. That's why he didn't file a report. He hired me Friday afternoon, and now you tell me he died last night. That's a record, even for me."

Scanlin shot me a dark scowl, letting me know my comments were in poor taste. That was a fault of mine; I was a blurter. I often blurted things out loud without thinking.

"Have you interviewed his acquaintances? What do they have to say for themselves?" Scanlin asked.

"Goldberg's crowd enjoys a good party. I was in Annapolis today and met a few of them, but I didn't learn much. I found it odd Mitch wasn't there until someone mentioned Crisfield. He was pretty cut up about losing his boat, so he must have done some snooping on his own. I planned to run down there tomorrow to check things out for myself."

"Help me understand, Miss Carella. Your client's yacht was stolen, then the yacht turns up, but now your client is dead, and tonight someone damn near snuffs out your lights. What's so important about one lousy boat that's worth murdering for?"

"I wish I knew, Lieutenant. It seems Goldberg got mixed up in something he couldn't handle, but I'm afraid I don't know what it was."

Goldberg was mixed up in more than a few things—he'd told me so himself—but until I found some hard evidence, I had no one to pin it on. Before I brought in the heavy hitters, like Scanlin, I needed solid proof.

Officially, the case was over since my client was dead, but when did I ever leave well enough alone? You could bet I was going to crawl all over Goldberg's buddies like an IRS agent on a Ponzi scheme. I'd bet the same yobbos who killed my client also tried to dust me off, but they missed. Big mistake. Somebody was going to squeal when I got hold of them by the short and curlies.

Scanlin had nothing more to contribute, and I wasn't about to elaborate further, so I thanked them again for coming to my rescue. I said I'd stop by the station in the morning to make an official statement concerning the attack and also Goldberg's involvement. We exchanged cards and agreed to stay in touch in case there were any fresh developments.

I must say, everything was so polite and civilized. They even showed themselves out while I searched for my little blind cat.

I had intended to find Marlowe, but as soon as the door closed behind the detectives, I collapsed on the couch. The assault had been more damaging than I let on. I was damn lucky I was not outright killed; however, a couple of severely bruised ribs were poor consolation.

The pain that I held in abeyance for as long as possible now had me doubled over. I could find no position that didn't exacerbate my agony. I wanted to hide away and sleep for about a week, but I didn't have that luxury.

I called Sally, who was like my big sister. She was always there for me whenever I got into trouble. She came right over, and her concern was clear from the moment she walked through the door. I appreciated being fussed over and the way she helped me get settled into bed with lots of pillows cushioning my tired, abused body.

She sat on the edge of the bed and gave me a look that said I'd better explain myself before she gave me hell. There were few facts in evidence, but I brought her up to speed to the moment Scanlin broke the news about my client.

I said, "Someone clued Goldberg that his yacht was in Crisfield. It was Boots Johnson who mentioned Crisfield to me, but I don't see him doing something like this."

"How can you say that? Surely he must have known Goldberg was already dead when you two spoke earlier. He could have set up Goldberg with the promise of locating his boat. That was easy enough."

"Then why put the hit on me?"

"Because he knew exactly where both of you would be at a given moment. Because he's decisive, and he works fast. You're messing around in his business, and he doesn't like it." Sally spread a quilt over the bed, but she hadn't finished with me.

"I told you to watch out for this guy. He's gotten to you, hasn't he? I can tell. Don't let this one get too close; he's dangerous."

With unerring accuracy, Sally prodded my one emotional sore spot. What could I say? When it came to my love life, my batting average was similar to the Babe's; I've struck out twice as many times as I've homered.

What she alluded to…well, I'm not proud of it, but the truth is, I had an affair while on active duty with the MPs. The affair was in bad form to begin with, and it did not end well. Just when I thought I had gotten my act together and all was going well for once in my life, I stepped right in it and nearly ruined everything.

There was no acceptable excuse for our behavior, and even less for a commanding officer to get involved with a subordinate under his command. It violated military regulations on many levels. With his career on the ascendency, he rectified that mistake with the stroke of his pen by having me reassigned to Germany, where I was no longer an impediment or constant reminder. It was a low point in my life that kicked off a losing streak I'd yet to surmount. Although, they say nothing lasts forever, perhaps even my crummy luck would change one day, or so I kept telling myself. Nowadays, I tend to keep things low-keyed while concentrating on being the best at what I do—within obvious limitations.

Sally dispelled my reverie. "Maybe Goldberg became a liability, and they couldn't trust him to keep his mouth shut."

"That's possible. He wanted to blab to the Feds about his friends when his boat didn't turn up. Murder generates a lot of scrutiny. If it was necessary to take out Goldberg, the stakes had to be extraordinarily high."

"That makes sense. Goldberg ran with a fast crowd who smuggled arms and people. Every one of them could be sent away for twenty years. I can only imagine how much cargo and how many people they had to shift to justify that kind of risk. I agree with you, murdering Goldberg complicates matters, but it stopped him from giving away their operations."

I tried to follow the thread of the argument as I fought to keep my eyes open, but it was a losing proposition. At some point, Sally slipped out so I could rest.

Drifting in that netherworld between consciousness and sleep, I still had the presence of mind to realize my dilemma. Since I hadn't found Goldberg's yacht, what should I do about his retainer? Should I contact the corporate attorneys handling his business affairs and return it?

In a panic, I wondered if he had a wife and kids, and whether anyone had contacted them with the sad news, but after a moment, I reconsidered. I doubted the wannabe party boy kept a family on the side. Still, I was in an ethical quagmire and unsure about what to do.

I swallowed another handful of aspirin before I drifted off. I turned on my side to find Marlowe curled up on the pillow next to my head. I'd figure out my next move in the morning after a good night's sleep. Like the song says, there's always tomorrow.

Chapter Four

The sun was up; it was a brand-new day, and my resolve to find those responsible for my client's death had intensified overnight, but unfortunately, so had my infirmity.

I had tossed and turned and groaned my way through the entire night. I finally gave up on getting any restful sleep, but I promised myself one day soon I'd even the score.

It was early, a little after eight o'clock, when I stopped in to see Scanlin. He was already in his office sipping his morning coffee. He took my statement, but offered no additional information about Goldberg's sudden demise. McAllister sat in on the briefing, but he didn't bother to speak at all. The man had no social graces; I suspected he merely grunted on cue.

"So, what's your next move?" Scanlin inquired.

"I thought I'd take a run down to Crisfield and check things out for myself."

"Even though you no longer have a client? Why bother?"

"Professional curiosity, I suppose. Besides, I don't like leaving loose ends."

"It's a long drive just to snoop around. What do you hope to find?"

"What I don't understand is how Goldberg ended up in southern Maryland. Someone must have tipped him off his boat was there."

"It could have been anyone."

"No, it had to be someone who knew Goldberg was desperate to get his boat back. He wasn't just ticked off that it got stolen; I believe he wanted to stir up trouble for those responsible. That is, until his boating pals put the fear into him. Possibly lured to his death."

They both sat on the edge of their seats, waiting expectantly. At the moment, all I could do was speculate; I had little to go on other than Goldberg's fantastic story.

Goldberg was antsy to retrieve his yacht, but I sensed he wanted a little revenge in the process. What better way to achieve his goal than to sic me or the police onto his former partners in crime? Although at the moment, I had no proof to support my supposition.

"Who would do that? What are you not telling us, Miss Carella?"

"I'm just wrapping up the details at the moment, Lieutenant. There may be nothing there at all, and if that's the case, I'll leave it to all of you, the police, to sort things out."

As I stood to leave, I caught the quick look they exchanged. I could tell they weren't happy with my answers.

I left the police station and headed for Crisfield, the southernmost point in Maryland along the Chesapeake Bay. It was a three-hour trip that took me through Salisbury, where I picked up Ocean Highway south to Somerset County.

I checked in with the county sheriff's office to let them know, as a professional courtesy, that I was working the Goldberg case. I explained my interest in locating Goldberg's yacht, and they directed me to the Crisfield Coast Guard station and suggested I ask for Chief Cloverman.

Twenty minutes later, I rolled into the historic seaside town and located the Coast Guard station along the picturesque Tangier Sound. As I entered the small building, a uniformed sailor came around the desk to greet me. Her uniform name tag read "Bowman."

"Hello. I'm Vic Carella, the investigator working the Goldberg murder. Is Chief Cloverman available?" I was purposely evasive about what kind of investigator I was, although I hoped she would make the wrong connection that I was police. No sense in giving away too much information without good reason, I always say.

Bowman's eyes went wide at the mention of murder. "I'll see if the chief is available." She scampered off to a back office where it was impossible to eavesdrop properly on their hushed conversation.

Soon a tall figure in an officer's uniform came forward, looking immaculate in what for him was probably everyday office attire. There's something about a man in uniform, wouldn't you agree?

I introduced myself and dived right in. "Thanks for seeing me on brief notice, Chief. I wanted to follow up with you on that murder victim, Mitch Goldberg. My office couldn't provide complete details, so I need to fill in the blanks."

Well, it was true…enough. Oh, don't start criticizing. This is how the job gets done.

He showed me into a tiny office crammed full of pictures of various craft at sea and other naval paraphernalia. Even to my untrained eye, everything was shipshape and Bristol fashion.

"Have a seat while I pull the report we sent over to the sheriff's department."

Chief Cloverman returned with a manila folder in hand and sat down at his desk. I wondered how he kept those sharp creases in his uniform from wrinkling while working behind a desk all day.

I pointed to a large map tacked to the wall. "How much area do you cover, Chief?"

"We handle most small boat traffic along the southern bay area." He pointed to an enormous expanse of open water along the Maryland–Virginia border. "For our mission, we have a forty-one-foot utility boat and a couple smaller craft for routine boarding inspections."

I wanted to establish a rapport with the chief, so I gave him a short rundown on my time with the 212th Military Police out of Fort Bliss, Texas. "I did one tour of duty stateside and another in Germany before returning to civilian life. I don't have much experience around water though."

Chief Cloverman laughed. "I've never been away from the Chesapeake Bay. It's been my home and my livelihood."

"Now there's a rarity."

"What information are you missing in particular?"

"When, where, and how was Mr. Goldberg's yacht found? My information mentioned Crisfield, but I need more specifics, if you don't mind."

The chief rifled a couple pages looking for the information I requested. At one point his brow furrowed, and he looked up at me with a steady gaze.

"Now I remember your name. As I recall, we found your business card in Mr. Goldberg's pocket and contacted the Metro police."

With flaming cheeks, I was forced into truthfulness, because the jig was up.

"Yep, you're right. You found my card because Mitch Goldberg was my client. I was helping him locate his stolen yacht, except somehow both he and his yacht ended up here at Land's End."

"You could have asked for that information, Miss Carella. We're not ogres down here."

"Sorry about the left-handed approach. Not everyone is as forthcoming as you."

Chief Cloverman closed the file and stood tall. I was being dismissed.

"Give me a break, Chief. Goldberg was my client for less than two days, and now he's dead. I feel responsible, and I want to find out who did this."

He cut me off, but then relented. "No more tricks, Miss Carella. As you are here, you may as well know the gist of it."

Cloverman sat back down and gave me a running summary of the report.

"At twenty-two hundred hours, my crew reported seeing Mr. Goldberg's yacht secured by a single line with no fenders deployed. With the changing tides, the boat could swing about, hitting the dock causing extensive damage. The crew chief boarded the yacht to speak with the boat's captain, whereupon he discovered the body.

We immediately contacted the sheriff's department, who came down to take charge of the investigation. Does that about cover it for you?"

"What was the condition of the body and the boat? Could you tell if there had been a struggle onboard?"

Referring to the file, he said, "The body was facedown at the foot of the steps leading to the VIP berths. According to the sheriff and the coroner, Mr. Goldberg was attacked from behind. Someone snapped his neck and pushed him down the stairs. I took their word for it since I don't do crime scene investigations. I do interdictions."

"Could you tell if anyone had searched the boat?"

"The contents of the cabin and cockpit were in their proper place. Except for the body, the boat was in perfect condition. It had not been ransacked as far as we could tell."

"Where is the body now?"

"The county coroner took it away. They're next door to the sheriff's office."

"I know where that is. And Goldberg's yacht?"

"It's moored in the impound area. We're waiting for instructions on what to do with it. Are you here to take charge of the vessel?"

"No, that's not for me to decide, but I'll let you know who will once I find out myself. Mind if I take a look at the boat?"

"Sure."

If everyone was as polite and helpful as the chief, my life would be easy. My earlier deception and subsequent embarrassment affirmed I had a long way to go when it came to being forthright with people. For too long, I'd relied on misdirection and omission.

The chief started for the door and then turned back. "By the way, has anyone broken the bad news to your client's significant other?"

"What are you talking about? From what little I know about him, I don't believe Goldberg had any women in his life."

"That's odd. We found four suitcases in one cabin, plus several boxes of new clothes in the other cabin, all of it women's clothing. The sheriff said to leave them until someone claimed the yacht."

Was Goldberg planning to make a run for it? Did he believe he could recover his beloved boat and clear out for good? Goldberg had held out on so many other details. Did he also neglect to tell me about some special person in his life? Was it possible there was someone out there waiting to hear from him, frantic with worry and not knowing Goldberg was already on that great *bon voyage* in the sky?

At the moment, I lacked insight into Goldberg's intentions during the last few hours of his life. I swear nothing about this case made any sense to me. Give me a straightforward divorce case, and I could predict with unerring certainty how people would act given certain stimuli.

"By the way," the chief said. "There's a hundred-dollar-a-day storage fee that adds up fast. Whoever is in charge of the decedent's estate might want to know that. When it gets to a certain point, we'll auction off the boat to recover our fees. Someone is going to lose a zillion-dollar boat over chicken feed."

"When I find out who's in charge, I'll let you know. May I see the yacht now?"

Petty Officer Third Class Bowman, recently promoted as I found out, was happy to escort me to Somers Cove, where they had Goldberg's yacht tethered. The marina was a short walk, so I solicited details from her point of view.

PO3 Bowman described how the news of the murder had electrified Crisfield, a small community of fewer than three thousand people, which hadn't experienced sudden death in over a decade. Crisfield was once world renowned for its record seafood production, but over time and with declining fortunes, the quaint seaside town was now a mere picture postcard of its former self. Crisfield had three centuries of history going for it, but its reputation was in jeopardy. The notoriety of murder threatened the bucolic lifestyle that was sacred to the local residents.

The *Bella Michella* dominated the small marina. Up close, the luxury pleasure craft did not disappoint; you couldn't ask for more. I could see why Goldberg got so excited over losing her. I envied how the one-percenters lived so well.

Bowman hopped from the dock to the gunwale and stepped down onto the aft deck among the luxurious comfort of cushioned lounges. I followed her lead, hoping I didn't make a fool of myself by falling into the water.

She unlocked the sliding glass doors, and we entered the opulent salon. To the left was an L-shaped sofa with a high gloss coffee table in front. Forward and to the right were freestanding chairs facing a flat-screen TV, and beyond that I could see the dining area and galley, complete with stainless steel appliances. There was even a dishwasher! To the right, the lighted stairwell curved down to the staterooms below deck.

I swear, if I owned a yacht like this, you couldn't pry me loose, but there wasn't a snowball's chance of that ever happening. I could forgive Goldberg for getting worked up over losing this floating Taj Mahal. The entire boat, inside and out, was immaculate to a fault.

We descended the teak stairs to the lower deck where the Coast Guard crew found Goldberg's body. There was nothing out of place to suggest how the former owner had met his demise. At the end of a short hallway, louvered teak doors led to the starboard and port VIP berths. I poked my head into the left-hand cabin, where I spotted the suitcases Chief Cloverman mentioned.

"Did anyone search these suitcases?" I inquired.

"We took a quick look, but no one's been on board since they wrapped up their investigations sometime Sunday morning."

I undid the latches, and a pile of women's clothes spilled out, clothes designed for the very young and hip. The revealing miniskirts, tank tops, and frilly off-the-shoulder blouses cried out "hot, hot, hot."

Upon inspection, I found each of the other three suitcases contained similar items. Next door, several boxes lay on the compact berth, each displaying the conspicuous gold logo of an upscale women's shop. The boxes contained more of the same stylish and provocative clothing; many still had store tags dangling from the hems.

What was Goldberg up to? I wondered whether he had some kind of unhealthy fetish. The idea of Goldberg as a cross-dresser flashed through my mind, but I crushed that idea in its infancy. Besides, these clothes were designed for someone fit and trim, so Goldberg's dignity remained intact for the time being.

"Have you ever seen the deceased or this yacht in the area before?"

"No, never. We'd have noticed a flashy boat like this one. All the watermen around here have working boats."

"Has anyone reported seeing several boats traveling together, maybe bar-hopping their way up and down the coast?"

"Not that I recall. Of course, we enforce DUI for boaters the same way the state police do on the highway. It's a bigger problem on the water than you can imagine."

"I see. How about a night spot, someplace that pulls in a lot of action? Is there a club nearby where a younger crowd hangs out?"

"Are you kidding? You tell me where and I'll meet you there. This place is Dullsville. The last time anyone partied in Crisfield was during World War II."

I thought about taking some of the new clothing to see if I could trace the stuff; it might be helpful to know what Goldberg was up to. In the end, I stuffed it all back into the suitcase and secured the clasps.

Why women's clothes? The thought returned that Goldberg might have a special girlfriend on whom he lavished his love and attention. Sabrina said she felt sorry for "the girls." Was there a link between Sabrina's girls and Goldberg's collection of hot-babe clothes? Like I said, so far, nothing made any sense to me.

When we got back to the station, the chief came out of his office.

"Everything satisfactory? Did you learn anything new?"

"All I can say is nice boat. I wish it were mine. By the way, Chief, perhaps you could advise me on something."

"How can I help?"

"How long would it take to sail a boat like Goldberg's from here to, say, Florida?"

"Why? Are you planning on taking charge of Mr. Goldberg's boat after all?"

"Just curious. Goldberg said he cruised down to Florida and back several times. I just wondered how long it normally takes."

"It's just a rough calculation, but given the size of the boat and estimating average cruising speed and fuel consumption, I'd say three days give or take maybe a half day. Of course, it depends on the weather and how long it takes to refuel. Let me know if you decide to take the yacht after all; I'll crew for you. I could use a vacation," he said with a laugh.

I'm sure you'll agree that from my perspective, three days on the water with a handsome and experienced sailor sounded like a pleasant way to pass some time, but regrettably, not likely to happen.

I thanked Chief Cloverman and PO3 Bowman for their hospitality and pointed my Audi toward home. On my way, I stopped at the sheriff's office to pay my respects to my departed client. The duty officer escorted me to the morgue next door.

I'd never lost a client before but felt ambivalent about Goldberg's death. Except for our brief encounter in my office, we didn't know each other at all. If I wanted to be noble about it, I suppose I should commit to finding his killer, or killers, and bring them to justice. Life could get so complicated.

Technically, it was a police matter now, but even as I told myself that, I knew me. I was constitutionally incapable of leaving things undone. The case had turned violent, and frightful, and dirty. He was a flawed man, yet when he got into trouble, he came to me for help. I confess, I had contributed little, but owing to a deepening resentment toward unseen forces, I now wanted to see this thing through for my client's sake. Besides, my overdeveloped sense of moral responsibility would not permit me to give up without a fight.

The visit to the morgue was worse than I had expected. The potent smell of formaldehyde coupled with the nauseous shade of green they used to cover the walls started my head spinning even before they wheeled out the body. They had him swaddled in white linen with just his face exposed. For the official records, and to satisfy the coroner's request, I formally identified the body.

"What happens now?" I asked the attendant as he rolled the body away. I was unsure of protocol in situations such as this.

"We'll attempt to locate his family, of course, but if no one claims the body in thirty days, we'll dispose of it." An inglorious end to a life not well spent.

"Let me know if you don't locate his next of kin." I gave him my contact numbers.

I left the morgue feeling depressed; the sight of Goldberg lying on that gurney affected me in a way I hadn't expected. I wanted to quit, turn over all my notes to Scanlin, and let him run with it. So much for the grandiose pep talk I had just given myself about following through.

A vision came to mind of that great oaf, Boris, when he bitch-slapped his girlfriend. I imagined an arrogant, boastful Boris and his gang as they plotted their secret excursions and made a fortune from smuggled contraband.

And what of Sabrina's concern for a group of heretofore unknown girls? Who were they? Where were they? How did they tie in? The fate of these mysterious girls, whoever they were, haunted Sabrina to a point that she agonized more over their plight than the immediacy of her own tribulations at the hands of Boris the Bastard.

A horrible thought came to me, which, if true, would cast the situation in a whole new light. Goldberg said they dropped off people at various locations, but I assumed he meant they helped illegal aliens get into the country. Once here, they no doubt blended into local communities to start a new life like so many others before them. In view of everything that had transpired, Goldberg's smuggling of illegals wasn't as altruistic as I first assumed. In all its ugliness and degrading forms, I suspected that the girls Sabrina alluded to were now sex slaves.

I theorized Goldberg got cold feet and wanted out but found the price of freedom too high. They stole his yacht to continue their smuggling operations, but Goldberg refused to accept the loss. He bucked the organization and even had the temerity to bring in outside help. That would explain why Goldberg had to be eliminated and, owing to our association, possibly me as well. His transgression forfeited both our lives.

It was pure conjecture, but as a working proposition, it made sense to a large extent. Second to money laundering, prostitution ranked as the primary revenue source for criminal activities in the US. Their lucrative operations depended upon a fresh supply of girls. It was just a theory, but it explained a lot that made little sense until this moment. I now saw the gang's entire operations from a new perspective, and it sickened me.

Something else occurred to me that made me just as nauseous. Provided my theory held together, what role did Boots Johnson play in all this? What was it Pete said? Boots was the negotiator; he brought the players to the table and facilitated the operation. Boris lacked the finesse to negotiate deals of that sort; he was the blunt instrument used to enforce discipline and keep everyone in line. The money angle required a smooth talker, someone with contacts, a dealmaker.

And there was me playing cutesy with the man who may have ordered my client killed. Without a twinge of conscience or a quantum of humanity, he condemned untold numbers of young women to a life of degradation, abuse, disease, and premature death.

Had he ordered the hit on me as well as Sally suggested? As she observed, he knew my intentions and my exact location last evening. This was my dinner partner from the other night, the one with the killer smile.

I pulled the car over to the side of the road before my stomach let loose. I wiped my lips with a tissue, but the vile taste remained.

Back at my office, it was after six by the time I finished typing the notes from my busy weekend and the trip to Crisfield. I still hadn't gotten over the shock of losing my client. I didn't know whether Goldberg had any next of kin, so I decided to contact his firm.

It was late in the day, but I decided to call Goldberg's office number. As the phone rang, I wondered who I should ask for, but the question became moot when a recorded voice came on the line directing all inquiries to the law offices of Warren, Sifkin, and Moore.

I chanced a call to the law office, and the receptionist put me through to James Warren, the senior partner handling Goldberg's affairs. I explained the reason for my call and inquired into Mitch's next of kin.

"As far as we know, Mr. Goldberg was a confirmed bachelor. He had no family, not even a distant cousin. It's most distressing, but at this juncture, it's a matter for the probate court."

As James Warren spoke, a certain inflection in his voice conceived in my mind an image of a wizened old-timer. Someone more comfortable taking his afternoon tea by a cozy fire, far removed from disturbing matters such as the sudden death of a client.

I summarized the Crisfield trip for him, told him where to recover the body, and also mentioned the mounting storage fees. The Somerset Sheriff's Department had already contacted the law office, but he assured me his firm would handle the funeral arrangements.

"There's also the matter of my retainer fee. I don't feel right keeping it since Goldberg located his own yacht. Shall I return the balance?"

"Let me ask you something. What are your immediate plans?"

"Once I turn over my notes to the Metro Police, it's their case. Why do you ask?"

"Your call may prove fortuitous and prescient. I, too, want closure to this dreadful affair. I'd like to commission you to carry on," he said.

His suggestion momentarily intrigued me, although I knew I was getting in way over my head. What did I know about arms smuggling and human trafficking? Ever since I got involved with the case, the threats had become increasingly personal. "I'm sorry, Mr. Warren, but it's a police matter now. They have all the resources at their disposal to follow through. Besides, it's not really my area of expertise. There's not a lot more that I can offer."

"Well, it was worth a try. Let's consider the matter closed and all debts settled, shall we? Thank you for your call. In case we don't speak again, I wish you all the best."

I disconnected the call and sat back. What started out as a promising case, far more interesting than the domestic trifling that normally came my way, had ended in total failure. It was time to close the books on this one.

Not every case was a winner, I thought to myself. I reached across my desk and was about to pull the chain on the desk lamp, but at that moment, my cell phone buzzed. I didn't recognize the number and was about to hit ignore, but then decided to take the call.

"Is that you, Ms. Carella?" a raspy voice croaked in my ear.

"No 'Ms.' It's just Vic. How may I help you?"

"It's not me that needs help, *Ms.* Carella. You're the one who needs looking after. If you know what's good for you, you'll forget you ever knew Mitch Goldberg. Do you understand?"

"It's no longer my case anyway, buster. The cops have it now. So you're too late."

"Smart girl. Just make sure it stays that way. Or else next time we won't be so gentle, not like before." The cackle in my ear sounded like a ghoul from some creepy old horror film.

"Kiss my ass, Jack! It's out of my hands now," I shouted into the receiver, but it was too late, because the caller hung up on me.

What was that all about? With Goldberg dead, there was nothing left to investigate except the murder itself, and that was definitely a police matter. So why the threat? Had I missed an important detail? And another thing—just who the hell did somebody think they were telling *me* to back off a case?

On impulse, I punched in a number and hoped that I wasn't too late.

"Mr. Warren? Vic Carella again. I've decided I want back in. Does your offer still stand?"

"I say, this is a pleasant surprise. What changed your mind in such a hurry?"

"Besides the fact that Mitch was my client, let's just say I now have personal reasons for wanting to see this through."

"Then by all means, yes, you're hired," he said. Then, like a field general dispatching orders, he added, "Report back to me when you find out who is behind this awful deed. And, of course, you'll let me know when funding becomes an issue, won't you? You'll have no problems in that regard, I promise you."

The rapidly changing events left me almost giddy with excitement, but I remembered to thank my new benefactor profusely for his generous support. With solid backing, I was back in the game. And I had my mysterious caller to thank for all of this. Right, like I'm really going to stay out of it. Puh-leeze!

Ever since I started nosing around inquiring about Goldberg's yacht, I knew Boris had a slow burn for me. I suspected Boris convinced Goldberg to meet him by dangling the return of his boat as incentive. When they were alone, Boris killed Goldberg outright; the brute-force solution was just his style.

And there I was crashing his little dockside party as the unwelcome guest, despite Boots's personal invitation. While I had assumed Boots sent his thug to rough me up and put me off the case, I now believed it was Boris all along. It was just his style, but it hadn't worked. Now tonight, the anonymous call threatening more violence if I did not cease and desist.

Well, too late, Boris, I thought. *I've accepted the challenge. Don't blame me for whatever comes next; it's all on you.*

Or so I told myself in a burst of bravado. I should have known Boris wouldn't take things lying down, but I'd soon find out.

CHAPTER FIVE

The next morning was almost a repeat of the previous day. I had intended to resume work with a vengeance, but the simple act of getting dressed nearly defeated me.

My bruised ribs had stiffened up overnight and reacted with violence to the slightest movement. Standing in front of my dressing mirror, I lifted my nightshirt to inspect the damage, only to find that I looked like I had been slammed into the glass by a pro hockey enforcer.

I suffered through the rest of my morning routine and finally arrived at a point where I could face the day. I did a quick mental review of where things stood.

Several lines of inquiry competed for immediate attention, such as why Goldberg would hoard a mountain of women's clothes onboard his yacht, which might coincide with young women being smuggled into the country. It was a cinch one overlapped the other, but I was determined to find out what was going on one way or another.

First things first, I needed to know when Boris and crew planned on leaving for their next Florida cruise. I assumed it was another procurement trip, and for the moment, I didn't have a clue about how to stop it. Following them was out of the question since I did not own a boat, nor did I have any knowledge of navigation. Besides, I think they would notice a lone boat dogging their trail all the way down the coast.

Before leaving my apartment, I went through my street routine once again and rechecked that my Glock pistol was securely in place. Unlike some people who carry concealed, I never minded the added weight. The way I figured it, you may need a weapon only once in your life, but for that one moment, you'll be glad it's there. I was ready for action.

I wanted to interview Sabrina, but first, I had to finagle a meeting away from the suspicious and ever-present Boris. Pete's earlier bio on each of Goldberg's friends also included their home addresses.

I headed back to Annapolis to locate the house that Boris shared with Sabrina, which turned out to be a comfortable Cape Cod. I drove around the block to get the layout of the neighborhood, and when I circled back, Sabrina and Katya Sevvin were climbing into a sleek blue Mercedes convertible.

I pulled alongside and called out, "Mind if I have a quick word?"

Sabrina appeared startled, and momentarily, I thought she might refuse, but then she acquiesced. "Not here. Follow me," she said and sped off. I had to go down the block a short way to pull a U-turn, and then drove like a demon to catch up.

We parked in the back lot of a diner just off Annapolis Road. I crawled into the back seat of the Mercedes and inhaled that distinctive new-car aroma. The dove-gray leather seats were buttery smooth and firm, a stark contrast to my modest mode of transportation. I didn't know where the meeting might lead, but at this point, I was flying by the seat of my pants and dangling in the wind. Or is that mixing my metaphors?

Sabrina and Katya half turned in their seats to face me. I didn't call attention to the black eye Sabrina sported, but I could empathize.

"The police found Mitch Goldberg's body," I announced, not bothering to sugarcoat it as I described the scene onboard the stolen yacht. The two women turned pale and got agitated, but it was important to short-circuit any useless discussion. It was time to confront the bad actors and their destructive behavior.

"Where is Boris?"

"Are you crazy? You saw what Boris is like. Why should we help you?" Sabrina said. Katya nodded in vigorous agreement.

"Here's what I think. Not only did that rat-bastard have my client killed, but he tried to have me whacked at the same time. I'm going to return the favor and burn down his little empire. I suggest you be someplace else before the fire starts."

"You don't know what you're talking about. Boris will see you dead first," Sabrina said, but it wasn't conviction that I heard in her voice. I waited her out.

"They're getting outfitted for another trip down south. We were told to stay away since there was no room for extras on this trip."

"Yeah, I overheard Anatoly on the phone with Boris," Katya offered. "They're taking three boats this trip. They've only done that one other time."

"What's so special about this trip?" I asked.

"All I know is Boris's contact says to expect an extra-large shipment of hardware." Katya squirmed in her seat to get more comfortable.

"Where are they now? At the Boat and Anchor?"

"No. They've got a little out-of-the-way place where they like to gear up," Sabrina said.

"The one off Riva Road, the Dirty Whaler?"

They glanced at each other and nodded in unison. "Yes, but how did you know that?" Sabrina asked.

"It's a matter of persistence."

I felt gratified to know my gut feeling about Mike Carver was correct. No wonder he didn't want to discuss Goldberg's missing yacht. The old second sight still functioned just fine.

"Tell me, how did Goldberg get coerced into all this? He didn't strike me as the adventurous type."

Katya said, "One day, out of the blue, Boris showed up with his new pal and introduced him around. The boys told him stories about the crazy parties, and they convinced Mitch he could make his brand-new boat pay for itself if he wanted to help. From then on, he was like a stray dog you couldn't get rid of."

Sabrina snorted at that. "Let me tell you about Mitch Goldberg, girlfriend. He was up to his fat ass in everything, just like the others. He didn't have much going for him in the looks department, if you know what I mean, but that dopey little guy sure knew how to make money! And he knew how to make it disappear too. Later on, he grew a conscience and tried to break away, but by then Boris had him under control...or thought he did until Mitch threatened to go to the police."

I shook my head. "That wasn't real smart. How did Boris react?"

"Boots Johnson was working a deal, and they still needed the *Bella Michella* to make it happen. When Mitch put up a squawk, Boris told him to pound sand."

Katya said, "Yeah, there are very few people in this world who can walk away from a multi-million-dollar boat, and Mitch Goldberg ain't one of them."

I perked up at the mention of Boots Johnson. "What was the deal?" I asked.

Katya said, "You mean what *is* the deal. It's still on. There's a big arms shipment coming from somewhere up north. It changes hands here, and eventually Boris and the gang rendezvous with their contact in Florida."

"Any plans for the return trip?"

Sabrina wagged her finger at me. "Hold on. We're spilling our guts to you, but what about us? I don't want the police showing up on my doorstep one day. Are you going to the police with all this?"

"Hell no. I just lost my first client ever, and I've seen what Boris is capable of. I don't want anyone else getting hurt because of my lack of involvement. I'm going after Boris and his crew, not you two."

"Me and my big mouth. I'm going to pay for this someday, I just know it," Sabrina lamented. "Mitch was harmless. I kind of felt sorry for him, but I guess it was inevitable."

"Why inevitable?"

"When Mitch threatened to go to the police, he sealed his fate, didn't he?"

"Tell me about Boris's operations. Is he dealing drugs too?"

"Boris doesn't do drugs, at least not yet. Smuggling girls and arms seems to be enough for now."

"Let me make a suggestion. In exchange for a fresh start, would you two be willing to testify against Boris and the others? You're in the unique position to shut down his entire operations."

Sabrina resisted, and then in a defeated voice, she said, "Do you realize what you're asking? Can you even conceive what Boris is capable of? I don't think you can. You've only seen the angry side of him, but trust me; you don't want to see his cruel side."

"Boris, Anatoly, and the others are into some heavy action, but I don't believe you want to be part of it. I'm going out on a limb here because I need your help to bust their smuggling racket. What do you say?"

Katya reached across the space between them and laid a hand on Sabrina's arm. "Go ahead, tell her. This is no life for any of us. Think of the young ones."

I waited while Sabrina decided whether she was all in. I didn't want to interrupt her train of thought, but once she started, the flow of words continued unabated. She described how Boris and his gang smuggled girls into the US and sold them on to other prostitution rings. The girls came from all over South America, Cuba, and the Caribbean islands. Setting foot on the golden shores of America wasn't as glorious as they were led to believe. Instead, it was the beginning of a never-ending nightmare.

"Dear God, I'm no better than Boris," Sabrina whispered. Her face was devoid of all expression. Her eyes were like dead things, staring into the past and revolted by what she saw.

Sabrina continued. "Suicide among the new girls runs high. And if they try to escape, Andre Adema hunts them down and hurts them so badly some of them end up…"

Now I understood Sabrina wanting to drink herself into oblivion night after night. In a low voice, I said gently, "It's not too late to make a difference."

"I've never lifted a finger to help any of those poor girls. I'm weak and too damned scared for myself."

They say confession is good for the soul, and I believed it. I could see Sabrina had made a decision, and from her reaction, Katya too.

"What can we do to help?" Sabrina said, as they awaited my instructions. The detailed information that I needed could only come from someone inside the organization. It was a dangerous proposition, but turning back was no longer an option. They both agreed they would find out as much as possible about the impending cruise and get back to me.

"One more thing along a personal line, if you don't mind." They waited in anticipation. "How does Boots Johnson fit into the organization? I don't understand his role in all this."

From the surprised expression on their faces, I now knew that, contrary to conventional wisdom, there *are* such things as stupid questions.

Sabrina asked, "You thought Boots was part of the prostitution ring?"

"Yeah, I mean, he and Boris are in this together, right? I figured Boots as the go-between negotiating the deals with Boris as the enforcer."

"You've got it all wrong. Believe me, no one is going to muscle Boris out of that lucrative spot."

"Then how is Boots involved?"

"Boots is a gunrunner, honey, not a pimp!" Katya said and laughed at the thought.

"Yeah, that's the other side of Boris's operations. Boris was running guns and military stuff on a small-time basis until Boots came along. Boots claimed he could arrange deliveries anywhere in South America."

Katya said, "That's why they're taking three boats on this trip; they're loading up on military hardware and other stuff."

"I thought you two were an item," Sabrina said, the inference being if we weren't then it was open season on one Boots Johnson.

"No, but I wasn't sure how he fit in. I assumed it had to do with prostitution."

"You've got Boots all wrong. He's the only one who keeps Boris in check, and that pisses him off because he heard what Boots is capable of. You've got to understand, Boris hates being told what to do, even when it involves a new gig, but then he doesn't control that end of the business."

"You mean someone else runs the show besides Boris? Who? Have you got a name?"

"Beats me. All I know is there's someone else higher up the food chain, most likely his New York contact. I know it's hard to believe, but when the word comes down, no matter how much he hates it, Boris gets off his ass and moves."

"When are they taking off? And where are they headed?"

"Andre Adema has a warehouse somewhere in St. Augustine where he imports fresh produce. They leave day after tomorrow. I'm sure that's where they're headed."

Damn! Only two days, but there was also the cruise time to factor into my schedule. I should have plenty of time to get in ahead of them to disrupt their plans. Whether they got busted for human trafficking or arms dealing, it made little difference to me.

I'm not sure where the feelings came from, but suddenly I had a pang of regret that Boots Johnson would get swept up in the sting. There was something about him that I couldn't quite figure out, but if he's going to cozy up to the likes of Boris, then on his head, so be it.

I left the two women at the diner and headed back into town. As I pulled out onto the highway, I thought I glimpsed a familiar face going in the opposite direction, but I didn't have time to worry about it. I was soon speeding back into town to work out my impromptu travel itinerary.

My ribs felt like they were on fire by the time I arrived at my apartment building. The painkillers had worn off, and I was hoping to catch a brief nap, but that thought went out of my head as soon as I saw Boots Johnson coming out of the lobby. He gave me a breezy greeting as if we hadn't seen each other in weeks. I'm no good at hiding my feelings, especially when I feel betrayed.

"Why the long face? Something I said?" he asked.

To avoid blurting out the truth, I stalled. "If you've heard about Mitch Goldberg, as I'm sure you have, then how am I supposed to act?"

Boots held up his hands in surrender. "That was not down to me. I simply heard he was nosing around Crisfield for his boat. I was as surprised as anyone when I heard the bad news."

I didn't know whether to believe him, so I changed the subject. "I'm thinking about taking you up on your offer to help, if it's still good."

"What's left to investigate? The police found Goldberg's body onboard his yacht. It's up to them from this point on."

I was on shaky ground here. I didn't want him knowing I was about to stick my nose into his business, since he'd been so ticklish whenever I broached the subject previously. My plan was to monitor him while letting him assume he was keeping an eye on me, although that kind of circular logic could land me in hot water. I attributed the fuzzy thinking to the continual pain in my side. Admittedly, it was not my best plan of action, but I had to shake something loose, so why not enlist my adversary in his own downfall?

"The police were here the other night when I got back from Annapolis. A Lieutenant Scanlin from DC Metro and his partner dropped the bomb about Goldberg."

"This is a Maryland case; what does DC Metro have to do with anything?"

"Apparently, the two departments are collaborating. They sent Scanlin to follow up after they found my card in Goldberg's pocket."

"Okay, so Scanlin mops up the details. End of story where you're concerned."

"It's not that simple. I…I just can't let it go. Not after everything that's happened. Look, do you mind if we go inside? I could use a drink."

We rode the elevator in silence. By the time we got to my door, sweat beaded on my forehead. The throbbing in my ribs let me know it was time for some more meds. Something in the way I held myself tipped off Boots to my condition.

Boots took the keys from my hand and opened the door for me. He helped me to the sofa and eased me down. I knew I had been pushing things a bit, but if this kept up, I might have to visit the emergency room for a little checkup.

"There's some medicine in the…" I started to say as Boots headed to the kitchen to see what he could find. He returned, holding the little green bottle that kept me going. I swallowed a handful of pills and lay my head on the cushions.

"What's the matter? Are you hurt?"

"I had a little run-in the other night after I left you. I was lucky Scanlin was already here and intervened before it got serious."

"What the hell happened?"

I gave him a steady look. Did he really not know, or was he merely being deceptive? I wasn't sure, and I didn't trust my instincts at the moment.

Boots leaned over and helped arrange the cushions so that I was more comfortable.

Really, if I just had a couple days, I'd be fit again. Why did I constantly push so hard? And what was in my DNA that made it so difficult for me to accept help when offered?

"How bad is it?"

"Like I went one-on-one with a truck and lost." I pulled up my blouse, and the rainbow of bruises attested to how I felt.

I could see the muscles tighten in his jaw, and his lips pressed into a thin line.

"Who did this?"

"I thought one of your Annapolis buds sent some-one to dissuade me from sticking my nose in where it didn't belong. The jerk came out of nowhere and hammered me good before Scanlin and his partner scared him off. Hey, it goes with the job."

"Don't be so flippant. This is serious. If I find out Boris or one of his boys did this, I'll make them pay."

"Don't go all Stallone on me. This isn't my first rodeo, you know."

We sat in awkward silence for a few moments. I thought, *I could like this guy, but if he insists on working the wrong side of the street, there is no future in it.*

"Listen, I've got to meet some people, but how about I pick up some Chinese takeout and meet you back here in a couple hours?"

"Wow, if I knew I could get this kind of service, I'd have jumped in front of that truck a lot sooner."

"Very funny. Stay put and try to get some rest. I'll be back soon."

With that, Boots went out the door without looking back. I stretched out and closed my eyes. I had things to do and people to see, but at the moment, I was too exhausted to care.

I had almost drifted off to sleep when my cell phone buzzed. So typical; just try getting a little shut-eye, and somehow the world will find you out. At first, I didn't recognize the number, but then remembered just in time.

"Mr. Warren, how are you?"

"Very well, thank you. I was hoping you could attend the memorial service I've arranged for Mitch Goldberg. It's rather short notice, but the memorial is tomorrow."

"Yes, you can count on me."

"Excellent. We'll meet at eleven o'clock at the Bethesda Memorial Gardens. It's on Arlington Boulevard."

"I'll see you there. Are you expecting many people?" I asked, wondering whether Mitch's boating buddies would dare show their faces.

"Under the circumstances, I suspect no one wants to be associated with the notoriety of violent death. I can't say I blame them."

"That's too bad. However, I'm looking forward to meeting you in person. Thanks for calling."

I lay back down and slept through the rest of the afternoon. I awoke when Marlowe kept pawing at my face and licking my hair. He can be an insistent little cuss. I rolled off the couch with a groan and went to fix his dinner. Behind me, I heard the lock rattle, and Boots came in, carrying way too many bags for just dinner. He set everything down on the counter and dropped my keys beside them.

"I picked up a few things, so you didn't have to go out."

"Thanks, I appreciate it."

Boots put the orange juice, milk, and eggs in the fridge. "Where does the rest of it go?" As I pointed, Boots quickly stored away the mountain of groceries.

I set the table while Boots laid out the feast. The smell of steaming Kung Pao chicken and beef broccoli filled the air, and I suddenly realized how famished I was.

I turned on the television, and we sat and ate mostly in silence as one presenter after another regurgitated the day's news. We caught a short blurb about Goldberg and his now infamous yacht, but there were no additional details we didn't already know.

"So, I was thinking—"

Boots interrupted before I could finish. "What are your plans now?"

"Why do you ask?"

"I was hoping you'd drop the case and let DC Metro or the Maryland State Police deal with Goldberg's murder. At this point, you're out of it, but if you keep snooping around, you're only inviting more trouble."

"I can take care of myself."

"Yeah, I see how that's working out."

"Hey, don't count me out yet. I'm just getting started."

"That's what I'm talking about. There's nothing more that concerns you. Let it go."

What was Boots driving at? He was getting awfully insistent that I butt out of the case. Was he worried that I'd screw up his big gun-smuggling deal? Was this his subtle way of warning me off? Or was he worried that I might piss off Boris more than I had done already?

We finished the meal in silence. The atmosphere was heavy with things left unsaid, questions that went begging for answers, but I knew we would not resolve things right then. We both were so heavily invested in our respective ventures it was impossible to walk away at a moment's notice.

I considered asking about the pending Florida trip, but something told me to keep *schtum* on that topic. That feeling of impending danger persevered. I still wanted to put Boris out of business, but with Boots in the picture, it only complicated matters. There was something there that I couldn't put my finger on at the moment. And I didn't trust my feelings just now; I worried I'd make the wrong decisions for the wrong reasons.

"You look tired," he said. "I should go."

I almost blurted out that he could stay, but caught myself at the last moment. What was I even thinking? It had to be the pain or the meds or possibly both. My head was all messed up.

"Don't get up; I'll let myself out. I may be out of touch for a few days, but I'll check on you when I get back. You have my number just in case."

"Stay safe out there. And thanks for everything," I said. It was weak, but it was all that I could manage at the moment.

CHAPTER SIX

I arrived at the funeral home fifteen minutes ahead of time to find a parking space, but I needn't have bothered because, as expected, the lot was vacant. However, had it been filled to capacity, it was impossible to miss the Rolls-Royce Phantom as it sat diagonally across three parking spaces. A chauffeur in full livery stood at parade rest next to the gleaming work of automotive art.

I received a smart salute from the driver as I crossed to the rear entrance that someone had left propped open. A hearse was parked under the portico with the rear doors wide open and ready to receive its forsaken cargo.

As I drew near, an elfin-like gentleman I took to be James Warren came out to greet me. The cut of his bespoke suit was flawless—was it Kiton or possibly Brioni? I couldn't be certain. Regardless, he and his tailor were fortunate to have each other.

"Ah, Ms. Carella, we meet at last," he said, taking my hand in both of his. "Come in—the service is about to begin."

"Please, call me Vic." As we started inside, I pointed to the Rolls. "I take it, that's yours?"

He gave me a crooked smile and shrugged his shoulders. "I allow myself a few extravagances. I admit to a weakness for the ostentatious, but I've worked hard all my life, and I cannot think of a single reason why I shouldn't permit myself the pleasure of being carted around in splendor." He gave me a wink and grinned like a mischievous boy getting away with something naughty. "It's over the top, isn't it?"

"We all dream, Mr. Warren, but it's the fortunate few who have the means to indulge," I said as I admired the ultra-stylish automobile. "You sure travel in style."

I followed him into the nondenominational chapel, where the sickly sweet scent of several floral arrangements assailed my nostrils. I stifled a sneeze just in time.

Inside, four somber men dressed in dark suits stood ill at ease near the coffin. By my estimation, they ranged in age from mid-sixties to late seventies. I had heard of people paid to attend funerals that would otherwise be underrepresented. I wondered whether James Warren had engaged professional pallbearers for the occasion.

Nearby, two stocky matrons in floral-print dresses and broad-brimmed hats stood alongside two younger women, one of whom wore a black pantsuit that accentuated her ample curves. The other was rail thin with an unhealthy pale complexion, as if by design she avoided all exposure to the sun. She wore a pleated black skirt, white blouse, short-waisted jacket, and the obligatory black hat to signify that she, too, was allegedly in mourning. They all were dry-eyed and grim.

James Warren conducted me to the front pew, and we sat down. His bony hand covered mine as he gave me a reassuring smile. He leaned close to whisper in my ear. "These ladies worked for Mitch at his investment company. It's sad, but I had to promise them bonuses besides their severance pay to get them to attend. The gentlemen are from my firm; I didn't give them a choice."

I got the feeling that had he wanted to, he could have filled the chapel to capacity at a moment's notice. I sensed no one refused requests from James Warren.

The group took their places in the pews behind us as piped organ music wafted from hidden speakers. A door to the left of the dais opened, and another somber gentleman entered the chapel, who I assumed was the funeral director. He gave a credible impression of a stork with his stooped shoulders and the way he clasped his hands behind his back as he approached the podium. He removed a sheet of paper from his breast pocket and began reading.

I won't bore you with the details. Suffice to say, the service was brief, almost terse, as the director read the scripted tribute to the life and times of Michael Quintus Goldberg. His monotonous voice droned on, and I confess I tuned him out.

Lost in thought, I considered the series of events that preceded this sad little scene, and I'm afraid emotion overcame me at the impersonal send-off. As I wiped away a tear, James reached over to pat my hand in sympathy. Besides us, there was no one to mourn his passing; even Goldberg's boating pals avoided his funeral. None of the clients that Goldberg had enriched bothered to attend, and no obscure relatives had come forward at the last minute to lay claim to his estate. It was a sad occasion, but after today, the memory of Mitch Goldberg would quickly fade into obscurity.

At the close of the brief service, the funeral director murmured a few words that passed for the closing prayer. Then we all left together. There was no graveside service; the funeral home had arranged a private interment.

As we walked together toward his Rolls-Royce, James asked, "Would you care to join me for lunch? You could fill me in on the details of your investigations to date."

"I'd like that. I've wanted to bounce ideas off someone, and you're better placed than most to advise me."

The courteous chauffeur stepped forward to open the car door, and I settled my derrière into the most opulent recliner seat ever made. The door closed on the ultra-quiet interior, completing the perception that the outside world ceased to exist.

James was like a kid at Christmas. With much fanfare, he demonstrated the many features he had installed in the Rolls, starting with the custom crystal ware, single malts, and built-in refrigerator.

He directed my attention to the original work of art he commissioned, which he mounted under protective glass on what you and I would call the dashboard, but the marketing folks at Rolls-Royce had transformed into a "gallery."

"Watch this," he said, indicating the paneled roof where hundreds of tiny pinpoints of light twinkled against the dark background. James manipulated a knob on the armrest, causing the blinking lights to morph into various constellations. It reminded me of the many peaceful nights I had spent stargazing while camping with my dad in the Shenandoah Mountains.

Overall, the Phantom was better appointed than many luxury homes I'd visited. It more than lived up to its reputation as the pinnacle in automotive achievement.

To say we drove downtown would be a gross understatement. The Rolls gently transported us as if on clouds through the busy streets of Washington and delivered us to the renowned Pascale-Dubois to sample some world-class French-Belgian cuisine.

I'd heard of it before, of course, although I've never had the pleasure. It was the kind of place where favored guests are greeted by name, and the chef catered to each according to their dining preferences. Little did James know I would have settled for something far less posh, but given what I'd observed about the old gentleman, I'm quite sure pizza and beer would have assaulted his senses.

James and the maître d' greeted each other like old friends. We sat near the stone hearth where a comfortable fire danced in the grate, and the murmur of conversation around us was not at all intrusive. The sommelier materialized and presented a bottle of Chateau Rieussec 2001 for James's inspection. While the bottle was being prepared, James offered a brief lesson in history.

"You'll like this vintage. The Carmelite monks founded the vineyard in the 1700s, and they knew a thing or two about wine. Tradition has it that a single vine produces a bottle of wine; however, when it comes to the Chateau Rieussec, the strict selection process might yield but a single glass. It's one of my favorites."

We touched glasses, and James offered a toast to a successful resolution to the Goldberg case as we sipped the excellent wine. He told an amusing story about how his father wanted him to follow in his footsteps and study law instead of the Bohemian, artsy-fartsy lifestyle he preferred as a young man.

"In the end, it came down to simple economics, as it always does. My father was specific about the disposition of his substantial estate, but it depended upon my circumstances at the time of his death." He chuckled as he reminisced. "The old man made it clear the choice was mine. I could follow my frivolous dreams and remain unencumbered by responsibility, or I could settle down and make something of myself . . . and inherit accordingly."

"I cannot picture you as frivolous."

"Those were crazy times back in the sixties. We all loved the hippie lifestyle as we chased after the elusive 'freedom' promised us. But, I assure you, I wasn't a complete fool. In the end, I made the old man proud."

"Given the two extremes, you made the right choice. I salute your foresight."

The server arrived to take our order. I didn't dare try to decipher the unpronounceable fare; instead, I let James order for both of us. He was a gracious host, and I felt comfortable in his capable hands.

James took another sip from his glass. "Now it's your turn. What is Vic Carella's claim to fame?"

I didn't know if he was genuinely interested in my background, but I gave him a brief summary of my time with the military police, and how, after leaving the army, Pete had set me up with a couple of Virginia firms that specialized in family law where I ran background investigations on potential clients and adversaries.

At the time, I wasn't sure where I was headed, but what started as part-time work evolved into a unique and lucrative service. These days, I'm the primary investigator for several firms, but it's taken every ounce of energy to achieve that modicum of recognition given that I am a squad of one and operate pretty much alone.

Although things weren't always as straightforward as I made it sound. I left out the part about growing up without a mother; cancer stole her away when I was twelve. My father, a career postman, did the best he could with a rebellious, wild child. However, a year after leaving high school, I joined the army, where a regulated lifestyle and good old military discipline had a dramatic influence on my life. Like they say, a little maturity goes a long way.

The server arrived, and I was curious to find out what my host had selected for us. The roast duck à l'orange was the house specialty, and the Chateau Rieussec was the perfect complement. We tucked into our meal with gusto.

"Have you identified who attacked Mr. Goldberg? I'm curious how he ended up in such evil company."

"I'm concentrating on the list of names Mitch provided me. He suggested they were into some shady activity, and I'm convinced that's what led to his demise."

I described meeting Boris and company in Annapolis, and ended with the police saving my bacon at the last minute.

As James Warren digested this information, I could see his distress as the creases in his lined face deepened, but he spoke with authority when he issued my new marching orders.

"I don't want you taking chances, Miss Carella. These people are little more than animals. Wanton, savage beasts. And they will stop at nothing to achieve their criminal ends. Promise you won't do anything that puts you in harm's way. You must contact me first. I can arrange any support you may need."

"That's very kind of you, but I can take care of myself. I've done so all my life."

"That may be true, but you are just one woman. An extraordinary woman, to be sure, but you cannot face this mob alone. I won't stand for it!"

His obvious concern touched me deeply, even though his request put me in a difficult position. Playing it safe wasn't my style, and it ran counter to getting the job done. Still, I'd hate to disappoint my benefactor, who expressed more concern for my well-being than anyone had in a long time.

"The thing is, Goldberg's friends are running a smuggling racket that I intend to bust wide open. The head honcho, a brute named Boris Zharkov, runs the show. Did Goldberg ever mention that name to you?"

"Not that I recall. Although, I'm aware he often looked forward to sailing with a new group of friends he'd met. I'm sure that's what prompted him to squander his money on such a foolish investment as a boat. Are you saying these people—these smugglers—are the same people Mitch mentioned to me?"

"I'm afraid so. They've been running girls and contraband up and down the East Coast for some time now."

"That's horrible. I'd never have done business with that man if I'd known the truth. Such depravity." Warren was red-faced and in danger of bursting a blood vessel if he wasn't careful. I tried to calm him down.

"The good news is I've got a line on their next jaunt down to Florida. If all goes as planned, I'll have enough evidence on their smuggling operations to turn the case over to either the Feds or the local authorities. I have a contact with the Metro police that may be able to help."

Warren looked thoughtful. "I'm still not convinced I should let you go off on your own, but you seem determined, Miss Carella. You remind me of myself in my younger days. Nothing could stand in the way of me obtaining whatever I wanted most. Ah, I envy you the thrill of the chase." His eyes twinkled again.

We topped off lunch with an excellent soufflé. If I never came back here again, at least I could say I'd dined at one of the finest restaurants in the nation's capital.

The chauffeur drove me back to Bethesda to retrieve my SUV. Even though I had a laundry list of things to do before I left for Florida, I made one more stop before heading home.

If things went sideways, I wanted someone to know where I was in case the unthinkable happened, and I was unable to contact anyone. I called Pete and told him to expect me.

Melanie met me at the door and handed me a glass of wine straight away. Not to be unkind, but she was rather nondescript in a mousy, intellectual sort of way. She was slim with straight brown hair and wide, round glasses perched on her upturned nose—not an unpleasant face, just somewhat forgettable. We'd never been close. She may have been unsure of my relationship with her husband or even jealous, but she'd always treated me in a cordial manner.

Pete sprawled in his easy chair, dressed in sweats and thick wooly socks. While he appeared casual, I knew his mind was always working overtime. He was impatient for the facts of the case. I filled him in as I had done with James Warren. When I got around to my pending trip to Florida, I could see the apprehension in his face.

"I plan to arrive in St. Augustine ahead of Boris and his gang. I need some hard evidence if I'm going to break up their little racket."

"I think we should call in the Feds. You may not grasp how dangerous the situation really is, Vic. Play it safe."

"There's no time for the Feds to mount a counter operation. I've got to act now."

"When do you leave?"

"I'm flying out Saturday morning. It takes about three days by boat, so Boris and his crew should arrive sometime on Sunday. That gives me plenty of time to get a line on their operation and possibly have them intercepted on the return trip. I couldn't care less about the hardware, but I am concerned about the human trafficking aspect. Why do you ask?"

Pete lowered the footrest on his recliner. "At least let me arrange backup for you."

I protested, but he waved me off. He went into his study to make a call. Melanie and I sat in companionable silence and sipped our wine.

Between you and me, the wine was okay, but I've always found Burgundy a bit too dry for my taste. I'd love more of that delicious wine James Warren had shared with me. It was unfortunate—or perhaps fortunate, as the case may be—that my tastes would forever remain quite pedestrian.

Pete looked pleased with himself when he returned. "I contacted a journalist friend of mine. He knows a retired Metro cop living in Jacksonville—Jimmy Courvelle. I called, and he agreed to meet you in St. Augustine to provide cover. You'll have to work out any compensation between you, but he's available. I'll email his contact details later."

"What happens if things get out of hand? Do we call in the local gendarme?"

"Follow Jimmy's lead; he'll know what to do. It's his territory."

I said I'd be in touch and got out of there in a hurry. The Burgundy upset my stomach, and besides, I needed my beauty rest. It was going to be a busy week, and I had a million little things to do before I left town.

On the way home, my cell phone chirped at me, and as I dug around in my purse, I wobbled in and out of my lane a couple times. I'm as guilty as anyone when it comes to distracted driving. It would be the death of me yet, I imagined.

"Vic? I'm glad I caught you." I heard the excitement in her voice.

"Sabrina, what's up?"

"There's been a change in plans. The Florida trip got moved up. They're leaving tonight."

"Tonight? Why the rush? What's happened?"

"I'm not sure, but Boris got a call earlier, and then he told the others to meet him at the Dirty Whaler to gear up."

"Is that where they stashed the shipment too?"

"I'm not sure, but they've already left. By the way, they're not using Andre's warehouse after all. Boris is meeting his contact at a small marina. From there, the stuff is heading to Miami and then will be smuggled out of the country."

"Sounds like they're improvising their plans. What's going on?"

"Beats me. All I know is they're hauling ass as we speak. I thought you should know."

"Wait. What about the return trip? Are they bringing back any new girls with them?"

"Nope, not that I'm aware of. Just down and back to offload the military hardware. And if I know Boris, he and the boys will hang around partying for a couple days before coming home."

"Is Boots Johnson cruising down with them?"

"Funny you should ask. I didn't hear his name mentioned, but I would imagine so since he arranged for the shipment to leave Miami by boat."

"I appreciate the info. I'll get back to you."

There was no question I had to follow them, but why the sudden change of plans? Had something or someone spooked Boris into action? I needed to get the goods on Boris before I turned him over to the police. This may be my only chance. I had three days at best before the window of opportunity closed.

I called Pete to let him know about the sudden change of plans. He voiced the same concerns that I had, but all we could do was adapt to the situation and hope for the best.

Well, damn, I thought, as I dropped my cell phone on the passenger seat. So, Boots was orchestrating this gig, was he? Too bad he was playing for the wrong team, but he'd have to live with the consequences when things didn't turn out as planned.

What's that? I know what you're thinking. So, yeah, maybe at one point I did have a soft spot for the big lug, but in case you hadn't noticed, he's working the wrong side of the street, so that's the end of that. I seemed to have a talent for picking the wrong guys. Still, I couldn't help thinking what a waste of a fine specimen of manhood.

Chapter Seven

The flight made a short stopover in Atlanta before reaching Jacksonville, where we were kindly treated to eighty-degree weather. I could appreciate why Northerners made the pilgrimage south each year. If I could trade drab Washington winters for these balmy southern climes, I might consider becoming a snowbird too.

Over the past couple of days, I spent a lot of time online familiarizing myself with the St. Augustine area. After I clued Pete about the schedule change, he came back with information that put things partly into perspective for me.

Sabrina confirmed there were no girls scheduled for the return trip to Annapolis. This coincided with the information Pete found out about the sex-trafficking trade, primarily controlled through Miami. And since Boris and crew weren't going anywhere near Miami, they could avoid the risk of attracting unnecessary attention and focus on the arms transfer.

The hour-long drive from Jacksonville to St. Augustine took me along I-95 until I eventually picked up US-1 that led me to the Southern Winds motel on San Marco Avenue across from the San Sebastian River.

I got checked in and headed to my room, which looked comfortable enough. Too bad I was only in town for one day. I'd love to spend a little time at the beach soaking up the sun, but I had to give it a miss this time. The local map conveniently provided by the front desk helped me get oriented with the locale. The Ponce de Leon Fountain of Youth was also nearby, another missed opportunity. I promised myself on the next trip I'd catch up on all the local delights.

I rechecked my notes. If Chief Cloverman's estimations were correct, Boris's flotilla should arrive in the next three to six hours, give or take a few, which would put them in the vicinity by late afternoon. However, I surmised they wouldn't attempt to move the hardware until well after dark.

I put in a call to retired police sergeant Jimmy Courvelle to see if he was available. He suggested we meet at the local pancake house nearby.

There was an empty booth along the front window where I sat down to wait. It wasn't long before a flashy Jeep pulled in. Clearly outfitted for rugged off-roading, the beefy tires munched loudly on the gravel drive. This being Florida, I assumed there were some serious backcountry mud trails to challenge the Jeep's four-wheeling prowess.

When Courvelle climbed down, I could see retirement had not affected the lawman one bit. He looked trim and fit and sported a Marine Corps high-and-tight haircut. His jeans were tight, and he wore a teal polo shirt that accented his tanned physique. And, of course, he had those ubiquitous mirrored shades perched on his nose. He looked like he was ready to roll out on the next shift. My kind of guy!

We made small talk as we waited for coffee. He had a certain aura about him, a calming effect that said, "Relax; I'm in charge now." Since I was in his backyard, so to speak, I'd have to depend on his knowledge of the locale. The waitress brought two steaming cups, but we declined her offer of menus.

I dispensed with niceties and dived right in.

"Boris and his crew should arrive sometime this afternoon or early evening. I expect they'll move the contraband sometime overnight. I want to setup surveillance ahead of time and record everything from the start."

"Can do, but why not have the Feds pick them up after they offload the junk? It would make things simple," Jimmy said as he slowly stirred his cup.

"So a handful of guys get busted for shipping some small arms, big deal. They'd make bail by tomorrow morning and flee the country in a skinny minute. I'm looking to shut down their whole East Coast operations from here to Annapolis, and possibly all the way to New York."

"Is this your doing, or are you working with someone?"

"I'm working alone on this, but to be honest, it's out of my league. I was hoping to secure enough evidence to hand off the case to a local cop I know, Lieutenant Alan Scanlin, Metro police. I owe him one. I'm not exactly equipped to handle this type of investigation."

"I know Scanlin, or rather I know of him. I heard he's a good man to have in your corner in a pinch."

"He's already helped me out of one jam. But by being here, I'm kind of treading on his toes, so I need some positive results before I go back and confess to meddling in his case. It's my case, too, although I'd prefer that he handled it."

"Where and when do you want to set up surveillance?"

I gave him the address to the Martinique Marina, the alternate location Sabrina provided where Boris would offload the hardware to waiting trucks.

"I know where that is. In fact, it's close by. I'll head over there now to scope out a good vantage point. We may need to improvise once I check out the setup. If necessary, we could always park a van nearby, but I'll let you know in a couple of hours."

I told Jimmy about Boris's other line of work, the human-trafficking aspect. "Supposedly, there are no girls slated for the return trip, so he may hang around and party for a couple days. But I must warn you; he's not someone to trifle with."

In a matter-of-fact tone, Jimmy said, "You let me worry about that."

I can't explain it, but suddenly I just knew, without a doubt in my military-like mind, that Jimmy Courvelle could deal with the likes of Boris Zharkov.

Jimmy said, "I'll call when the area is secured. It could be a long night, so make sure you eat something. And I suggest you dress warmly; the breeze coming off the water at night can get quite chilly."

We left the diner, each going in opposite directions. Back at the motel, I laid out the gear I'd need for the surveillance gig this evening, which included my Sony FDR recorder, the one with night vision. It's been useful on more than one occasion when gathering evidence on cheating spouses.

Divorce brought out the ugly in people and caused normally rational people to lose their ever-loving minds. It amazed me how inventive and devious people could be when defrauding their significant other of their rightful share of the family's community assets. Ah, the tricks one has to resort to just to make a living, but believe me, there was no shortage of clients or opportunities; everyone was at it one way or the other.

I also laid out dark clothes that would allow me to melt into the shadows. My blonde hair was a problem but easily solved with a wooly cap pulled down around my ears.

I ordered a pepperoni pizza for delivery but didn't devour it like I normally do, barely managing a couple of slices. I took a quick nap. If it turned into a long night, I wanted to be rested and alert for all eventualities. I was already feeling the anxiety of the moment.

When I awoke a short time later, my room was in shadows. It was only half-past six, but the autumn sun had nearly disappeared. I rechecked my gear for the umpteenth time and then turned on the television, but the local news was all too familiar despite the change in venue; robbery, murder, political corruption—nothing ever changed no matter where in the world you found yourself.

I switched off the TV and went to stand by the window. Finally, my cell phone chirped, and I fairly leapt on it. It was Jimmy letting me know the coast was clear. I left immediately for the marina just off the Vilano Causeway.

Jimmy had instructed me to park near the entrance to the marina on the west side and meet him in front of the St. Augustine Sailing Society near the dock.

The building was dark, and the parking lot nearly deserted when I arrived. I shouldered my backpack and quickly covered the short distance to the club. Jimmy emerged from the shadows as I approached. He dressed for the occasion, too, only he opted for the military look, complete with black fatigues tucked into the tops of his combat boots. He had refrained from camouflage facial paint, which might have been a bit much to take.

The AR-15 that hung muzzle-down from a single-point sling was an impressive-looking rig. He outfitted the short-barreled black rifle with a night scope, silencer, and thirty-round mag. It was the ideal weapon for close-quarters combat. It never occurred to me we'd encounter trouble of this magnitude, but obviously, Jimmy wasn't leaving anything to chance. No doubt about it, Jimmy Courvelle was ready to rock and roll.

Silently, he motioned for me to follow him. He parted the hedge surrounding the front of the sailing club, and we stepped into the dark recess close to the wall of the building, where we were completely surrounded by the thick shrubbery. Peering through the branches, we had an unobstructed view of the small marina from our strategic position. It was perfect for my needs; there was just enough room for us to maneuver, plus we had a direct line-of-sight to the docks along the bulkhead.

I removed the folding tripod from my backpack and threaded the recorder onto the mounting plate. I set the device to record to check the focus and ambient light, made a few adjustments to the aperture setting, and then placed the device on standby. I even remembered to cover the red recording light next to the lens with black electrician's tape. I didn't want to give away our position inadvertently; Boris might not react too kindly.

While we waited, we remained silent, knowing sound easily carried over water. Someone standing on the other side of the small harbor might detect our presence. We settled in for the wait, not knowing how long before Boris and company arrived or whether he would show at all.

As we huddled together in the confined space, I considered whether Boris was the devious type who might set up the marina drop as a double-blind, not trusting his own people to keep their mouths shut. He might be sufficiently paranoid or suspicious to have a last-minute change of heart and redirect his crew to another location.

Paranoia was the bane of investigators; you could never be sure your quarry would follow through on projected plans or suddenly change direction in a constant vigil to avoid capture. The uncertain world inhabited by terrorists and drug lords was replete with stories of fugitives so infected with paranoia that they were constantly on the move, never staying two nights at the same location. However, based on available information, we were committed, and now only time would tell.

I found myself constantly rechecking my watch, which, of course, made the time drag by even more slowly. It was a little after nine o'clock when Jimmy reached out and touched my arm. He motioned toward the mouth of the harbor, where we observed three cruisers silently making their way single file into the marina.

The lead boat was outfitted with a spotlight, and someone constantly swept it back and forth across the marina. The beam flashed once across our hiding spot, but there was nothing to give away our position. I switched on the recorder to capture what I hoped would be the damning evidence I needed to drive a stake through the heart of Boris's operations.

The two trailing cruisers came to a halt while the lead boat maneuvered parallel to the bulkhead. Two men leapt onto the dock with lines in hand to secure the boat.

Behind us, we heard heavy vehicles approaching the marina from the main road, and right on cue, three cargo vans turned into the marina parking lot. In turn, each swung about and backed toward the dock. Several men emerged from each truck, flung open the sliding doors, and waited expectantly.

Boris disembarked, but even in the dim light, his massive hulk was identifiable from a hundred yards. He approached one of the truckers, a short man in coveralls. They shook hands and chatted a bit. Boris turned, waved his arms, and pointed, and then everyone jumped into action.

From below deck, crates appeared and were handed off to the men on shore, who quickly stored them in the waiting vans. They worked smoothly, and with such efficiency, you'd think they had done this sort of work before. Yeah, probably hundreds of times.

I caught a glimpse of Boots Johnson high up on the flybridge as he looked down on the men at work. Not one to get his hands dirty, Boots appeared content merely to observe the activities.

As the men finished unloading one boat, the next one quickly took its place, and the transfer continued unabated. They worked tirelessly from start to finish and completed the transfer in about forty-five minutes.

Other than alerting me to the flotilla's arrival, Jimmy was silent throughout the dockside activity. The pair of binoculars slung around his neck remained glued to his eyes during the transfer. He swept the harbor to ensure there were no hidden dangers on our flanks.

Finally, the last of the crates were stored in the vans. The sliding doors were noisily slammed shut and locked, and then the men scrambled into the cab of the trucks.

Jimmy and I watched the short trucker approach Boris. Boots jumped down from the boat to join them. There was a brief conference, and then they shook hands all around and quickly separated. The small man hopped into the cab of the first truck, and the small convoy pulled away. Boris made a circular hand signal above his head, and all three boats fired up their powerful engines in preparation to head back out to sea.

In the commotion, I lost sight of Boots Johnson, but I assumed he was already onboard. The trio of boats glided out of the marina and soon disappeared from sight.

Jimmy broke our enforced silence at last. "Did you get what you came for?"

I assured him that I had indeed. He held the backpack for me as I repacked my gear.

"It wasn't much to watch, but I now have proof Boris is smuggling arms. I'll let the police, or possibly the Feds, make the case. Let's get out of here."

"Um, if it's all the same to you, I think I'll head back to Jacksonville tonight. Not that it hasn't been fun—quite the opposite actually—but I'm going to hit the road."

"What can I say? It's been a pleasure meeting you, and thanks for backing me up tonight," I said. "I'll drop you a check when I get back. Are you sure I can't buy you a drink or something?"

"You go ahead. But the next time you're in town and feel like a little sun and surf action, call me. I'll be glad to show you around."

It was a gentle pass, not in the least offensive; besides, there was no harm in trying. Who knows, maybe a little time on the Florida beaches is what I needed. I told him I'd keep it in mind, leaving the prospect of a return visit open for the time being.

Jimmy carried my backpack to the car and placed it on the passenger seat beside me. With a quick wave, I made a U-turn and headed for the exit. I tried to remember the reverse directions that would lead back to my motel as I scanned oncoming traffic before pulling out.

I threw a quick glance in the rearview mirror and saw Jimmy still standing near the sailing club, watching as I left. In that brief moment, I saw a shadowy figure cross the parking lot and approach him. There was something distinctive in the way he moved. I hesitated for only a second, and then gunned the engine to merge onto the Vilano Causeway.

What the hell? What was Boots Johnson still doing here? And what were he and Jimmy Courvelle up to?

As I pulled away, I took a quick look over my shoulder and saw the two men heading toward Jimmy's Jeep.

I sped up and eased into the left lane, and about a half mile later, turned into the Vilano public boat ramp. I whipped the car around, facing the causeway, then killed the engine and lights. The parking lot was empty at that time of night. I hoped I wasn't too conspicuous sitting alone in the deserted lot.

About a minute later, I watched as the Jeep passed by the public facility. The headlights of approaching traffic briefly illuminated the vehicle, and I could make out two passengers in the four-wheeler.

Confused and worried, I couldn't get my head around what I just witnessed. Was I being set up? Was Jimmy part of Boris's crew? Did he rat me out to the opposition?

It was risky, but I made a fast decision. I cranked up the little Toyota rental and tailed the two of them to see what I could find out.

If indeed I had been betrayed, it meant that throughout the entire surveillance, I was in proximity to someone who quite possibly had orders to keep me quiet—at all costs. I thought of Goldberg, and a cold shudder coursed through my body.

Was it possible Jimmy knew Boris and was sent to keep an eye on me while the arms transfer took place? Was there even any incriminating evidence in those crates in the first place, or was it all an elaborate setup? Perhaps Boris and crew had already offloaded the hardware elsewhere, and they staged this for my benefit to put me off the case.

I toyed with the idea of contacting Pete, or possibly Scanlin, to have the Florida authorities intercept the convoy before it reached Miami, but I doubted they could mobilize local law enforcement that quickly.

Up ahead, I kept an eye on the Jeep's distinctive taillights. I hung back in traffic far enough to avoid being spotted, but not so far as to lose sight of my quarry.

At the light, the Jeep turned left onto San Marco Avenue, heading south. I sped up as I approached the intersection. I was afraid if I got too close, they'd spot me, but I couldn't risk being left behind if the light suddenly changed. Tailing someone on a busy street was a lot harder than it appeared in the movies. Of course, anything was possible when carefully scripted in the make-believe world of the cinema. This was life on the streets where, more often than not, things hardly ever went as planned.

The Jeep continued on San Marco, which eventually changed names to become Castillo Drive, although we were on the same stretch of road. We appeared to be headed for the historic district. As we approached the Bridge of Lions, the street name changed yet again to become Avenida Menendez.

Suddenly, brake lights glowed, and without signaling, Jimmy made a tight left turn ahead of oncoming traffic into the St. Augustine Municipal Marina along the Matanzas River. I went right and parked in the Coastal Motor Lodge opposite the marina. Retrieving my camera, I quickly attached the bulky telephoto lens before stepping out of the car.

Palm trees lined the Avenido Menendez, and I tried to make myself as inconspicuous as possible as I peered around a tree. From this vantage point, I watched Boots and Jimmy descend the metal gangway to the floating docks and head for the center console fishing boat tied up in the first berth. At the helm stood a slim man in jeans wearing a sports jacket over his white T-shirt. From their casual greeting, I deduced a certain familiarity between them.

I assumed this was the South American contact Boots was using, and that they were about to conclude their arms deal. This was the part in *Miami Vice* when Sonny Crockett showed up with a briefcase full of cash, but nothing so dramatic happened here. I still couldn't figure out how Jimmy Courvelle fit into all this. The more this case played out, the more it didn't feel right.

Through the viewfinder, I got a good look at "Lanky," as I had dubbed him. He was tall and skinny like a basketball player and had a lean, clean-shaven face. He kept his dark hair clipped short. I snapped a string of shots as Boots and Jimmy climbed onboard. Soon everyone had a beer in hand as they lounged on the cushions and talked…and talked.

An hour later, they were still at it as they happily downed one beer after another. I don't know what I expected might happen, but I felt conspicuous standing along the busy thoroughfare holding a camera with a telephoto lens. From anyone's perspective, it was obvious I was keeping watch on the marina, but there was no way I could approach without being seen.

Well, no kidding, genius, I thought. It was the ideal spot to hold a guarded conversation. They could quickly spot anyone approaching their position and change the subject as necessary.

Across from me and next to the marina was a restaurant erected on pylons. Late-night diners crowded the deck tables. I considered taking up a position there to get a closer look, but it was impossible to conduct surveillance in such a public place. Right then, I'd have given anything for a parabolic microphone so I could hear what the three men discussed. I wondered if my name came up in conversation. Not out of vanity, you understand, but I'd have bet yes.

I was having trouble figuring out the dynamics between a retired cop, a hood, and a man with a boat. I doubted Lanky was merely an old fishing buddy given the company he kept and the hour of their clandestine meeting. Was he also part of the smuggling racket? How were these three related to one another? Again, not being vain, but what did they have in common besides me and my ongoing investigation into Boris's affairs? And if Jimmy was in league with Boris and company, why did he let me walk away with all that footage? Was I in danger?

They continued talking quietly as if they hadn't a care in the world, but I was tired. I wasn't sure how much longer I could keep up this vigil. I'd already gotten some curious looks from people out for a late-night stroll. It would be just my luck to get busted as some kind of pervert or peeper.

I was almost ready to pack it in when I caught movement onboard the boat. I zeroed in with my long-distance lens once again just as Boots and Jimmy stepped onto the dock. I took a few more candid shots, but the party had broken up, so I got out of there myself.

Back at the Southern Winds, I prepared for an early morning departure, but that took hardly any time at all. I was too wired to go to sleep right away; instead, I wrote up a few notes to hand off to Scanlin when I got back.

I replayed the video footage of the gang unloading the hardware, noting the names of those I recognized along with the number of crates they shifted. The surrounding buildings and landmarks were easily recognizable despite the dim lighting.

I also reviewed the pictures I'd taken with my digital camera. There really wasn't much to see as I scrolled through all the shots—just a dull beer party from my point of view.

Near the end, something caught my eye. I reversed several times and went forward frame by frame, looking for the one oddity that I felt sure I'd missed earlier.

At first, I hadn't realized what I'd seen, but I spotted it in a shot of Lanky shaking hands with Boots as he prepared to leave. There it was again in the next frame when he and Jimmy shook hands.

I enlarged the images and reexamined each in detail, but there was no mistake. The flap of Lanky's jacket was open, and I could see a badge attached to his leather belt.

Well, what do you know? Lanky, or whoever he was, appeared to be a lawman.

After supervising the transfer of illegal arms, presumably on their way to South America, here was Boots and Jimmy having a friendly beer with a cop. I pondered the ramifications, wondering whether Boots had a couple of crooked cops running interference for him, or conversely, could this be a legitimate meeting between law enforcement agents?

If that were true, what was the nature of their relationship? Did that make Boots a snitch? Inexplicably, I found that distasteful, even though it should have cast Boots in a more positive light. But somehow I could not see Boots ratting out his colleagues, no matter how loathsome he found them, unless, of course, the cops had something on him that forced his cooperation.

If Lanky and Jimmy were legitimate lawmen, then I found it strange that the police hadn't swooped in to round up everyone once they completed the transfer. I mean, the trucks carrying illegal arms were easily identifiable and could be stopped anywhere along the highway. And they could impound the three vessels used to smuggle the arms along with the arrest of Boris and his entire crew. By anyone's standards, it was a huge bust.

Another thought occurred to me, but with everything else I'd learned in the last few days, I didn't know whether I could trust my judgment.

What if Boots was working undercover?

That would put a fresh perspective on everything; it would explain how he moved in and out of the country so easily, and why his name appeared on so many law enforcement databases. And now this clandestine meeting with a couple of actual lawmen, as if they were old friends.

Perhaps Lanky was Boots's handler, his liaison to one of the three-letter agencies that investigated international smuggling. But how could I confirm my suspicions without tipping my hand? This was not the kind of information that was handed out freely.

I needed to contemplate this confusing development a while longer. There were others more familiar with these matters than me I should talk to. This was way outside my scope of expertise, not to mention my limited resources.

When I got back to DC, I'd ask Pete; no doubt he'd know who to contact. Or perhaps I'd go straight to Scanlin and let him run with it. Or even James Warren; I was sure he could advise me on the best course of action. He would know who to contact and how to present the information in a way that kept me out of the line of fire.

One thing was for certain: the case had suddenly become more complicated. Rather than coming up with answers, I now had lots more questions.

Chapter Eight

Monday morning I was back in the office documenting my trip down south. I had spent all day Sunday being lazy and catching up on some needed sleep. Later on, I got myself organized for the coming week. Marlowe seemed glad to have me back home; he followed me from room to room as I puttered around the apartment. Midafternoon, he curled up on my lap, and we both had a long nap.

After typing up my notes, I put in a call to Scanlin, but he wasn't available. I left word for him to get in touch; I wanted to hand over everything and put this case behind me as soon as possible. What with Goldberg's death, Boris's smuggling operations, and the personal threats, by comparison, my old life of chasing delinquent spouses and staking out divorcees looked damned attractive to me right now.

It was time to put Pete into the picture as well, and besides, I had a bone to pick with him.

When I arrived at the *Statesman*, I caught him between meetings, but he insisted on hearing all the gritty details. I ran down the whole routine from the surveillance setup through the arms transfer. It was hard to glamorize a boring stakeout for the benefit of my friend, who had suddenly become an armchair detective. Poor old Pete needed to get out from behind his desk more often.

Then we got down to cases.

"How much do you know about Jimmy Courvelle?"

"Hardly anything at all. He's a friend of a friend. Why?"

"Do you know if he's still active or truly retired from law enforcement?"

"He was a Metro cop for nearly twenty-five years, then suddenly put in his papers and moved down south. There's a reporter here with the *Statesman*, Rayshon Marshal, who put me on to him. Again, why do you ask?"

"Oh, no reason, really, except that he's in cahoots with Boots Johnson."

Pete squawked at that and demanded more information. I laid it out for him from the moment the arms transfer concluded until I left Boots, Jimmy, and Lanky at the public marina.

"Boots may have a couple dirty cops working for him, or else he's compromised, and they're using him to get to Boris. Regardless, they've got a sweet setup going for them, but you'd need a program to tell who's on which side."

"I could dig deeper into Courvelle's background, but I trust Ray. He wouldn't do me wrong, and by extension, you either."

"For crying out loud, Pete, for all I know, I was sitting next to a guy who had orders to slit my throat. And then he and his bud casually go drinking with some other dude whose affiliations are still suspect. Gosh, I want to do that all over again."

"Take it easy, Vic. I truly believe you weren't in any real danger."

"Oh, you believe that, do you? You weren't there."

"You gonna let me explain? There's a story going around this morning that hasn't hit the wires yet about a big bust near Miami, just outside US territorial waters. Seems the Coast Guard intercepted a shipment of small arms and antitank missiles. Missiles, Vic! What does that sound like to you?"

I knew exactly what it sounded like, but it also sounded too convenient.

"If that's true, then Boris is in a lot of trouble, and not only with the Feds."

"So it's possible that Jimmy Courvelle, Boots, and this other player, who may or may not be a legitimate lawman, tipped off the Coast Guard, and *viola!* They get a big result," Pete said with a flourish.

"For that to happen, Boots Johnson would have to be working with the Feds."

"Or he could be a federal agent himself," Pete observed. "Did you ever consider that?"

"As a matter of fact, I did. How do we find out for sure?"

"Leave it with me; I'll ask around…quietly, of course. There may be other factors in play we're not aware of."

"Okay, but get back to me as soon as you can. I need to know once and for all which side Boots is playing for. I just hope it's for the home team."

"Oh, you do, do you?" Pete leered at me and gave me a look like I'd just revealed some big truth.

"Let's just say I've got this certain vibe about the guy. He's different."

"Different in what way?"

"With Boris, I'm sure he'd like to get me alone and do to me what he did to Goldberg. I don't get that same feeling with Boots. Call me strange, but I feel secure around him."

"Be careful, Vic. You're running with a tough crowd. Remember what I said about the Feds maintaining surveillance on your boy. There's got to be a reason for that."

Actually, I hoped Boots wasn't in the tank with Boris and his crowd. It didn't feel right, but then what do I know about the smuggling business other than I still planned to hit Boris where it hurt most—in his fat ass where he sits on his fat wallet.

We speculated on the repercussions Boris would likely face. The blame for losing the shipment so soon after the transfer would undoubtedly fall to him. I mentioned the likelihood that a gang war could erupt.

"No big loss as long as Boris and his crew are the ones getting whacked," I said.

"Careful, Vic. Don't lose your perspective, or you might find yourself as jaded as the crooks you're trying to take down."

"No chance of that," I said as I headed back out on the streets. But Pete's words echoed in my head, and I wondered if he was right. Often he acted as my alter ego and saw things more objectively than me.

Was it merely wishful thinking that Boris would finally get his comeuppance, or was I in danger of becoming a cynical, hard-bitten bitch? No, I wouldn't let it happen, not as long as I kept my eye on the goal.

Exactly what was my goal now that Boris had lost his precious shipment? How did I see the case playing out? So what if Boris lost one shipment? There likely would be others. And what about his involvement with sex trafficking; that hadn't stopped as far as I knew. What happened to the young women caught up in the world's oldest and still lucrative profession? Who spoke for them?

I needed to assess my motivations for continuing this case. Was I pursuing Boris truly for the sake of the unfortunate women involved, or had I become too involved? Given Pete's astute observations, along with everything else that had happened to me lately, it felt an awful lot like I had turned into a crusader after all.

I suddenly realized just how obsessed I'd become with putting an end to Boris's operations. The man was living rent free in my head and clouding my judgment to the point nothing else mattered. Too many questions were spinning through my mind. I needed to slow down and analyze the end game.

It wasn't a matter of having access to resources. There were plenty of options available to me, and any of them could easily put a stop to Boris's filthy business. There was Scanlin and McAllister, two able cops standing in the wings who would love to know what I knew at the moment. If not them, there was a plethora of government agencies equipped to handle the situation. I could easily hand off to any of them, knowing they could produce results faster than me. There was my new friend and mentor, James Warren; an old-school warrior who certainly knew his way around bureaucracies and the law. Overall, there were plenty of resources at my disposal to hasten the demise of Boris's illicit operations.

I tried to reach Scanlin again from my cell phone, but it was still a no-go. I headed over to my favorite watering hole for a beer.

Each Monday night, the football crowd rolled into the Old Market Grill, but I didn't plan on hanging around long enough to join the raucous fans at the bar come game time.

Sally took one look at me and shook her head. Given my line of work, she sometimes got overly concerned for my safety. Believe me, it was nice having someone looking out for your welfare, but she needn't have worried so much.

"Did you get your cat back in one piece?" she asked, knowing how my neighbor coveted Marlowe in a big way.

"Yep, my big guy's back at home."

Marlowe often stayed with my neighbor, old Mrs. Shepherd. She didn't care for me or the hours I kept, and she was always telling me how Marlowe deserved a better momma. Despite her low opinion of me, I was grateful to have someone look after my baby whenever I couldn't get home on time or had to leave town in a hurry.

Without asking, Sally placed a Corona on the bar as I sat down. Okay, so I'm a creature of habit. Who isn't?

"Was it worth it? Did you get whatever it was you went after?" she asked while keeping an eye on her crowded bar.

"Easy-peasy," I said. "Not a single hitch. I can't wait to hand it off to the local authorities. As far as I'm concerned, I'm through chasing down Boris and his crowd."

The relief showed in Sally's smile. "Good. I was afraid you were getting in deep with people you had no control over."

"You should have seen it. They offloaded a ton of hardware destined for who-knows-where. And right in the middle of it all was my boy, Boots Johnson.

"Um, Vic…" Sally started to cut me off but was a beat too late.

"Did someone mention my name?"

I swiveled my barstool around and came face to face with Boots Johnson. He looked like he'd just come from an executive board meeting with his dove-gray silk suit over a light-pink shirt and steel-gray tie. He motioned for a Corona as well.

"Oh, hi. We were just talking about you," I admitted, trying to cover my embarrassment at being caught out. "I was telling Sally about the not-so-great party in Annapolis; quite a strange collection of people."

I wasn't sure he bought my line of bull, but I plowed on. What the hell was I doing talking out loud about things that could get me whacked? Had I suddenly lost all perspective?

"I hope you don't mind, but I took a chance that I'd find you here. A lot has happened since Sunday, but I never got a chance to apologize for Boris's behavior. He went crazy for a little while."

"You can say that again. I thought Boris was going to clobber me right there in the bar. Whatever happened to his girlfriend? I felt sorry for her." I was backpedaling as fast as I could, but I didn't sense any hostility from him.

Boots eyed the rapidly filling bar and happy-hour crowd. Sally hovered nearby, mixing drinks. He clearly wanted a private word with me.

"Let's get a table. We need to talk. There are things you should know that will help keep you alive."

He caught me by surprise, but put that way, how could I refuse? We carried our drinks to a booth in a remote corner of the restaurant. Boots came straight to the point.

"First, you need to understand that, out of necessity, I do business with people who have no conscience when it comes to murder, torture, or personal destruction. Are we clear on that?"

"I kind of figured that out for myself. Boris isn't exactly the subtle type."

Boots picked at his beer mat, tearing small pieces from the frayed corner. "He's only part of it. I'm afraid that, from my end, things are accelerating way too fast. I came to warn you; it's imperative that you be on your guard at all times from now on. Do you understand?"

"I appreciate the concern, but why? What's happened?"

"The fact is Boris has gone berserk. He's in deep trouble and lashing out at everyone he sees as a threat. You should know your name is at the top of his hit list."

"You mean because I started poking around and suddenly the Coast Guard confiscates his arms shipment?"

"You appear to be well informed. That just went down within the last twelve hours. How did you find out?"

"Friends with deep connections."

"Oh, yeah, the reporter fellow. I should have known." Boots shook his head.

Something was in the air, but I wasn't sure what. On a hunch, I took a chance.

"I think it's time we were honest with each other. I was in St. Augustine and watched as they offloaded all that hardware. But, of course, you know that already courtesy of your pal, Jimmy Courvelle."

"That's right. I knew you were there all along, but it's not what you think."

"So straighten me out on what I think. Tell me, are you a federal agent?" It was his turn to be caught by surprise. The look on his face removed any doubt to the contrary.

"What we discuss here goes no further, okay?"

"Sure. What's the story?"

"We've had Boris under surveillance for quite some time now. He came to our attention via our Miami contact. He was picking up illegals as fast as they came off the boat, but sex trafficking is not our mission; we left that to other agencies."

"That's disgusting. If the Feds knew Boris was into human trafficking, then why didn't they shut him down? Why was he allowed to continue?"

"I can't speak for other departments; it's a convoluted situation. Boris first appeared on our radar when he agreed to move guns down south. He frequently delivered a small cache of arms, then returned with a boatload of girls and literally sold them to various organizations between here and New York. Boris kept pushing for more; he was looking to expand his operations. Later, they brought Goldberg onboard to create a false money trail to launder the proceeds. I got tagged to infiltrate Boris's organization."

"Goldberg said they coerced him into helping."

"That's bullshit. He was a greedy little toad from the beginning. He thought he was clever and loved the idea of being a gangster. The Feds were already investigating him for suspicious financial practices, and that was well before Boris got his hooks into him."

I sipped my beer and stared across the restaurant at the boisterous crowd that kept Sally busy as everyone enjoyed a fun night out. It felt almost surreal; the two of us calmly talked of murder and human suffering while the other patrons went about their normal lives, clueless about the turmoil going on around them. If ignorance was bliss, the self-indulgent crowd at the bar ought to be in ecstasy.

Boots continued, "Goldberg showed Boris and his gang how to launder payments through each of their private businesses. They filtered dirty money through several legitimate businesses into offshore accounts, and clean money came back in. It was going beautifully until Goldberg got cold feet."

"What was your mission besides keeping tabs on Boris?"

"To trace the arms deals back to the source. That's where it got fuzzy. We thought they handled shipments out of New York, but we haven't identified who called the shots. We knew it wasn't Boris; he was just the middleman, although he kept a tight rein on the others."

"Sabrina and Katya mentioned that before, something about Boris not being the decision-maker. That he always jumped whenever new orders came down."

"One time I thought we were close to nailing the source, but it didn't happen. With this last shipment heading out of the country, we had to make a fast decision. We couldn't have US-made materiel ending up in the hands of terrorists and used against our own troops. It was important to seize the shipment before it could reach its destination."

"Some good news at last."

"Yeah, but the downside is we unleashed the Bear. Boris has been on a tear ever since he got word the Coast Guard intercepted his shipment."

"What does that mean?"

"He's got to make up the loss somehow. I don't think he has the funds, but just in case, he's preparing for retribution."

"If somebody whacks Boris for losing the shipment, is that a bad thing?"

"Not necessarily from my point of view, but only if we confine the trouble to just Boris. He may not be the brightest bulb on the tree, but he's an expert at self-preservation. That's why I'm warning you to take extra precautions. Boris is on the warpath, and anyone even remotely connected to the bust is a target. Myself included. I'm sure he never trusted me."

I decided to take his warning seriously. An unhinged Boris "the Bear" Zharkov was far more dangerous than anything you'd find in the wild.

"So tell me, how do you know Jimmy Courvelle?"

A faint smirk passed across his face. Boots said, "What a coincidence, huh? Jimmy occasionally works with the Coast Guard handling inland investigations. He was already working with our outfit, and when you turned up on his doorstep, it couldn't have been more providential."

"Seeing you two together gave me quite a shock. I didn't know what to think. You know, I followed when you two left the marina."

"I should have figured as much. We had to get things organized to pick up the shipment once it left Miami. We didn't have much time."

"The hell you say. I watched you guys drink beer for over an hour like you had all the time in the world."

He grinned at that. "Well, we might have had an extra moment or two to spare."

"What's the story on your friend, 'Lanky,' the skinny guy with the boat?"

"He's a guy I can't discuss with you. That you even saw him could compromise ongoing operations. Just know he's one of only a handful of people on the planet that I trust completely."

"What happens now?" I wasn't sure how or even whether I should proceed with the case.

"We still don't know who's financing Boris's operation, so I'm following up on that angle. I may never get close to him again; he's rabid with paranoia."

"I might be able to help with that. Leave it with me."

Boots objected. "Seriously, Vic, the dynamics of the game have changed. Just remember this: if you see Boris, or any member of his gang, don't bother asking if they're coming for you, because they are."

I remembered the sheer ferocity when the Bear smashed his girlfriend's face for talking out of school. I could only imagine the tender mercies he'd visit upon me.

Boots drained his beer and said he'd be in touch. He left me at the bar and exited through the revolving doors.

I was glad things were out in the open between us. Now I could concentrate on Boris and not get distracted about covering my flanks. Briefly, that business in St. Augustine had me worried, but no longer. It helped to know who was on my side and who was not, although I never doubted for a moment where I stood with Boris.

Sally came over with a big grin on her face and handed me another beer. "That looked like it went well. What did Mr. Nicebody have to say for himself?"

"Would you believe we've been working the same side of the street all along, but from different angles?"

"That's interesting, but still hard to believe. What now?"

"I've got some follow-up work to do before we wrap up Boris and company and deliver them to the Feds."

"Just remember what I said about being careful," Sally admonished.

"Funny, that's what Boots said just now. But I promise I will, *Mother!*"

I hung around just long enough to finish my beer and then headed home. I was afraid if I stayed away too long or too often, Mrs. Shepherd might just kidnap my darling Marlowe for herself. I grinned at the thought, knowing that it would never happen. Besides, I'm pretty sure I packed more heat than old Mrs. Shepherd.

Marlowe and I settled down to watch a couple of shows, and then I stayed up late to catch the eleven o'clock news. There was no report of the arms bust off the coast of Florida, at least not in the Metro area news cycle. Perhaps it got reported in the local Miami news. Regardless, as Boots had said, it was a new ballgame now.

While still getting used to the idea, I felt more confident now that Boots and I were not at odds over this smuggling business. I never fully believed he was the villain he pretended to be, but somehow, I couldn't shake the notion I was being played. That was then, and this was now, and I was looking forward to new beginnings.

I brushed my teeth and put on my nightshirt before cuddling up with my big guy, Marlowe. He always slept on the pillow next to me.

The last conscious thought I had before falling to sleep was of the hunky Boots Johnson and me frolicking in the surf on some deserted island. It was a very pleasant dream.

# # #

I awoke to the sound of my cell phone as it vibrated across my nightstand. I grabbed it before it fell off the edge.

"Miss Carella? Detective Scanlin. Are you there?"

I glanced at my clock perched on the dresser. It was nearly three o'clock in the morning. "I'm here. Why are you calling so late?"

Scanlin said nothing for a few seconds, and I was about to chew him out for disturbing my beauty rest when he finally spoke again. "Boots Johnson has been shot."

No! Boots shot? The conversation we had earlier came back to me in a rush. He warned me to be careful that Boris was out to get anyone connected to the arms transfer and subsequent seizure. Had the raging Bear finally caught up with Boots?

"Miss Carella, did you hear me?" Scanlin's voice was insistent.

A feeling of dread, like a cold, wet blanket, came over me. "What happened?"

"It was a drive-by shooting. I'll give you the details later, but I thought you should know."

"Tell me, how… how is he?" My voice got stuck in my throat.

"It's not critical, but he's in surgery. He's at Sibley Hospital. How soon can you get here?"

I told him I'd be there in fifteen minutes but managed to do so in ten. The hospital was located a few blocks west of my apartment. I parked in the visitor's parking lot outside the emergency center and hurried into the building.

Sergeant McAllister was waiting for me in the lobby, and without so much as a hello—trust me, the man almost never spoke anyway—he escorted me to the emergency ward.

Down the hall I saw Scanlin talking to someone in a green surgical gown, who I assumed was a doctor. As I approached, the medical person stepped away, and Scanlin turned to face me.

"He's resting now. They removed a slug from his upper arm and stitched up the graze along his ribs. He'll be okay, but he's going to be hurting for the next several days."

"I know what that's all about. Can I see him?"

"No, he's sedated and in recovery. He's going to be just fine."

"When did this happen? And how?"

"He was perfectly lucid when the EMTs arrived on-site. He told them he got ambushed as he approached his building. A black SUV pulled up, and someone started blasting away. We have no tag number to go on, and as of yet, no witnesses have come forward. It was a clean getaway."

"I'm curious . . . Why did you call me?"

"We had him flagged as an associate of Goldberg when we ran the initial background check, so when his name came up on a 911 call, they alerted us, and I came down to interview him. Before he went into surgery, he asked the nurse to contact you."

"I saw him earlier tonight at the Old Market Grill. And yes, he is involved with Goldberg and Boris Zharkov."

"Like I said, we knew about the Zharkov connection. Did he happen to mention where he was going, or if he planned to meet someone after leaving you?"

"No. We had a couple beers, and then he left. I assumed he was going home."

"That was true enough. What did you two talk about?"

Briefly I thought about holding back on Scanlin, but this didn't seem like the right time to play it cute. I suggested we find a quiet place to talk. One of the duty nurses directed us to a suite of cubicles that people sometimes used to pray or grieve in private while emergency staff attended family members. McAllister shut the door of the tiny room, and we sat in crowded proximity to one another.

Scanlin said, "When you two talked earlier, did he express any concerns about threats or impending violence?"

"Yes and no, Lieutenant," I said and quickly continued before he could object. "Let me explain."

I summarized my trip to St. Augustine and how I witnessed Boris delivering what I believed to be illegal arms, and that Boots was there as well. I didn't mention the other two lawmen since Boots was reluctant to discuss any details about his colleague, "Lanky" or Jimmy Courvelle. I wanted to clear that with him first.

In short order, my involvement with Boots had become quite complicated. I didn't want to throw a wrench into the works early on by talking out of school to the police. I would wait until Boots clued me in to what I could or could not disclose.

Scanlin and McAllister remained expressionless as they absorbed the details. Finally, Scanlin said, "Do you recall our earlier conversation? The one about keeping each other informed?"

"I know you're mad, Lieutenant, and you have a right to be. Believe me, I wanted to keep you in the loop, but things escalated way too fast."

"Don't even go there; that's total BS. You deliberately withheld information related to an ongoing investigation. Do you realize the implications?"

"That's the irony of it all. When I got back in town, I planned to turn the case over to you. I've already prepared my case notes for your review. Check your voice mails. I called you several times, and now this."

Scanlin looked unconvinced. He could make things difficult for me if he chose to, but I hoped he wouldn't. He exhaled a long sigh.

"There's nothing more any of us can do tonight…or rather this morning, but I expect to see you in my office later today, and we'll pick it up again."

"Thanks, Lieutenant. I appreciate it."

"Don't go thanking me. You're still not in the clear, not by a long shot."

"I meant thanks for letting me know about Boots."

I exited the Emergency Center and headed to my car. Once Scanlin had my case notes and corroborated my story, I felt confident it was only a matter of time before he had Boris and crew rounded up.

With Scanlin representing local law enforcement and Boots representing the Feds as an undercover operative, it was a race to see which agency got to Boris first. Guess who was the toad in the road and most likely to get run over? That would be me, running between two camps while trying to stay out of Boris's line of fire.

I just wanted to be out of the picture once and for all. In my mind, that's how I saw myself at the moment as I waited for the endgame to play out. How could one person be so wrong?

CHAPTER NINE

The persistent knock at my front door eventually roused me from a restless sleep. I glanced at the clock and saw it was straight-up noon. The gentle tap suggested it was old Mrs. Shepherd being as unobtrusive as possible while attempting to get my attention.

I opened the door to find her staring at me through thick lenses. I must have looked a fright, but she tactfully refrained from commenting on my disheveled appearance and the dark circles under my eyes.

"I'm sorry to disturb you, Vic. You know how I don't sleep well anymore. I couldn't help hearing when you got in this morning. It was awfully early. Is everything all right?"

"Everything's fine, Mrs. Shepherd. I was visiting a friend in the hospital and stayed late."

"Oh, my. They've certainly relaxed their visiting hours. How wonderful for you."

"Well, it was special circumstances."

"Nothing serious, I hope?"

"All is well. And you? How are you feeling?" I felt I had to be a little sociable.

"Oh, don't ask. My feet hurt, my back aches. It's always something, but then you'd know all about that. I mean, with the hours you keep and the people you associate with. How is Marlowe, by the way? If you're very busy, he could stay with me for a few days."

"Thanks for offering, but we're fine for now. I'll let you know if something comes up."

I could have told you she was only interested in Marlowe, but I pretended I believed her concern extended to me as well and thanked her. She shuffled back to her apartment across the hall from me, where she resumed her duties as the self-appointed sentinel for our floor.

I felt ratty and slightly disoriented. I squinted at the bright sunlight filtering through pull-down shades that made my eyes feel like they were full of grit. I'd gotten home in the wee hours but couldn't fall asleep right away, not with so many competing images setting my brain on fire.

I put the kettle on to boil and dialed the hospital to check on Boots's condition. My call was timely, because I learned he was kicking up a fuss about an early discharge. I instructed the nurse to keep him there until I arrived. Although I desperately needed my morning coffee, that nectar of the gods and regenerator of life would have to wait.

Boots was sitting in a wheelchair having a heated debate with a couple of determined nurses when I arrived. He had his street clothes on like he was prepared to leave right then and there.

Exasperated, one of the nurses slammed down a file and turned her back on Boots. She saw me coming down the hall and called out, "Are you with him?"

"Maybe. What's going on?"

"He's all yours, girlfriend. Perhaps you can talk some sense into him."

Boots had a stubborn look on his face as he debated the state of health care practices with the two nurses. Both sides dug in their heels, and neither would give an inch.

I said, "Where do you think you're going?"

"Home, where else? There's no way I'm staying here."

"You need rest. You're as pale as the proverbial ghost."

"Everybody knows you can't get any rest in a hospital. They stick you and prod you all night long, and then have the gall to ask how you're feeling," he said. He was dangerously close to sounding like a whiny old man.

The nurses glared at him, and Boots gave it right back.

"It's a matter of protocol, sir. It's for your own good," said one of the nurse combatants.

"If a guy's been shot, he's entitled to a little rest—*undisturbed* rest, that is!"

I'd had enough of this kiddie hour bullshit. "Okay, buster, let's go. You're coming home with me for a few days."

"The hell I am."

"That's right, the hell you are. Now put up your feet and shut up."

I kneeled down to help position his feet on the wheelchair footrests. A nurse handed Boots a clipboard, and he signed the attached release form. I rolled him down the hall toward the bank of elevators. Funny how none of the nurses wished him well. Can you believe it?

Back at my building, I parked underground, and we rode the elevator in silence to the second floor. There were no courtesy wheelchairs available in my apartment complex, so Boots had to lean on me as we slowly made our way down the hall. I helped get him settled on the couch where only last week he had attended me; the irony was not lost on either of us. I placed a carafe of iced water and a glass on the coffee table.

"Lieutenant Scanlin gave me a brief account of the drive-by. Is there anything else you can add?"

"Yeah, he sent a note saying he wants to meet with me, but I don't think my superiors will approve of that. I hope you believe me now when I say Boris is out for blood."

"I never doubted you. Do you think he suspects you had something to do with hijacking his shipment?"

"Probably so, since I was the one who arranged the transfer in Miami. I think I covered my tracks, but you never know. Besides, he's always been a suspicious son of a bitch. Since I'm not part of his regular crew, he may clean house to be on the safe side."

"What a world you live in," I observed. "So, what happens next?"

"My friend on the boat, the one you called Lanky, I need to get in touch with him. By the way, he goes by Donker Dave."

"Why Donker?"

"It's a nickname he picked up while in the Marine Corps. I'm sure you can draw your own conclusions about how he came by that name. By now, he'll have new orders for me."

"I think I prefer Lanky, but never mind that. For the time being, you're not going anywhere. You will stay put until I say differently." That's me, the ex-buck sergeant taking charge of her troops.

After a light lunch, Boots stretched full length on the couch. He'd taken more pain pills and was fading fast on me. I didn't fancy sitting around watching Boots snooze all afternoon, so I headed over to Scanlin's office to sort things out.

It was a short ride downtown on the subway, and I walked the last couple blocks to police headquarters. It was late afternoon, and the sidewalk was crowded as nearby offices emptied and people headed for home. I waited for a break before I dashed across the road against traffic. I'd never been one to worry about jaywalking fines.

As I approached the entrance, I saw Marvin Bocci come strolling out of the building. I twirled around, hoping he hadn't noticed me. He came down the steps and turned east away from me, moving rapidly despite his immense bulk. I wondered what he was doing here. Seeing him startled me until I remembered he worked for the mayor's office and was probably there on business.

At the front desk, I gave the sergeant my name and asked for Lieutenant Scanlin. I didn't have to wait long. McAllister soon appeared and led me upstairs to their office. Scanlin stood as I entered and indicated the chair in front of his desk. I sat down, not sure what to expect next.

"Where did we leave things before?" Scanlin asked.

McAllister was suddenly Mr. Chatty as he helped prod my memory. "I believe Miss Carella was going to explain why she deliberately withheld vital information about an ongoing investigation."

"Wait a minute. Instead of jumping down my throat about procedure, why don't you ask me what I found out?"

They both bristled at my opening gambit. If they expected me to come in all meek and mild and begging forgiveness, then they were dead wrong. You know that's not my style.

"Let's face it; you wouldn't know a damn thing about that arms shipment if I hadn't followed Boris and his crew to St. Augustine and then told you about it. Besides, it was totally outside your jurisdiction. And unlike you, I'm not wrapped up in bureaucratic red tape. I did you a favor. I did for you what you couldn't do for yourself. Admit it, fellas."

With that, I tossed the thumb drive containing my case notes, images, and all the details pertaining to the Goldberg case onto Scanlin's desk. He caught it as it slid across his blotter.

"Don't think this lets you off the hook. What you may or may not have found out about Zharkov and his arms shipment may be totally worthless when it comes to filing proper charges in a court of law."

"I was working a legitimate case for my client. That my client was already dead is immaterial. I had valid information that I intended to follow up on, and I did just that. You're now in possession of the entire case. I'm turning over everything I have on Goldberg, his damn yacht, and his slimy friends as well. What more do you want?"

Scanlin and McAllister exchanged glances. The beginning of a sneer appeared on McAllister's face. *Oh, goody*, I thought. *Here it comes.*

"Miss Carella, we're formally charging you with obstruction of justice during an ongoing investigation and tampering with evidence. Stand up, please." McAllister whipped out a pair of handcuffs and snapped them around my wrists.

Of all the ungrateful…I couldn't believe this was happening.

"Your problem is they confine you, boys, to a pigeonhole and you can't see the bigger picture."

"You can't go around breaking the rules whenever it suits you," Scanlin said. "I don't like this anymore than you do, but we have to follow orders as well."

"Orders? On whose orders am I being arrested?"

Neither offered an explanation, and then it suddenly dawned on me: Marvin Bocci, the assistant to the assistant to the mayor. Now I knew where the pressure was coming from. Bocci has a quiet word with the captain; the captain has a quiet word with his detectives, and so on.

Pardon me, but you're familiar with that old saying about something stinky always rolls downhill, right? Well, there I was at the bottom of the hill, knee-deep in doo-doo. Under the guise of violating police procedures, I was suddenly swept up in the bureaucratic machinery.

"I'm entitled to a phone call. I want my attorney present."

"In due course. After you're booked, you can make your call. Come this way." McAllister took me by the arm and guided me from the room. When I looked back at Scanlin, I sensed the whole affair embarrassed him.

McAllister led me down the hall and placed me in a dingy cell. At least I had the place to myself, for the time being anyway. The six-by-eight cell comprised a double bunk, toilet, and sink. It was a drab and filthy space. I was convinced they painted the walls dull gray to dampen the spirit and extinguish all hope. I sat on the edge of the lower bunk, not daring to move for fear of touching something disgusting.

They say the wheels of justice turn slowly. Well, three hours later, following the humiliation of being formally charged, photographed, and duly fingerprinted, I finally got my one and only phone call. A guard took me back to Scanlin's office. McAllister was nowhere to be found, which was just as well.

Scanlin pushed the phone toward me, and I dialed James Warren's number from memory. The receptionist put me through to him immediately, and in short order, I explained my predicament. To my everlasting gratitude, James made appreciative noises about soon having someone's head on a pike and said that he was on his way to bail me out.

We sat in awkward silence while we waited for my attorney to arrive. Finally, Scanlin broke the quiet.

"You realize you brought this on yourself, more or less. So don't get pissed off at me."

"You're not really going to lecture me, are you?" I said, slowly and deliberately.

"The thing is, we already knew about the smuggling operation, and we were about to mount our own investigation. With you flying off to Florida to suss out Zharkov, things could have backfired with serious consequences."

"Excuse me, but it's my ass that would suffer the consequences, not yours."

"Still, things could have gotten out of hand."

"The arms smuggling is only part of the problem. Are you also aware he's into human trafficking as well? Prostitution?"

The look on Scanlin's face said this was new information to him.

"You never mentioned that before," he said lamely.

"If you bothered to read the file I gave you, it's all in there. Boris frequently transferred guns and military hardware to someone in Florida and later picked up boatloads of young women and brought them back here. God alone knows where they went after that."

"No, I wasn't aware, but it explains a lot." Scanlin avoided eye contact. "Listen, for what it's worth, I'm sorry."

"Yeah, you're sorry. Big deal. You're still doing Boris's dirty work for him via that fat toad, Marvin Bocci."

"Hey, don't tell me about doing someone's dirty work. Not with the attorney you've got working for you," he retorted. "I've heard a few things about your pal, James Warren—"

From behind me, a familiar voice said, "Hello, detective. How can I be of service?"

Intent as we were on taking our respective shots at one another, neither of us had noticed James standing in the doorway.

James addressed me directly. "My colleagues are securing your release as we speak. Come along, my dear, and let's get you out of this awful place."

"Uh...hold on, sir—" Scanlin objected, but James cut him off.

"By the way, Officer, I'm filing a complaint with your superiors about this whole affair. Your charge of obstruction of justice was premature."

"Technically, she withheld information vital to an ongoing investigation. That's a fact."

"Let's talk facts, shall we? Actually, it's all a matter of timing."

I could see James was just warming up.

"I believe you'll find that during her investigations, my client received a tip regarding an alleged illegal arms shipment. She had no substantive knowledge, just a tip. Now that she's handed over proof of an actual crime, it remains to be seen whether you can—or can't, as the case may be—do something about it."

"We will look into all the details, I can assure you."

"See that you do. And another thing, Officer. I expect you to expunge this frivolous charge from her record, or there will be consequences. Let's go, Miss Carella," he said. His jaw was set in a hard line as he spat out the words. "We're finished here."

I'd never seen anyone so thoroughly put in their place before. When James Warren finished speaking, there was nothing left to be said. Full stop.

I signed the inventory release form to get my belongings back. Before leaving, I checked they had not confiscated my firearms during my short internment. That would have kicked off a whole new round of trouble that I was glad to avoid. I just wanted to go home and hit the shower to wash away the smell of this place.

By the time we left the station, the sun had gone down. The cool night air felt refreshing after being locked up in that squalid cell; the prospect of being put back there was abhorrent to me. I'd always been the one on the outside, never the house guest. The overwhelming sensation of being powerless was an unfamiliar experience for me, one that I hoped to never repeat.

That old nagging feeling of failure was never far from the surface, and I realized, as I often did in situations like this, that I was only one step away from dropping the ball. And once fumbled, it was a sure bet no one would take me seriously again. I was not about to let that happen, no matter if it killed me. Doing the job—it was all that mattered to me at this point.

"Allow me to give you a lift home, my dear. I know how distraught you must feel."

"If it's all the same to you, I think I'll take the Metro. I just want to walk and think for a while. That business with the police unnerved me, to say the least. A walk would do me good."

"As you wish, but call me in the morning, so I'll know you're all right. We need to talk."

He started to say something else but just shook his head. I kind of knew what was coming, but it would have to wait. He shuffled off to his gleaming Rolls that stood proudly in front of the police station, attracting envious looks.

Perhaps I should have taken him up on the ride home, but I wanted to shake off that feeling of entrapment, of being enclosed in a confined space. The Metro stop was only a couple blocks away, and the walk made me feel better; it was good to be out and about. That minor incident with Scanlin showed me just how fast the tables can turn, and suddenly you find yourself on the wrong side of the law.

I took the train to the Tenleytown station, which put me within a few blocks of my apartment. I rode the escalator to street level and walked along Wisconsin Avenue.

Now, I know this is just an opinion, but would you say there is something strange about me? Perhaps an aura or latent scent? I certainly don't know what it is, but I seem to have an uncanny knack for attracting the wrong kind of people, as if I was some kind of shit magnet.

A mug in a black hoodie came out of the shadows to block my way while two of his buds circled behind me to close off any retreat.

I quickly sized up the situation. "Guys, please, this is not a good time, okay? I'm having a really bad day. Can you just let it pass for once?"

"What a shame. My baby don't want to party with me? Then gimme the bag, bitch."

To these lunkheads, I guess this looked like one of those crime-of-opportunity moments. Too bad for them, because that old army training kicked in when I needed it most. In an instant, I had the little Kel-Tec .32 pointed at his head, so he'd know I meant business.

"That's real cute. Looks just like a gun, only smaller. What are you going to do with that, little lady?" asked the dumbest punk on the planet. Either that or it truly did not intimidate him. I'd have put money on the former.

I raised the weapon and fired into the sky. The loud report reverberated off the canyon walls of the surrounding apartment buildings.

I shoved the muzzle of the gun in his pimply face and said, "The next shot is going through your thick skull, dumbass. Back it up."

The prospect of actually checking out of this world early finally engaged his two-celled brain, because the punk held his hands up and pleaded with me not to dust him off.

I sidled around him, so I could keep the other two in my peripheral view. I walked fast, turning around every couple of steps to make sure they did not follow me until I was out of sight of the three young punks.

My hands shook as I slipped the little pistol back into my pocket. I thought, *If I had actual live rounds instead of blanks, would I really have shot the teenager over pocket money?*

I wasn't sure until I considered the odds were not in my favor: three against one. So yeah, I might have done it out of necessity, but luckily, I didn't have to prove it this time. I was grateful things hadn't escalated to where I had to resort to real firepower, but it was damn close.

When I got back to my apartment, I found Boots still racked out on the couch, sound asleep. I dropped my purse on the table and headed to my kitchenette for a shot and a beer to calm my nerves.

Out on the streets, all hell was breaking loose, but at the moment, all I wanted to do was curl up and hibernate. Yeah, I'm usually all decisive action, just not tonight.

Despite my abrupt and needless arrest, I didn't enjoy withholding information from Scanlin. He had a job to do the same as me, only I held most of the cards at the moment. It might not always be that way, and one day I might need a friend in police circles, so it wouldn't do to antagonize the guy.

Still, I had given him all the information he needed to bust Boris's operation wide open, so technically, he no longer needed my help. And there was the human trafficking business to contend with. Even though I was willing to let Scanlin follow up on the arms smuggling angle, I'd be damned if I was going to stand idly by while Boris continued to force vulnerable young women into a life of prostitution. Something had to be done.

One thing was crystal clear to me. The attack on Boots confirmed Boris was lashing out and cleaning up loose ends, and I was likely next on his list. With my luck—my continual crummy luck, that is—it was a sure bet that I'd come up craps eventually.

My mistake was underestimating Boris—big time! I wouldn't make that same mistake twice. I decided it was time to improve the odds in my favor.

I got out the Kel-Tec and emptied the magazine of the remaining blank cartridges, then replaced them with jacketed hollow points. No matter how much of a deterrent they may be, blanks would not save my ass in case I ran into another jam. In addition to my standard Glock, from now on, I was going fully armed. Although a .32 caliber was not the most effective man-stopping round, a backup piece, even the tiny Kel-Tec, was better than nothing at all.

I decided to report the mugging in case some concerned citizens were frightened of being murdered in their beds because guns were going off in their neighborhood.

I went into my bedroom and closed the door before dialing Scanlin's cell phone. I didn't want to end up on his wrong side so soon after our recent encounter.

When he came on the line, I apologized for the intrusion, then gave him the details concerning the night's event. He sounded both intrigued and amused when I described how the use of blank cartridges actually defused the situation.

"That's a new one on me. I'd have opted for the real deal. The idea of a decoy pistol is unique, but most people wouldn't waste their time. However, I'll make a note of it in your file for reference. Tell me, why do you carry blanks in the first place?"

"I don't believe every situation calls for deadly force."

"Yes, but think about this: if the perp had lunged toward you, you wouldn't have had time to ditch the decoy gun and go to your primary piece. You'd be dead."

"You're right, Lieutenant. It was a personal preference, and in hindsight, a poor choice on my part. After tonight, and with the escalating feud with Boris, I've already made appropriate changes."

"It's probably best. I appreciate you letting me know about this. Since no actual rounds were discharged, I don't see the need for a formal incident review. And, uh, listen, I'm sorry about the earlier fiasco. We were suddenly getting heat from several directions, and all of it concerned you. I should have known this was a frame-up job. I hope you believe me when I say it was not my doing."

"I've already forgotten about it, Lieutenant. Besides, I'd much rather work with you than against you. Let's focus on the bad guys from now on."

I went to check on Boots before heading to bed. I found Marlowe curled up on his chest, both snoring contentedly. I turned out the lights.

Chapter Ten

The smell of frying bacon permeated my apartment and roused Boots from a deep sleep. With his arm still in a sling to keep it immobilized, he struggled and groaned as he rolled upright. I knew that feeling all too well.

"Morning, glory. Want some breakfast?"

He merely grunted as he shuffled off to the bathroom while I set a couple of mugs on the counter. Boots came out of the bathroom and wiped a washcloth across his face. The bloodstained bandage on his left bicep was visible below his T-shirt sleeve.

"What time is it?"

"It's after eleven. Why, you got a hot date or something?"

"I guess I was more out of it than I realized." He sipped gratefully at his coffee.

"No kidding; you slept right around the clock. How are you feeling?" I set a plate of bacon and eggs in front of him and placed the salt and pepper shakers within reach.

"I've survived worse. I'm still kicking myself for not paying more attention. We're trained for situational awareness, but for one brief moment, I let my guard down," Boots said and dived into his breakfast like he was famished.

While he ate, I filled him in on how the mayor's fixer, Marvin Bocci, spread a little unwelcome pressure among the police hierarchy that ultimately landed me in a jail cell.

As I continued my narrative, Boots shook his head when I mentioned the confrontation with the street punks. He sounded like Scanlin when he lectured me on the futility of carrying blanks.

"Okay, I get it now. That's why I'm fully geared up from now on. Besides, there has been way too much drama in my life lately, so I figure I'm better off if I remain well armed."

I felt gratified when Boots handed me his empty plate, and I piled on more. He said, "I never heard. Did the police get a line on the vehicle or the shooter?"

"According to Lieutenant Scanlin, no one came forward. By the way, he called when they admitted you to the hospital. Apparently, you asked the nurse to notify me. Why me?"

"There was no one else close by. I couldn't very well have the hospital contact my agency. And then that cop, Scanlin, suddenly turned up out of nowhere and started asking questions before they took me into surgery. I couldn't risk talking to him, not with months of undercover work at stake."

"Still, why me?"

"I figured if things went sideways, someone from my team would eventually reach out to you, and I believed you would have assisted if at all possible."

"That was highly presumptuous of you."

"Sometimes you have to take a chance on people," he said and gave me a steady gaze.

I nodded in acknowledgment of the compliment. An awkward silence descended on us as we continued eating. After we'd cleaned our plates, I put them in the sink for later.

Boots sipped his coffee. "What are you going to do next?"

"I need to check on Sabrina and Katya. If Boris is running wild, they could be in big trouble."

"Just be careful and stay out of sight—"

The knock at the door startled both of us. Boots looked at me and gestured with his hand, simulating a gun. I reached for my purse and handed him the Glock while I checked that the Kel-Tec was fully charged and ready.

We separated and crossed the room, staying to one side in case someone started shooting through the door. We held our weapons in the low-ready position, just in case.

I called out, "Who's there?"

A muffled voice answered, "Ms. Carella, my name is Dave. I'm a friend of Boots Johnson. I need to speak with you."

A big grin lit up Boots's face as he unlocked the door. "What the hell, Donker. You had us going there for a minute. Get in here."

Donker Dave—I definitely preferred Lanky—was a tall drink of water, all right; more height than bulk, although I sensed his lean frame belied an underlying quiet strength. He took one look at the firepower and put his hands up in mock surrender.

"Hey, don't shoot. I'm on your side."

"I thought that was just a rumor," I said as the tension in my shoulders relaxed. "Come in and make yourself comfortable."

Donker pointed to the bandage on Boots's arm. "How bad is it? The scuttlebutt says you stopped a couple bullets."

"I won't be doing one-armed push-ups anytime soon," Boots said and patted his rib cage. "The other is just a scratch. I'll be fine in a few days."

Donker grinned at me. "Some people need constant supervision."

"Oh, sorry, let me introduce you two. Donker, may I present Vic Carella, my guardian angel of late."

"Pleased to meet you, at last, Ms. Carella," he said as we clasped hands. "I heard you enjoyed our little show down in St. Augustine."

"Please, call me Vic. And good on you for busting that arms shipment before it got into the wrong hands. I take it the hospital told you where to find Boots. It won't take Boris long to figure it out as well."

"Not to worry. We've had a team covering the place since you arrived home early yesterday morning."

This was surprising news. "I never noticed anyone about, but thanks."

"You weren't supposed to," Donker said.

"What are you doing in town?" Boots asked.

"The director called and said you'd been hit. As soon as I could, I snagged a military hop out of Jacksonville. I thought I was coming to bail you out of trouble, but now I see there's no need. By the way, didn't anyone teach you to duck?"

Donker faked a boxing move like he was going to punch Boots on his wounded arm, causing him to flinch. I admired the easy camaraderie between them.

"Where's Boris?" Boots asked.

"He's gone underground, but we'll flush him out soon enough. So, you didn't get a tag number or anything, huh?" Donker sat on the back of the sofa, crossed his arms, and stretched those long legs.

"It happened too fast. A vehicle pulled up behind me, and just as I turned around, I heard several shots. I remember being hit and falling on the steps."

"Did you get a look at the shooter?" Donker pressed for details.

Boots laid the nine-millimeter pistol on the counter. "Just a glimpse. He was sitting in the rear passenger seat with a gun sticking out the window. I'd put him at about forty, dark-haired, stocky build. Nothing unusual, but I might recognize him if I saw him again."

What the hell—it was worth a try. On the off chance Boots might identify him, I told them about Mike Carver, the taciturn bartender of the Dirty Whaler. I remembered at our initial meeting, I sensed Carver was holding back more than he was telling. And later, Sabrina confirmed that the Dirty Whaler was where Boris and company geared up for their routine trips down to Florida and back.

"If you can get it, I'd like to see a photo of this guy, but for now, it's not much to go on," Donker said. "I've already checked with the local police; they're as clueless as we are."

"You didn't speak to Lieutenant Alan Scanlin by any chance?" I asked.

"No, but I know who you're talking about. The guy's been raising a ruckus because the director won't allow him anywhere near Boots. It's vital we maintain his cover." To Boots he said, "And you're not to have any contact with Metro; those are the director's orders."

"Aye, aye, Captain. Besides, I don't talk to anyone outside the agency."

Donker gave him the hairy eyeball and nodded in my direction.

"Present company excepted, of course."

"Make sure you don't," he said with finality. "Ms. Carella…Vic, I must insist on total information blackout from you as well. We're at a critical stage in our operations, and any loose talk at this point could get someone killed."

I described how Scanlin tried to pump me for information while Boots was in surgery. I made it clear their collaboration in St. Augustine, including the contributions by one of Metro's own, namely Jimmy Courvelle, never made it to Scanlin's ears. Besides, I wasn't exactly a rookie when it came to following orders.

Boots spoke up. "By the way, I just remembered the weapon that was used in the drive-by. It was a bolt-action hunting rifle with a scope."

Donker shook his head. "Isn't it funny what people focus on in a crisis? But it fits; the hospital said the slug they dug out of you was a .243 small game caliber."

"Hey, who are you calling small game?" Boots retorted in mock indignation.

I've often heard humor helps people deal with near-death experiences; something to do with survival instincts. I don't know that I could remain so nonchalant.

I noticed Donker looking around my apartment, taking it all in, and suddenly remembered my manners. "Can I get you anything? Would you care for some breakfast?" I invited them to relax in the living room as I started for the kitchen, but Donker was insistent they had to leave.

"Nothing for me, thanks. I'm not staying long…and neither are you, soldier. The old man wants a briefing this afternoon, so I suggest we get moving."

"Sheesh, I just got out of the hospital."

"And am I glad of that; saved me a ton of paperwork."

"What a pal. He really cares."

They both thanked me for my hospitality. Boots grabbed what little he brought with him, and just like that, the pair of them hurried out the door.

I was thinking if taking a bullet for the team didn't warrant a little downtime, what did? Remind me not to get shot around these guys; I couldn't stand the excitement. If it were me, I'd tell the "old man" exactly what I thought of his briefing.

I tidied up and soon had the place back in order. Marlowe finally came out from under the bed and showed himself. He's shy around strangers and usually finds a quiet spot to hide until things return to normal. He hates having his routine disrupted. Talk about a creature of habit; Marlowe put me to shame.

I decided to go for a run to loosen up and clear my head.

As I jogged along the path between my apartment complex and the next one over, I breathed in the earthy smell of autumn leaves and fresh mulch. While my feet pounded the pavement, I let my mind wander back over recent events. In spite of the all-too-brief encounter, I learned a few things about Donker and the organization he and Boots worked for. They impressed me at the speed with which their director responded to the attack on Boots by mobilizing a team to set up a perimeter. It must be nice to have resources at your fingertips. I wondered what form of retaliation Boris could expect, and then remembered I needed to contact Sabrina and Katya. I hoped that the crazy Russian had not inflicted his rage on them.

When I got back to my apartment, I dialed Sabrina's number, but it went straight to voicemail. I hung up without leaving a message. Maybe I was reading too much into an innocuous call, but I sensed it was not a good omen.

Meantime, I had other calls to make, starting with a big one to thank James Warren for his timely intervention with the Metro police. My God, was it really only yesterday I was sitting in a DC jail cell wondering what had just happened? Suddenly, I felt like my world was spinning out of control, and I was just along for the ride.

Also, I was hoping Pete could tell me how much political pull Marvin Bocci really had, and whether his reach included the police hierarchy. If he had the juice to influence precinct captains, then I'd have to steer clear of Scanlin from now on; he'd be more of a liability than an asset to me. One problem after another kept piling on, and my days were running together. I punched the redial on my cell phone.

"Hello?"

"It's me. Are you free to talk?" I wanted to give Sabrina a chance to bail out in case Boris was nearby.

"I'm good; go ahead."

"I was just checking on you and Katya. I heard Boris was raising hell after his shipment got intercepted and wanted to know if you two were okay."

She lowered her voice as she spoke into the phone, but I could hear the urgency. "Vic, you gotta get us out of here! Boris is acting all weird; he scares the hell out of me."

"What do you mean, weird? What's he done?"

"He's been out of his mind over losing that shipment. He tore through our house and destroyed the place; you should see it. And now he's threatening to kill everyone he's ever known just to get the one who ratted him out."

"Tough. I told you I was going to blow up his empire. This is only the beginning."

"Sometimes I think you're as crazy as he is. He despises you and calls you all sorts of names."

"Ouch, that really hurts, but I think I'll get over it."

"Seriously, Vic, he blames you for the trouble he's in right now, so be careful. He'll kill you if he gets the chance. He's insane!"

"He didn't hit you again, did he?"

"No, at least not yet. This is the creepy part. He carries on like a wild man, and then suddenly he's real calm and friendly toward me. Vic, I'm scared to freaking death. I swear he knows you and I talked. I keep wondering when he's going to flip the switch and come after me."

"Have you talked to Katya? How is she doing?"

"She's still with her husband, but she doesn't trust him either. You've heard the expression 'thick as thieves'? Well, she thinks Anatoly and Boris are closer than Anatoly is with her, his own wife!"

"Now that is weird. Where is Boris now?"

"Right this minute, I don't know. The night before last, when he got the call about the shipment being intercepted, he raged around here trashing the place, and then he went out. He supposedly went to meet Anatoly. I thought it was about some new business, but I don't know that for sure."

"What time was that?"

"It was after nine o'clock, and I haven't seen him since. He's out there, and he's looking for someone to blame for losing all that hardware."

I quickly filled her in on the drive-by shooting. On its surface, the timing of Boris's sudden disappearance and the attack on Boots Johnson corresponded.

"Katya said she overheard Anatoly complaining to Andre Adema about how they're expected to make up the loss, but there's no way the guys have two million dollars stashed away. They're scared someone's going to step out of the dark and pop them as well."

"*Two million!* Holy crap! No wonder he's gone crazy."

"His contact has been pushing him to cough up what he can to offset the loss, but Boris doesn't have the money. He spends every dollar he brings in."

"No chance you've got a line on that contact, have you?"

"Wish I did, but no. Can you help us out, Vic? I'm afraid."

She was patently begging for my help. Frankly, I didn't know what to do. I could hide the two of them for a couple days, a week maybe, but after that, I wasn't sure.

"Give me a little time, and I'll get back to you. In the meantime, do you have somewhere you can go temporarily? Perhaps a friend's house or a motel off the beaten track?"

"We'll find a place. Just help us get away from Boris before it's too late."

My mind was in turmoil about how I could help, considering I had limited personal resources. I thought about contacting Boots and Donker to see about placing the women in witness protection. It was a long shot, but worth looking into. Meanwhile, I decided to call James Warren. He was well connected and could advise me on what to do.

"I've been waiting for your phone call, young lady. How are you today?"

"Fine, Mr. Warren. I wanted to thank you again for getting me out of trouble. I didn't know the cops were so testy about their precious jurisdiction."

He chuckled at that. "Not to worry. As we say in the legal profession, it's all about ruining the opposition's day more than they're ruining yours. Just wait until the mayor gets my letter, and then the fur will fly!"

Oh, hell! I started a turf war with the cops. I never intended to antagonize Scanlin. In fact, I was hoping to smooth things over once he took over the investigation.

"However, I am perturbed with you for going off to Florida like that and getting involved with those smugglers. Nothing good will come of it."

"I know, I know. It wasn't my best move, but I'm through with all that. I turned over what little evidence I had to the police; it's their case now."

"Evidence? What sort of evidence?"

"I recorded the entire arms transfer at some marina in St. Augustine. Metro police have the information, and they can deal with it. I'm well out of it."

"As you should be. I feel better knowing you're no longer involved with that crazy Russian and his gang of thugs."

I didn't know whether to tell him how things actually stood at the moment. Even though I had relinquished all interest related to the arms smuggling, I still intended to disrupt Boris's sex trade operation. I decided not to mention that for the time being.

"Actually, Mr. Warren, I called you on another matter. Something to which I hope you will give serious consideration since it involves helping a couple people out of a tight jam."

"You intrigue me. Tell me more."

"I have a couple of contacts who helped me enormously regarding Boris's arms smuggling deal, but right now, I'm afraid for their safety."

"Who are they? And how can I help?"

"That's where it gets sticky. They're related to the two primary gang members, but they don't have the means to break free. They're good women at heart, but they desperately need help to get out of town and disappear. I know this is a big ask, but I was hoping you'd consider underwriting their escape so that they can start a new life free of Boris and his henchmen. Trust me; you'd be saving their lives."

James did not respond immediately. I was sure I'd just overstepped the boundaries of propriety, but then his voice came back on the line.

"I must say, it's an unusual request, but not impossible. I can see where not helping might end in tragedy for them. I appreciate your concern, and I'm glad you brought this to my attention. If it means helping someone get a fresh start in life, then I'm happy to offer my assistance. There are conditions, of course. What sacrifices are you prepared to make?"

"Me? I'm not sure what you mean."

"I don't want anyone to come to any harm, and I certainly don't want a death on my conscience. If I help these women get a fresh start, I want to know you're safe as well. Are you willing to let the proper authorities handle the case from now on?"

"I suppose so. Technically, the arms smuggling is already out of my hands; however, there's the matter concerning the prostitution ring. It's still an ongoing operation."

"Then let the police handle that as well; they're better equipped than you. I suggest you go back to your normal routine and put this terrible business behind you. Getting involved with that blasted Goldberg has been nothing but a curse!"

"I have to agree with you on that point. My life's been on a downward spiral since the day he walked into my office."

"Then it's settled. Pardon me if this sounds condescending, but if I may say without offense, Victoria, I've grown quite fond of you. I dread the thought of something terrible happening to you, of one day getting a call that you're injured, or worse. Am I asking too much?"

I was christened Victoria, but no one has ever called me that, not even my parents when they were alive. It sounded peculiar, and yet pleasant at the same time.

"Mr. Warren, you don't know how much I appreciate you saying that; it means a lot to me. Yes, I agree it's best to let the police take over, so I'll stay out of it from now on. It's the least I can do."

"Excellent! I'm pleased to hear that. I feel better already."

"So you'll help my contacts? They're rather desperate to get away as soon as possible."

"You figure out the plans, my dear. Let me know what you need and how much, then leave the rest to me."

"Thank you, Mr. Warren! Literally, you have spared two lives. You are one hell of a gentleman!"

"Really, Victoria, there's no need to butter me up. I've already agreed to help," he said, but I could hear the embarrassment in his voice.

First the lion, then the lamb. He was certainly a mercurial character.

I hung up, feeling ecstatic. At long last, here was a chance to put a plan in motion that would actually make a difference in someone's life. I hadn't felt this pumped in a long time. With resources readily available, the planning process should run smoothly.

I dropped in on Sally to relax a bit. The events of the past two weeks had my nerves wound up tight.

When I arrived at the Old Market Grill, my favorite bartender and all-around best friend was hard at work as usual. I knew I could always count on Sally; she and Pete were the only constants in my life. I hoped they didn't think I took them for granted. I'd have to do something special for the both of them, because friends like them were too few and precious.

Sally had a Corona on the bar before I even sat down. "Your usual, madam?"

"Yes, and put it on my tab, my good woman."

Sally gave me a dubious look. "What tab?"

"Don't all the cool people say that? I mean, we high rollers have no need to mention vulgar things like money. One assumes the tab gets paid, eventually."

"One assumes… Forgive me, Miss Bond. I didn't know you were on assignment in my humble emporium,"

Sally said, laughing at my terrible attempt at humor. "You're in a good mood. Don't tell me—you hit the lottery, and you're flying off without me. Say it ain't so."

"Not with my crummy luck. Who do you think you're talking to? No, I just solved a tremendous problem for someone, and I'm feeling pretty good about it."

"Well, hallelujah! And here's me thinking you were in over your head and going down fast. Are you going to give me the details, or is that classified?"

"I'll clue you in all right, just not here. If you ever get a night off, I'm taking you out to a fancy dinner, and I'll tell you all about it then. For now, keep the Coronas coming, because today I'm celebrating."

I ordered extra spicy Buffalo wings to go with the clean, crisp taste of the Corona—my two favorite food groups. As I worked my way through the hot wings, I reflected on how quickly events had progressed in a matter of days.

At least I could relinquish further involvement in good conscience, and I'd soon have an escape plan in place for Sabrina and Katya—such relief! And now I could return to what I did best.

Things were looking up from my rosy perspective as I sat on my barstool, happily swigging my way through a few beers. That is, until a tiny thought in the back of my mind nagged at me and finally wormed its way free to spoil my brief moment of blissful peace.

CHAPTER ELEVEN

I rode the elevator up to my office from the gym in our building after I finished a high-impact workout. My hair was still damp, and I needed a shower, but since I wasn't expecting any clients in the office, I thought I'd get back to work.

There were a ton of backlogged emails, outstanding bills, and calls from exasperated clients demanding immediate attention, but it felt good to be back at the helm. I worked steadily for a couple of hours, making a bit of headway, when I saw Pete's number pop up on my phone.

"Where are you?" he asked without so much as a "how do you do."

"I'm at the office. I'm trying to restore order to my life and get back in the groove."

"Do people actually say 'groove' anymore?"

"Whatever. What's up?"

"I've been waiting for your call. It's been all go-go action, and then I don't hear from you. How's the investigation going?"

"Sorry. There have been big changes on that front; it's no longer my problem. On advice of Mr. James Warren, Esquire—and my new attorney, for your information—

I've turned over my case notes to Lieutenant Scanlin. It's his show now; he's running with it."

"Wow, Vic. What's gotten into you?"

"It just makes sense. The whole thing with Boris was way over my head. I'm back where I belong, and the most dangerous thing I have to face is the dirty looks from cheating spouses when I catch them with their pants down."

"What happened with your cowboy friend? Are you two getting together or what?"

"That's filed under 'nunya,' as in none of your damn business."

"I thought you had a thing for the guy, that's all. If you don't, then fine, but just in case you do, Melanie said to invite you guys to dinner one evening. But, like you said, you're not an item, so forget it."

"Not so fast. I only said if we were, it's still none of your business. However, since you're asking, I'll inquire whether Mr. Johnson's schedule is open."

"Oh, *Mister* Johnson, is it? You don't fool me. I know you've got the hots for the guy."

"Don't push it, buster. To show you where things stand, we're not even at the hand-holding stage yet. So, there."

Pete said to get back to him about dinner and then hung up. I resumed work on the escape plan to relocate Sabrina and Katya. Basically, with sufficient funding from James Warren, they could set up housekeeping in a remote part of the country and quietly fade from memory. With the two of them safely out of the way, it would be a cinch for Scanlin, or for that matter even Boots and company, to finally put Boris out of business.

I couldn't get over the extreme generosity of my benefactor agreeing to help Sabrina and Katya. James had access to resources that I could only dream about. Things were certainly looking up.

It was such a straightforward plan, I couldn't see how it could fail; all the risk was in the execution. The plan called for them to be ready to move at a moment's notice. No hoarding of sentimental items that might tip off Boris of their impending departure, no sudden changes in routine that might make him suspicious. Asking someone to pick up and leave behind all they have and all they know was the hard part, but there really was no alternative given their current predicament.

I called the law office to speak with James, only to learn he was in court. I tried Sabrina next.

"Can you talk?" I inquired automatically.

"No problem. What's happening?"

"It's almost time for you and Katya to get out of Annapolis."

"Holy cow, Vic! I don't know how to thank you. We didn't know what we were going to do if Boris came back."

"You haven't seen him or talked to him since he left?"

"No, not a word. What have you heard?"

"Nothing on my end. Just so you know, I turned over the case to the police. I'm completely out of it; it's in their hands. Me, I'm going back to what I do best, and it ain't chasing down gangsters."

"How did you manage all this? And so quickly too?"

"I'm working with the most generous person I've ever met. Actually, he used to represent Mitch Goldberg, and recently he helped me with a petty matter involving the police. I told him about the two of you, and he's generously agreed to resolve your little problem."

"Mitch's attorney?"

"Yeah, why?"

"It's odd, because I thought he was also… Oh, never mind. This is great news. Just tell me when we're leaving."

"It's going to happen in the next few days. I've still got a few details to wrap up. Here's the deal. When I call, you must be ready to drop everything and walk away immediately. There's no time for dillydallying around. When you two disappear, Boris will go all out to find you. I want you far away and safe before he realizes you're even gone. Understand?"

"We'll be ready. How are we traveling? By car, plane, or what?"

"I'll let you know. Just be ready."

We hung up, but not before Sabrina said again how much she appreciated my help. The relief in her voice was palpable.

I tried his office again, but James was still in court. Oh well, he was a busy man, and I shouldn't expect to monopolize his time.

I had nearly completed the escape plan, and it was a solid one. Sabrina and Katya could look forward to a new life somewhere far away from Annapolis, wherever that may be. The two women could work out their own arrangements to relocate together or separately. After that, it was up to them to keep a low profile as they eased into a new life, totally anonymous and free of retribution.

It felt good to do something positive for a change. I'd been on edge with this case from the very beginning, but now, at last, there was some visible light at the end of that long, dark tunnel.

My cell phone buzzed at me.

"Hello?"

"Hello, you. Got time for lunch?" My heart did a little leap when Boots's smooth voice came over the line.

"I've always got time for you. When and where?"

"How about we meet at my newest favorite restaurant? I hear they serve great beer."

"You're on, buster. Race you there."

That was the beauty of running your own shop; when the really important things popped up at the last minute, you could take off in the middle of the day without a lot of hassle from the boss. I grabbed my purse and headed over to the Old Market Grill where, hopefully, we could get in ahead of the noon rush.

As I entered, I caught Sally's eye and waved, but she was busy as always. Half the people at the bar were there just to see her. She brought in a lot of admirers.

I headed for the reception desk to put my name on the waiting list, but then saw Boots rise from a table down the center aisle. As I approached, I noted several women swiveled in their seats to get a better look at him; he looked good enough to eat. He wore a light gray herringbone jacket over a black shirt open at the collar, black slacks, and of course, he had on those trademark Western boots of his. I expected no less. He had ditched the sling, but I could tell he still hurt from the gunshot wound by the way he kept his arm close to his side.

"Are you slumming today? No three-piece for the executive board meeting?"

"Gimme a break. A guy can't dress down without taking a lot of heat? How's it going?"

I was filling him in on the plans to get Sabrina and Katya out of town when I noticed the worry lines crease his forehead with concern.

"Is there something the matter?" I wondered whether I had jumped the gun, so to speak. I had assumed responsibility for the security of the two women and was determined to see it through, but had I inadvertently stepped on someone's toes in the process?

"That all sounds great, but I need to clue you in to a couple things." The seriousness in his voice got my attention. Something was brewing.

"Okay, what did I screw up this time?"

"No, nothing's screwed up. Just that you may be a little ahead of yourself. Donker and I met with the US District Attorney, who's preparing indictments against Boris and his crowd. The DA plans to offer Sabrina and Katya reduced sentences for their testimony."

"What are you talking about? Reduced sentences? What for?"

"They're about to be charged as co-conspirators and accessories before and after the fact. C'mon, Vic, it's not like they were on a pleasure cruise the whole time. They were present when contraband was shipped across state lines, and also when illegal immigrants were transported up north."

"They had nothing to do with that. You can't bust them for what Boris and Anatoly and the others were doing. That's not right."

"You don't want to admit it, but let's be honest; they were just as involved. Let me put it into perspective. Say a bank robber shoots and kills a guard, and because of his participation during the commission of the crime, they charge the getaway driver as an accessory to murder, even though he didn't pull the trigger. It's the same thing here. You can't expect the agency to turn a blind eye."

"In this case, that's exactly what I expect. Boris will have both those women killed the minute they agree to turn state's evidence against him. Why do you think I'm working so hard to make them disappear?"

"I'd hold off if I were you. You're bordering on interfering with a federal case."

"Gee, it's not like I've never done that before."

"True enough, but it won't end well if you persist. You know I'm right about this, so just drop it, okay?"

"Easy for you to say. I'm the one who put them in jeopardy. Tell me, have you located Boris yet? Do you have a solid fix on him or any of the others?" Boots avoided eye contact as the accusation hung in the air.

"Listen, I know you're worried, but we've got over a year invested in this investigation, and it's quickly coming to a close. Don't put that at risk. Let us handle it."

"You know damn well what Boris will do to Sabrina and Katya if they testify against him. Why are we even debating this?"

"It won't come to that, but if necessary, we'll place them into witness protection. Just don't blow up our case."

"I'll think about it."

"I've never told you how to do your job before, but this time I am. We've got a lot riding on what happens in the next couple weeks. Do I have your word you'll stay out of it?"

I'd been holding my breath, but I let it out in one long sigh. "Of course," I said, although capitulation was not my strong suit.

"One other thing," Boots said as he took a pull of his beer. "You'll need to come down to the federal courthouse to provide a deposition. Hopefully, it will be the last time you need to involve yourself where Boris is concerned. Once the DA drops this load of indictments, Boris will be so busy trying to stay out of jail he won't have time for you three. Soon we'll have him put away for good."

"When do I meet the DA?"

"Tomorrow morning. In fact, Donker and my director will be there as well. I'd like you to sit in on the meeting. As I said, this thing is wrapping up fast, and we want to put Boris away as quickly as possible."

"But you don't even know where he is. What if he has already left the country?"

"We're following standard protocol. Once they hand down indictments, we ramp up the resources to pull in the entire gang. For now, they've gone underground like the rats they are. Soon they'll be in a cage where they belong. It's only a matter of time."

"I just hope you're right. I'd feel better if we knew Boris's whereabouts."

In the morning, I'd ride over to the courthouse to take care of business with the DA. Events were indeed moving quickly. We both drained our beers and left the Grill. Boots grabbed a cab and headed across town while I went back to my office.

What a load of…I hated being put in this position—conflicting loyalties, that is. Logically, I had to admit Boots was right; this was a big bust for his agency, and I could compromise not only their case but possibly his career as well.

Yet taken together with what I knew about the precarious position Sabrina and Katya were in, I didn't know if I could let it go so easily, at least not without creating problems for one side or the other. Isn't that just life all over? It called to mind the line from Robert Burns: "the best-laid schemes of mice and men" and all that.

Boots had me over a barrel, but at least he didn't strong-arm me on the finer points. I knew he was walking a fine line where the two of us were concerned, and I appreciated it. We were just two people approaching the same problem, but from vastly different viewpoints.

Even though I preferred to put a different slant on it, I had to be honest. I knew that, technically, Sabrina and Katya were guilty. It's kind of hard to plead innocent when serious crimes are being committed in your presence as you enjoy a leisurely cruise down to Florida and back time after time.

There was no avoiding it; the day of reckoning had arrived. Perhaps the two women could angle for immunity in exchange for their testimony against Boris and company. Witness protection couldn't be all that bad, could it? I mean, here I was orchestrating my own version that they were willing to accept, so why not get the real deal sponsored by the government?

Any offers would have to come from the federal prosecutor handling the case, but I wondered how Sabrina and Katya would react to such a proposal. It certainly was better than the alternative. I shuddered to think of the consequences if Boris or any of his friends ever caught up with them.

It was no use fighting it; my continued involvement was at an end. It was time to let the pros in law enforcement take the lead. Wasn't that what everyone had been telling me all along? Sometimes I'm slow to give up on a project when I'm fully invested, but this was one of those times I needed to acquiesce.

I had committed the fatal mistake of the professional investigator: the case was compromised, and all objectivity lost, because I had become personally involved with the suspects. That pretty much described where I stood at the moment.

I needed a new perspective and a little time to rethink my position. But, let me ask you something. Have you ever heard of being overcome by events?

Chapter Twelve

I got off at the Judiciary Square Metro stop located across the street from the District Court building. When I arrived, Boots Johnson was outside waiting for me. We breezed through building security and rode the elevator to the third floor.

The outer office was a hive of activity with the sound of ringing telephones a constant backdrop. A dozen or more people busily typed at their computers while an office clerk pushed a cart down each aisle, depositing fresh stacks of files on various desks.

As we entered the DA's office, Donker Dave and another gentleman rose to greet us. I gave Donker a nod. I assumed this was their director and approached him with my hand outstretched. His stout frame contrasted with that of the gangly Donker, and he was at least a head shorter. He had a ready smile, and I got the impression of an easygoing personality.

"Pleased to meet you, Ms. Carella. So you're the one keeping my department jumping at all hours. Jerome Peters. For lack of a better title, I guess I'm the liaison with headquarters for these two rogue warriors."

"The pleasure is all mine. And no formalities here; call me Vic."

I glanced toward the woman sitting behind a gleaming desk about the size of a tennis court. The zestful aroma of lemon furniture polish permeated the office.

At a glance, the similarities in our appearance struck me. For this meeting, I had opted for what I considered my chic corporate look: a classic Hugo Boss black jacket and skirt over a white blouse. However, it looked as if we got dressed out of the same closet this morning, because the DA's attire was almost identical to mine. I wondered whether the glare she gave me was for mirroring her appearance, but hey, how could I have known?

Rather curtly, she said, "Marge Kavanagh. Take a seat, and let's get started."

Kavanagh arranged four chairs in a semicircle facing her desk. Miss Smarty Pants was clearly running the show, so we all waited expectantly while she read over a couple of documents.

Addressing Director Peters, she said, "I understand you're ready to proceed with arrests as soon as we issue the indictments?"

"We have several gang members in our sights as we speak. And we'll round up the others soon thereafter."

She raised her eyebrows in surprise, and said, "I thought you had everyone under surveillance. Who's missing?"

Peters shifted in his chair, but before he could answer Boots spoke up. "We're ready to move on most of the gang members right now, although we're still searching for Boris Zharkov and Anatoly Sevvin. They've gone to ground, but we're confident it's only a matter of time before they turn up."

"Zharkov is the prime target in our petition, and you don't even know where he is? You've got to be kidding me."

"To be fair," Donker interjected, "he disappeared the same night as that drive-by attempt on Boots here. He obviously expected immediate retaliation and dropped out of sight. He can't have gone far."

"Tell me about this John Doe," Kavanagh said, reading from a long document she held with her crimson-tipped fingers. "What's the status on this character?"

Peters said, "We're still investigating the link between Zharkov and someone we believe is heading up the organization. As yet, we haven't identified him by name."

Kavanagh slowly shook her head. "Gentlemen, I can't see that we're ready to issue indictments after all, if this is the best you can do. Tell me you've at least identified the perp who killed this…Mitch Goldberg person," she said, again reading from the sheet.

"We have not positively identified the culprit, but we're certain it was Zharkov. The method of dispatch was just his style." Peters looked grim; the interview was not going as planned.

With unerring accuracy, the DA homed in on what appeared to be several nebulous points in the case. Their discomfiture was not a pretty thing to witness.

The DA dropped the charging document on her desk and laced her fingers across her stomach. The uncomfortable silence stretched on until finally she swiveled her chair around to face me.

"And how do you fit into this Kabuki theatre?"

The others were seeking arrest authority from the DA, and protocol may have dictated a certain amount of kowtowing to the queen bee. However, I didn't see a need to play along. I stuck to the bare facts.

"It was my case to start with. Goldberg enlisted me to help locate his stolen yacht. He mentioned the smuggling operations at the very beginning and was trying to extricate himself from further involvement when his boat went missing. In the course of my investigation, I followed Zharkov and his gang to a marina in St. Augustine." Indicating Boots and Donker, I continued, "One thing led to another, and soon we realized we were all working on the same case, but from different angles."

"So you were actually on-site when Zharkov delivered the military hardware?"

"Boots can corroborate my story. I recorded the whole transfer on video, so there should be no doubt about Boris's involvement."

The DA pondered that for a second, clearly not impressed, but going through the pretense that she was getting to the bottom of things. She was getting on my nerves. It must be nice to sit back in your comfy office and second-guess all the fieldwork that ultimately justified your position.

"Do you have anything more to contribute?" she asked.

"I guess not, unless you're interested in how close I am to finding out who is the force behind Boris and his gang. My contacts are working on a couple of angles for me."

"Oh yes, your infamous informants, Sabrina Farkas and Katya Sevvin; I heard about them. Is it true you're helping them relocate, to disappear as it were?" Her tone of voice clearly conveyed her thoughts on the subject.

"Yeah, that's the plan. Hopefully, they'll be out of town before Boris loses what's left of his mind and tees off on the two of them. Right now they're sitting ducks and at risk."

"Let me be clear. Now that you're a potential witness as well, you're to avoid all contact with anyone connected to this case. Someone from my office will reach out to the others. If you interfere, I will have you charged with tampering with my witnesses."

"Okay, I get that. But I suggest you get busy and do something about their security, and be quick about it. You want their help, but you've left them dangling in the wind."

Jerome spoke up. "That was our thinking as well. We're looking into witness protection for both women. Once they're in a secured location, we can concentrate on Boris and company."

Kavanagh nixed that idea. "I don't agree. I don't see the need for further expense to the government by placing these women in witness protection."

"What's the alternative?" I asked. "You know damn well once Boris gets word his girlfriend is testifying against him, he'll have her killed. And there goes your precious case."

"At least we'll still have you, won't we?" One corner of her mouth curled up in a lopsided grin. "Leave the details to me. I know how to squeeze people to get what I want. I had planned to offer them immunity for their testimony, but the more I dig into this case, the more I find they're highly culpable themselves. I'm reconsidering all options."

"If I may make an observation, following the drive-by attempt on Boots, I'm surprised at the lack of urgency by your office. From my viewpoint, it looks like you have little interest in protecting the very assets needed to bring down the heavy hitters."

"I suppose you believe that by testifying, they're doing us a big favor. Well, I've got news for you. Those two are guilty as hell, and they're going down like the rest of them. They'll get no breaks from me. I'm not about to go soft on a couple of skanks."

"I've got news for you as well, *babe*. Those 'skanks,' as you so rudely called them, will probably make your case for you. You're better off placing them in witness protection because they have firsthand knowledge about Boris's operation that will nail this case shut."

As soon as I opened my mouth, I could see the others rolling their eyes and shaking their heads at my unrestrained outburst.

No one dared breathe a word. Kavanagh and I stared each other down until the DA shifted her gaze, as if she suddenly remembered there were others in the room.

She addressed the three agents dismissively. "Until all of your suspects are located, I'm not presenting any of this to a grand jury. I'm not going into court with a weak case. On your way out, have Gloria take her deposition," she said and jerked her head in my direction. "Make sure you get every detail. We don't want anyone saying we didn't do our jobs properly."

The deliberate snub hung in the air as the three men stood to leave. The smartassed bitch wouldn't make eye contact with me, which was probably just as well. Kavanagh ignored us and went back to reading a file.

Outside, I couldn't contain myself any longer.

"What's with the DA? Is she even playing on the same team as you guys? What's her major problem?"

The three of them awkwardly shuffled their feet and looked embarrassed. The office activity came to a standstill as everyone zeroed in on our conversation. Jerome Peters detached himself from our little group and approached a pretty auburn-haired woman that I assumed was Gloria and gave her instructions about taking my deposition on the Zharkov case.

The young woman led me to a private office where I provided as much detail as I could muster. She asked that I not leave until she transcribed the text for my signature.

Back in the anteroom, I found Boots and Donker waiting for me. Jerome Peters made his strategic retreat to parts unknown. It didn't take long to type up the deposition; I signed it straightaway, and we all left together. We took the elevator to the ground floor and exited the courthouse without so much as a single word between us.

Out on the street, we all took a breather. I hoped my little tantrum hadn't fouled things up for them, but honestly, I couldn't see that we had accomplished anything with all that legal foot-dragging. The DA seemed awfully reluctant to move forward with the case. It wasn't as if the culprits had to be in handcuffs before they could issue the indictments; it was up to the lawmen to make the arrests. I didn't understand why the DA was stalling and said as much.

"I told Donker we were going to have problems as soon as I heard Kavanagh was handling the case. She won't stick her neck out for anyone because she's more interested in maintaining her stellar conviction rate." Boots paced back and forth with nervous energy.

Donker said, "The fact is, without Boris, it's a crap case. We need to step up the search for Zharkov and Sevvin. I suggest we start by notifying ports and airport authorities. Let's get moving."

Turning to me, Donker said, "Thanks for coming down today, Vic, despite the 'Kabuki theatre' aspect. We'll keep you informed of any fresh developments." He shook my hand and edged away discreetly to give Boots and me a private moment.

"I'll call you when I can," Boots said. "Now that you know what the DA is like, watch yourself. She'd like nothing better than to make your life miserable, so stay well out of it from now on, okay?"

"I'll think about it. I'll feel a lot better once you've located Boris."

We parted, and I took the Metro across town to my office. I was still fuming about Kavanagh's sorry performance. I'm a hyper suspicious person by nature, and that little drama in the DA's office had me wondering whether Boris somehow had gotten to her. To my way of thinking, her contrary actions were nothing short of aiding and abetting the enemy. Deep down I knew it was preposterous, but I could think of no other reason that would excuse her attitude.

I sat next to the window and rocked gently in my seat as the train trundled down the underground tracks. Do you ever get that sixth sense you're being observed? I had that feeling. As we pulled away from each stop along Metro's Redline route, that creepy sensation stayed with me.

The train was crowded with commuters, yet I couldn't shake the uncanny notion I was being watched. I tried to spot whether someone had taken an unusual interest in me, but I didn't catch anyone looking my way surreptitiously. Maybe it was nothing, and I was just being paranoid, although in the past, I'd learned to pay attention when that perceptive spider-sense of mine tingled.

I rode the escalator to ground level and stalled for a bit to see if I could spot a tail. At the corner, a street vendor had set up shop, so I bought a bottle of water from her. I took a sip and scoped out the pedestrians for any telltale signs of imminent danger, but no one stood out as a potential threat.

I was about to cross the street when I saw a familiar hooded figure coming up the escalator. I had noticed that same dark-green hoodie on the train.

In a clumsy and amateurish attempt at being nonchalant, the dude projected precisely the opposite effect. I knew he was definitely following me by the way he meandered in my general direction while pretending to be invisible. When he was almost even with me, he veered at the last moment to block my path.

He started out by hustling me for some spare bucks like he was a homeless person down on his luck. He certainly had the smell down pat; the odor emanating from him was almost overwhelming.

When I didn't respond, the punk leaned in close and shouted obscenities in my face. He had a lot to learn about the give-and-take world of panhandling. I took a step back and casually shifted the water bottle to my right hand and slowly unscrewed the cap.

Then the punk said something strange. "You were warned, lady. Now you're gonna pay."

As I raised the bottle to take a swig, he dropped his shoulder and drove his fist, like a piston, straight at my jaw. But I had already anticipated this move.

I pivoted my torso to block with my left forearm, then countered by jamming the open mouth of the water bottle into his eye as hard as I could. He shrieked like a soprano as I grabbed a handful of greasy hair and held on while I twisted and ground that bottle into his eye socket. Water, mixed with blood, covered his face, causing him to choke and sputter. I wondered if this was what it felt like to be waterboarded.

As he stood off-balance, fighting to save his eye, I shoved the punk backward, smashing his head against an aluminum light pole that rang out like a bell. I swept his legs out from under him and planted him on his back. With a looping overhand punch, I shattered the bridge of his nose like fragments of fine bone china, which took the fight right out of him. Out of an abundance of caution, I stepped back to a respectful distance just in case he turned animal on me, although there was little chance of that.

He pressed his hands to his nose to staunch the flow of blood while the circular cut around his eye gushed freely. He coughed and spat so much blood that I had to help him sit up. In spite of his attack on me, I didn't want him to choke to death. Several people nearby had their cell phones out, recording the street scene. I doubted anyone had bothered to dial 911, so I did.

The EMT squad arrived in short order and got the bleeding under control before transporting my assailant to the emergency room. A patrol car pulled up just as the ambulance drove away, and I gave the officer my version of what happened. He would get the B-version later when he interviewed the "poor old victim" at the hospital. But I wasn't worried because several witnesses came forward to corroborate my story. I suggested to the officer that he route his report directly to Lieutenant Scanlin to save time, since the detective would hear of the incident in due course.

If I knew my man, there was a slim chance of linking Boris to the little pissant who tried to sucker punch me just now. Boris would have covered his tracks, no matter the outcome.

The attack was not a one-off. The warning Boots had drilled into me came back in a flash. I was being watched and followed, and when the opportunity presented itself, I would be taken out of action or possibly killed outright. It was as simple as that. It seemed Boris had me cornered in our own version of the *Danse Macabre*—the Dance of Death. But then, when it was all said and done, wasn't death the great equalizer after all?

# # #

Back in the office, I glanced once more at the escape plan I had drawn up for Sabrina and Katya. I contemplated deleting the file, considering my new marching orders from the DA and my promise to Boots, but then changed my mind at the last minute.

It was a good plan yesterday, and it was still a good plan today. I decided to sit on it a while longer to give the DA time to work out details from her end. In the back of my mind, I held out hope of doing things my own way, which was usually how I ended up in trouble, but why break the habit of a lifetime?

I found it difficult to pick up the threads of my old routine; too many competing thoughts running through my mind distracted me. After a short while, I lost my ability to concentrate on detailed matters, so I closed up shop for the day. Besides, the shadows on the wall had lengthened considerably, which was usually the signal that it was time to make a pit stop at the Old Market Grill. I hadn't spoken to Sally in what seemed like ages, so I thought I'd drop in for a quick visit.

I had just locked the door to my office when my cell phone buzzed inside my purse. I fished it out in time before it went to voicemail.

"Hi, there. I was just leaving the office."

"Oh, Vic. I'm so glad I caught you. Something terrible has happened!"

"What's wrong?"

"It's that animal, Andre Adema. You've got to stop him."

"Calm down, Sabrina, and tell me what's happened."

"He's at it again. We just heard one of the girls tried to escape, but Andre picked her up at the bus station before she could get out of town. I'll bet he's taken her to that farm of his way out in Virginia somewhere."

Was this the break I'd been looking for? If I could tie Andre Adema to the sex trade, and link him directly to Boris, the DA would have to move on them.

"What does that mean?"

"It means he'll likely beat the hell out of her. He always takes girls out there when they get out of line. I've heard about his brand of discipline. I also know sometimes they don't come back."

"Give me the address. I'll look into it."

Sabrina gave me the location and general directions to a farm out past Front Royal, Virginia. I punched in the directions on my cell phone. As it turned out, it was about a seventy-five-mile drive west from here at the north end of the Shenandoah Valley, on the crest of the Blue Ridge Mountains. The farm wasn't specifically listed on any maps, but I got a sense of the general area.

I called Boots to see if he would act as backup, but he didn't pick up. For about a half a second, I considered calling Scanlin, but that was a nonstarter since Andre's farm was outside his jurisdiction, and things could get sticky between competing bureaucracies. I decided to wing it on my own. The DA's warning echoed in the back of my mind, but it did not deter me. Besides, I wasn't exactly tampering with her witnesses; I was merely responding to a tip.

Yeah, I know; it was pretty thin, but what else could I do?

I headed back to my apartment and quickly geared up for the trip to the Virginia countryside. It was two hours later and well after dark by the time I found myself among the rolling hills and farms of the Shenandoah Valley. I slowed to a sedate thirty miles per hour as I searched for a certain disused dirt road along Route 55 west of Front Royal.

I approached an ancient general store that looked like it hadn't changed much since the 1950s and decided to gas up. After topping off my tank, I went inside to confirm that I was in the right neighborhood. You've gotta love country directions. The man said to continue down the road apiece and look for the gigantic tree with an old Wonder Bread sign. It could have been worse; at least I wasn't searching for the "brown cow standing in the pasture" or some such nonsense. I don't mind a drive through the countryside every once in a while, but give me the city any day.

At last, the familiar carnival-colored sign flashed in the headlights, and I slowed to make the turn onto a deeply rutted back road. After a short bumpy ride, I killed the engine and lights and continued on foot.

The night was cool, not cold, and quiet, too, because the sound of insects one normally heard during the summer had dissipated here in early fall. With only a half moon to illuminate the unfamiliar territory, I walked about a quarter mile until I came upon an overgrown cornfield on my right that hadn't seen a plow in years.

If my calculations were correct, this was the remote farm owned by Andre Adema where he brought girls to "break them in" and discipline them. I could only imagine what that entailed, but Sabrina had given me a pretty good idea. The farm was well off the beaten path and completely isolated. Andre had chosen this site well to avoid unnecessary attention.

I climbed the three-bar fence that ran the perimeter of the deserted pasture and stepped into a minefield of abandoned farm equipment left to rust in the grassy field. This required careful navigation, since I could not remember the last time I had gotten a tetanus shot.

The dilapidated farmhouse looked like it was ready to fold under its own weight, but I knew Andre was there by the flicker of candlelight coming from a second-story window. He had parked his white paneled service van on the far side of the house, nearly out of sight; soft ticking sounds could be heard in the still night as the engine cooled.

I crept along the side of the house and found a window that was missing most of its glass. As carefully as I could, I picked out the remaining shards until I could safely crawl over the sill and into the darkness beyond.

Once inside, I remained crouched along the wall and waited while my eyes adjusted to the deepening shadows. The room had a dank smell from continual exposure to the weather. Soon I discerned the outlines of a wingback chair, a steel-tube and Formica table, and an old sofa that spilled its stuffing on the floor.

As quietly as I could, I crossed the room to the hallway and ascended the narrow staircase. In turn, I tentatively lowered my weight onto each tread to avoid as much noise as possible. The soft, dancing candlelight grew brighter as I neared the top step. I peered cautiously over the edge of the floorboards to find a single attic room crowded with broken and abandoned furniture from prior generations of residents.

Andre Adema was there. He had his back to me and was oblivious to his surroundings as he hurriedly packed what looked like an old wooden footlocker.

I glanced to my right to the far end of the loft and nearly spewed lunch all over myself. The naked body of a young girl was splayed out on the bare wire box springs of an ancient bed. Her hands and feet were bound to the four corners, and a gag covered her mouth to muffle her screams. And I bet she screamed her head off, because the bloody red welts that crisscrossed her pale skin bore witness to the exquisite agony she had suffered, and recently, too, for the blood had not yet fully congealed.

I watched closely and prayed that I might detect the slightest rise and fall of her breathing, but it was no use. I soon realized she was mercifully beyond this world. For a brief moment, I mourned the waste of her young life. No one deserved to be treated this way. A surge of disgust, like bile, backed up in my throat that forced me to either choke on it or cough it up.

Andre Adema whirled about when he heard me gag. In his haste, he tried to turn, back away, and grab for his gun all in one motion, but I already had my Glock up and in the classic two-handed combat hold. And I had the perfect sight picture, too, as I drew a bead on his contorted, sweaty face.

What kind of monster did unspeakable things like this to another human being? It was beyond my comprehension; I couldn't get my head around it. Seriously, what kind of depraved mind took pleasure in inflicting pain and suffering on helpless victims?

In a kaleidoscopic flash of memory, all the nightly news stories I'd ever heard and all the police reports that I'd ever read from years past came back to me. Scores of defenseless women paraded through my mind's eye—living, breathing, feeling human beings. The poor women were sexually abused and discarded like so much trash simply to satisfy the pathetic lust of some perverted sonofabitch who wouldn't know how to function in a normal relationship.

It was at this precise moment that I dispensed with any internal debate with myself. I freely admit it was a conscious decision on my part, but I vowed, right then and there, this particular animal would never harm anyone again.

Andre Adema took one look at me and correctly interpreted my slow and deliberate movements as I stepped into the attic to face him. He raised his hands in surrender and cried out, "Don't shoot. I give up. Look, my hands are up. For crying out loud, don't do it!"

In a futile attempt to outgun me, he went for his pistol, and I let him nearly make it. For the longest time afterward, I could recall with absolute clarity the high-pitched hysteria in his voice as he screamed at me while trying to free the gun from his belt.

Captured in my memory like a snapshot in time, the instant that I pulled the trigger, I had the rare and unexpected pleasure of witnessing a plume of crimson exit the back of his head before he hit the floor.

I left the creep lying where he fell. Sadly, I had to leave that poor girl too, but it was necessary that I got out of there as quickly as possible. I hurried down the stairs and went out the front door. I breathed in deeply, and the cool nighttime air helped clear my head.

Oh, don't get me wrong, I didn't feel the least bit of guilt about dusting off Andre Adema. Not one damn bit. Actually, I wished I could have done so several times over. What got to me was the pure evil that had pervaded my life ever since Mitch Goldberg walked into my office. From that first moment, I knew there was going to be trouble. Didn't I say so?

I don't remember the long ride home. My little Audi SUV was like a homing pigeon, and before I realized it, I was in the underground garage at my apartment building.

In spite of the time—almost two o'clock in the morning—I got out my armorer's gear and went to work on my nine millimeter. That's the beauty of Glock pistols; they are easy to maintain. The weapon broke down effortlessly into its basic components.

I scrubbed the slide and frame inside and out with cleaner and replaced every internal component using the spare rebuild kit that I kept on hand, including a new firing pin and ejector. I also installed a used spare barrel that I had picked up at a swap meet. I knew enough to replace all the parts that could leave telltale signs that it was my gun used to eliminate that pile of excrement back at the farmhouse. I even remembered to swap the magazine. I didn't want some sharp forensic expert linking me to Andre Adema.

Ammo was a different problem, however. I had a couple boxes of the same brand sitting on a shelf in my closet. Tomorrow I'd replace it with an altogether unique brand. I wasn't worried about the brass shell I'd left behind at the farmhouse, because it had always been my habit to reload mags using gloves, thus no fingerprints.

Sometimes you have to think like a crook, or perhaps I watched too many crime thrillers. Nevertheless, when I finished, I went to bed secure in the knowledge that the world was better off without Andre Adema, or so I rationalized to myself.

# # #

I awoke to find the pull-down shades illuminated by bright sunlight, which gave the bedroom a warm glow. In my mind, the events of only a few hours ago had already taken on the feel of yesterday's news.

Wasting precious little time, I quickly completed my morning routine. My immediate task was to dispose of the old gun components and surplus ammunition.

I took the George Washington Parkway into Fairfax, Virginia, and followed the two-lane road west all the way out Route 7 past Leesburg. I wanted to see an old army friend of mine, retired Sergeant Major Gene Godfren.

The Sarge ran a small, exclusive shooting range where quite a few federal and state police officers passed through Godfren's capable hands, as well as military and a certain unnamed black ops team. By the time they left his range, the Sarge had every one of them honed razor sharp, like precision instruments, and ready for specific combat missions.

Set back from the main highway was a nondescript building that you didn't notice unless you knew to look. The vestibule was arranged with a double set of doors that formed a mantrap, along with multiple surveillance cameras. You couldn't get into the sergeant major's shop unless you belonged there.

The small shop had row upon row of glass-topped cases featuring all manner of firearms, knives, holsters, and other accessories available to those whose livelihood revolved around security and self-defense.

Godfren was behind the counter when I entered but came over with a big grin on his face. "It's about time you came to see the old gray-haired Sarge," he said and gave me a crushing hug. "Come to knock the cobwebs off your aim? You know, accuracy is a perishable skill," he reminded me. The old Sarge was always in training mode.

"Yeah, I need the practice. Also, I've got some spare ammo to donate if you want it."

Sarge laughed at that. "If you know how much ammo you've got, then you don't have enough."

"I have some parts I'd like to dispose of too," I said and dropped a plastic bag full of components on the countertop. "They all need to be reworked before they're used again, but I'd like the barrel recycled into oblivion, if you don't mind."

He looked at me sharply. "Trouble?"

"Let's just call it trouble avoidance."

I didn't have to say more; sometimes knowing too much only complicated matters. With a nod, he grabbed the bag of spare parts.

"Follow me, troop."

We went into the tool shop behind the front office, where he kept his gunsmithing gear. He fired up an acetylene torch and heated the gun barrel until it glowed cherry red. Using a small sledgehammer, Sarge reduced the molten metal to a flat lump. He repeated the process several times until the steel was unrecognizable and beyond worthless.

With that small chore completed, he said, "You're still running close to the edge, I see."

"Most definitely this time, sir. But I'm about to close the file on some wicked people."

He didn't probe further. We spent a few minutes catching up on old times and reminisced about people we used to know, and then Sarge set me up on a firing lane. Over the next several hours, I put a couple hundred rounds through my newly rebuilt rod to break in the fresh components and refine my shooting skills.

Without constant practice, it was easy to lapse into bad shooting habits that affect accuracy. Sarge observed my progress and made several adjustments to my stance, head position, and grip. Soon the hits on center mass and head shots were consistently tight.

Before I left, I also stocked up on a new batch of personal defense loads as well. This time I opted for Hornady's Critical Duty 9mm+P ammunition. It was the FBI's newest standard defense load, and if it was good enough for them, then I could get by with it too.

"Sorry I can't stay longer, Sarge. Got some villains to catch, but I'll be back soon."

"You'd better. You owe me a beer." He gave me a quick hug, and I got out of there. Sarge had been the senior enlisted man in our unit and always looked after the troops like we were his kids, and in my case, a wayward kid bordering on delinquency. The old Sarge was good people.

I always felt better after putting in some range time. There is something calming about blowing up a couple boxes of ammo on the firing line; it never failed to relieve my stress level. I headed back into the city, confident there was no longer a connection to the events from the night before.

Hold it right there. You cannot make me feel bad about this, so don't even try. You're going to argue that I took the law into my own hands last night, right?

Well, sort of, and we can debate the finer points on that. But was it justified? I'd like to think so. And I'd damn well do it again if faced with a similar situation. Besides, who else was going to defend those poor girls?

It is a tragic fact human trafficking has flourished for centuries and will probably carry on long after we're all dead and gone. But at least there was one less purveyor in the game, namely Andre Adema. And I was just getting started.

This is my story, and I'm sticking to it—it wasn't me. And besides, the rat had it coming.

#

Monday rolled around all too soon. The office had a dusty smell of disuse, so I cranked open the windows to let in some fresh air and sat down at my desk to catch up on the stack of mail that had piled up beneath the slot. The red blinking light on my answering machine alerted me to several messages, and I'm sure my email in-box was chock-full of time-wasting junk.

I didn't like all this access to my time. It was intrusive, but then it went with the job. There was nothing too pressing at the moment, just a couple of new prospects inquiring about my availability, which I had to blow off for the time being.

Lieutenant Scanlin had left a voice message stating he needed to speak to me. If he already had a report on the farmhouse, then that was fast. It never failed; these old places could remain deserted for years but let something happen in the middle of the night, and suddenly, everyone knows all about it. Was this the case, or was Scanlin still pursuing the arms smuggling angle?

If you thought my guilty conscience was nagging at me, you'd be wrong. Although, I had to be careful around Scanlin or I might find myself confined to a sterile room—the one with the two-way mirror and tape recorder—as I tried to explain a suspicious homicide.

I called Scanlin and caught him in the office. He suggested we meet somewhere other than the station, which was fine by me. We agreed to meet at Georgetown Park, a nearby mall where we could talk over a latte.

The afternoon traffic was unusually heavy, and it took over twenty minutes to cover the six blocks. I arrived to find Scanlin already seated at the bistro with two steaming cups in front of him.

"I took the liberty of ordering for you. I hope you don't mind."

"Not at all."

"By the way, I heard about your little run-in."

"Yeah, some punk tried to sucker punch me. I assumed it was Boris sending his regards."

Scanlin nodded his head. "The beat cop reported you put your man down hard. Good for you."

"Hey, I've been trying to mind my own business and stay the hell out of your case, but some people didn't get the memo." I took a sip of coffee and sat back. I watched as throngs of people strolled by, intent on a leisurely afternoon of shopping.

"How goes the investigation?" I asked.

"Like you, we've been told to back off. I guess the Feds don't care for the competition."

"Yeah, the DA wasn't exactly subtle about it."

"By the way, where's your friend, Johnson? I need to speak to him."

"What about?"

"I need to clear up a couple points about his involvement with Zharkov and the shipment they took down to Florida, but he seems to have disappeared."

"Even though the DA forbade further contact?"

"Just closing out the books. What does it matter now?"

"Honestly, I don't know where he is, Lieutenant. I heard he's been quite busy since he left the hospital."

"Funny how uncooperative certain agencies can be when it involves one of their own. If he contacts you, let him know we merely want to fill in some blanks. We're not asking for a deposition."

"When I see him, I'll pass along your request."

"You're not fooling me, Miss Carella. I know you're still going after Zharkov, so let's not be coy with each other. We got into an unpleasant situation the other night—not of my doing, by the way—however, I want you to know there are no hard feelings. I believe we can help each other and remain independent in our respective investigations. What do you say?"

"I did promise to stay out of your way regarding the arms smuggling, but I said nothing about the prostitution ring. And regarding Boots Johnson, I cannot speak to what he may or may not be involved in, so don't put me in the middle. If you need to contact him, you have official channels; use them, not me. I just want to be clear on that."

"Fair enough. Now that we've drawn the lines of demarcation, allow me to throw a little information your way."

"If it pertains to the prostitution ring, then go right ahead."

"Yeah, it does. Ever heard of Andre Adema?"

The warning bells started clanging loudly, but I kept my composure and stuck to the bare facts. "I met him in Annapolis; he's part of Boris's crew. He supposedly imports and exports fresh produce. Why?"

"He was found Sunday morning on his farm in Virginia. Someone blew his brains out."

"You don't say… Killed, was he? By whom?"

"That's the sixty-four-thousand-dollar question. What do you know about it?"

"Why should I know anything? From what I've heard about Andre Adema, it couldn't have happened to a more suitable bastard. No loss as far as I'm concerned."

"I thought you might take that attitude. Just for the record, you're saying you have no knowledge concerning Adema's death or who may have killed him?"

"Nope, nothing at all," I said, as clear-eyed as a church deacon.

Scanlin nodded his head and gave me a crooked grin that was neither amused nor sincere. He didn't believe a word I said, but could you blame him? I mean, we'd been doing this dance from day one, and neither of us willing to give an inch. I'd have to add Scanlin to my growing list of people to watch out for. And what was that bull about working our respective investigations? But then he segues right into the sex-trade angle. As they say down South, Daddy may have raised a hellion, but he didn't raise a fool.

We had reached the end of our give-and-take session, and neither of us came away with anything useful to our "respective investigations."

I admit I was a little worried that Scanlin had somehow linked me to Adema's death. Going over all the details in my mind, there was nothing that could implicate me directly.

Okay, I admit I wasn't squeaky clean on this, but I could make a damn good case for self-defense if pressed to explain myself. I just didn't want to get caught up again in the slow grind of bureaucratic machinery. I'd already had a taste of that, and it wasn't fun.

And now for the really tough job.

I left the mall and headed over to the law offices of Warren, Sifkin, and Moore, hoping to catch my benefactor in the office for a change. For personal reasons, I dreaded this meeting because I knew how it was going to end. However, since the DA banned me from further involvement in either of the two cases, there was nothing more I could do on Goldberg's behalf, and I was no longer responsible for the safety of Sabrina and Katya.

To my mind, things were progressing as they should. Who was I to argue with the federal government or local law enforcement? It is the wise person who knows their place and their limitations. Or was I merely trying to convince myself? So much had happened in such a short time frame, but at least things were quickly coming to an end. Or so I hoped.

Regardless, I was not looking forward to this conversation with James Warren.

I'd never met anyone quite like him before; I found him to be openly generous and willing to help others just for the asking. In a short couple of weeks, he'd come to mean so much more to me than I could have imagined.

When I arrived, the receptionist ushered me into his office after inquiring whether I wanted coffee or tea. I declined and sat down in the plush leather wingback to wait.

I looked around and noted James had decorated his office with the usual legal tomes and other paraphernalia. I was impressed, however, by the number of framed pictures featuring a young James Warren in a polo kit. There were the obligatory group shots with team members celebrating their wins, but there was one of James that I particularly liked: the one of him mounted on a gorgeous stallion. The camera caught him as he leaned forward to pat the animal on its broad neck. In this shot he was decades younger, but the image captured what I considered to be the classic James Warren: it depicted a man of quiet confidence in control of his destiny.

The door opened, and James strolled in as masterful as ever.

"Good afternoon, Victoria. What brings you here? Nothing the matter, is there?"

"Sorry for the intrusion. I should have made an appointment, but I was close by and needed to see you. I have additional information about my two lady friends."

"By all means. What's on your mind?"

"It turns out your generous help is no longer required regarding their escape. The Feds have preempted those plans."

"Oh, really? How so?"

"They threw me off the case and ordered me to stand down because a slew of indictments are pending, which makes me a potential witness. The two women I told you about—Boris's girlfriend and Anatoly Sevvin's wife, by the way—are also being called to testify. Thereafter, they will probably disappear into the witness protection program if they aren't outright indicted themselves."

"I see. So, you don't need my help after all. It appears your altruistic plans are for naught. Well, at least they'll be in excellent hands if I'm to believe what I've heard about witness protection. Where does that leave the gang of smugglers?"

"Once the Feds take the gang off the street, it's all down to the prosecutor. That will put a stop to their arms smuggling and sex trafficking rings once and for all, and I'll be glad of that!"

James turned his head and gazed out the window, deep in thought.

"I, uh . . . I cannot thank you enough for all your generosity, Mr. Warren. You've been incredibly helpful throughout this entire ordeal."

"Don't go embarrassing me again, Victoria. I have to believe any decent person in my position would do as much or more. Your friends are safe; that's all that matters. Now you can relax and quit worrying."

"We've collaborated on some big issues over the past couple weeks, but things are wrapping up quickly. I cannot help feeling we've come to the end of something fantastic, and it's time to move on. Am I wrong in thinking that?" I said, feeling as if the curtain was coming down on the last act of a memorable and powerful performance.

"Come now, cheer up. You're not going to get all sentimental on me, are you? Fate threw us together, and we faced some tough challenges. Thankfully, it's all worked out for the best. Of course we'll always remain friends if that's what's worrying you. Of that I'm quite certain."

"I hope so, Mr. Warren. Without doubt, this has been the most intense and frightful case I've ever taken on. Going back to routine domestic cases will seem almost pedestrian by comparison, like taking a giant leap backward. To be honest, I prefer it, but it has been one hell of an adventure."

"Was there anything else?"

"Not really. I guess this is goodbye—for now. I just wanted to let you know about the change of plans, and to thank you in person for all you've done. You're an incredible man. It's been a pleasure meeting you and working with you."

He took my hand in both of his and held on tightly for a moment. I thought I detected a trace of moistness around his clear blue eyes.

"Goodbye, my dear. Stay in touch. And stay out of trouble," he admonished one last time.

Sage advice, but when did life ever work out the way we hoped?

Chapter Thirteen

I was beginning to wonder how I got any work done in the pre-Goldberg days. Lately, every time I sat down to catch up with old clients, something pulled me away. Since I was no longer involved with the smuggling case, I was determined to get back into my normal routine, even if it killed me. And who knows, it just might.

By midafternoon, I had three fresh cases lined up requiring background investigations on pending divorce litigation. These days, assembling documentation on community assets is a huge part of any divorce settlement. It's a matter of knowing where to look and how to dig out information in spite of secured databases and privacy laws designed to protect individuals from prying eyes such as mine.

The difficulty in hiding assets lies in eliminating the paper trail, which is virtually impossible. Your average citizen fails to realize just how many nongovernmental databases contain their private information, including cable companies, magazine subscriptions, and charities, to name a few. The trick is they all share that information among themselves.

My best sources were the big-box stores and online retail sales. Once I get onto that line of inquiry, it's only a matter of time before I've got your entire financial history laid out before me. It comes down to cross-referencing enough related databases to discover how and where uncooperative spouses tried to squirrel away community assets that they refused to share with their soon-to-be ex-significant other.

For example, I was having particularly good luck tracking down one wayward deadbeat. Here's a tip: don't transfer assets into your brother's name, not even going back a year or more, for those contemplating long-term plans. It's still a dead giveaway. And if the hapless brother commingled his relative's assets with his own that makes him vulnerable to a visit from the taxman. Not a good move for either of them, but from my perspective, so easily traceable.

As I probed for each new tidbit of information, I documented the missing assets I found all along the information trail. I'm nothing if not an expert at research and recordkeeping. It was an amateurish attempt by the lying little jerk to hide assets from the wife and her attorney—wait a sec; this sounds so familiar. Have I said this before? Perhaps I'd become so jaded that I perceived all of these conniving spouses in the same light.

Nevertheless, for me, it was like an Easter egg hunt as I blithely skipped along, collecting treats here and there, and filled my basket to the brim with goodies.

Trust me, if you're going to hide assets, it's best to leave it to the professionals; your chances for success go up exponentially. Then your only worry is whether the so-called professional will keep their mouth shut. It's a never-ending nightmare of lies and deceit that eventually spirals out of control. I suggest you do not try this at home.

My cell phone buzzed, and I picked it up before the second ring.

"Hi, Vic. Sorry I missed your call. We're running a bit late, but we'll be there as soon as possible," Sabrina said. I could tell she was on the road from the background noise.

"What are you talking about? We had no plans to meet," I said.

"I thought you said meet you at the diner, you know, the one on Annapolis Road where we first met. We'll be there in ten minutes. And have we got some good news for you, but we prefer to tell you in person. We'll see you soon."

"You realize I'm not allowed to have contact with you guys anymore, right? The DA threw me off the case. She made it abundantly clear, practically under penalty of death."

"After I tell you what we found out, you'll want back in, I promise," Sabrina said excitedly.

"In that case, I'm on my way—wait, wait!" Something clicked into place in my mind. "You said 'missed my call,' but I never called you. You called me just now. What's going on?"

"Actually, it was your text message saying you wanted to meet. It's a lucky coincidence, because we just found out Boris and Anatoly are planning on leaving the country… Oh, darn, there goes my big surprise. You made me tell you anyway. But guess what else? I think we've finally identified their principal contact as well!"

"You must be mistaken, Sabrina. I didn't text you. Check again. What was the number on the text message?"

Sabrina's voice trailed away as if she handed off the phone. I waited while Katya checked the number on the text message while Sabrina drove. I heard Katya respond but couldn't make out what she said owing to the road noise.

Sabrina came back on the line. "That's funny. I thought it was your number because it starts out with the same area code and prefix. I didn't bother reading the whole thing; I just assumed it was you. Besides, the text was specific about where to meet."

"Where are you now?"

"We're close by. We're on Route 50 and approaching the exit now."

It was an obvious hoax but a disturbing new development. Who else, other than the three of us, knew about our earlier rendezvous at the diner?

Then I remembered. At the conclusion of our first meeting, I thought I'd recognized a familiar face just as I pulled into traffic. At the time, I had a vague feeling that I saw Mike Carver whizzing past me, heading in the opposite direction. But, if not him, then someone else spotted me in the area and figured out I had met with Sabrina and Katya.

A sudden stab of fear went straight through me. I shouted into the phone.

"Sabrina, stop what you're doing. Stop the car! Get out of the car now!"

"Why? What's wrong? I don't understand—"

For a nanosecond, I heard the explosion at the other end before the line went dead. I silently prayed over and over to the good Lord above that nothing had happened to them as I hurriedly hit redial, but Sabrina's number went unanswered.

I quickly dialed Lieutenant Scanlin, and as soon as he answered, I started blubbering about this strange turn of events. I practically ordered him to dispatch someone to check on the two women. I knew it was out of his jurisdiction, but he could cut through all the red tape with a minimum of explanation and get results faster than I could. I was desperate to know whether Sabrina and Katya were all right.

I waited and waited. I could have screamed at not knowing what had happened, but I dreaded the answer. Finally, after what felt like an eternity, Scanlin came back on the line.

"What did you find out?"

"I'm sorry, Vic. There are people already at the scene reporting on the explosion. A blue Mercedes convertible was blown to bits. I take it that was the car Sabrina was driving?"

Words failed me. What had just occurred here? What had I done? My face crumbled as tears welled up and spilled down my cheeks.

Images of our initial meeting flashed through my mind when Sabrina and Katya first made their big commitment to help me bust Boris's smuggling operations. In the beginning, they were afraid because they knew the risks, yet they were still willing to put themselves out there to help me. And now they had paid the ultimate price. And it was entirely my fault.

"Vic? Can you hear me?" Scanlin's voice finally disrupted my thoughts.

"Yeah, I'm here," I said. My voice cracked.

"Where are you? I'll come to you."

"I'm—I'm still downtown. I'll come to your office." With that, I hung up. I couldn't talk anymore; I wasn't capable of coherent thought at the moment.

I took a cab to police headquarters, not trusting myself to navigate DC traffic. The cab deposited me in front of the station, which stood out in stark contrast in a neighborhood populated by small shops huddled together among aging brownstone-type apartments.

The wide granite steps led up to the brass double doors. There were so many, and I didn't feel like making the effort, but I forced myself up the steps one at a time until I finally reached the top. I pulled on the heavy door and ducked inside. I don't know what I expected might happen, but at this point, there was nothing that any of us could do to help poor Sabrina and her loyal friend, Katya.

I couldn't stop thinking about it. What had I done? Look at the trouble I had wrought. Even though my initial investigation and subsequent actions were well intentioned, I had caused more harm than good. What a fool I was to get involved in the first place.

The desk sergeant was expecting me because he immediately escorted me to Scanlin's office. His sidekick, Sergeant McAllister, was there as well. They stood as I entered; the grave looks on their faces said they understood what I felt at the moment. It was much appreciated.

Scanlin spoke first. "We got word it was a pretty powerful explosion; the car completely disintegrated. If it's any consolation, I'm quite certain they died instantaneously."

"I'm sorry too. This can't be easy for you."

I was surprised at the expression of sympathy coming from McAllister, but he sounded genuinely sincere. I suppose even this rugged giant had a heart deep down inside somewhere. I mumbled my thanks.

Scanlin continued. "Why were you even talking to Sabrina Farkas? I thought the DA forbid any further contact."

"They were set up. It was a trick."

"What do you mean?"

"They received a text supposedly coming from me that said to meet at a diner where we met once before. It was a hoax, of course, but they didn't know that. They thought I wanted to meet with them. They called to tell me they were running late."

McAllister sprang into action. "I'll pull the phone company records. We'll find out who sent that text." He left the office on a mission.

Scanlin didn't push it, and we sat in silence for a brief interval. I was on the verge of losing it again and fought to control my emotions. The women were trying to help in the only way they knew how. And now they were dead.

Sabrina and Katya, you didn't deserve this. I'm so sorry. I let you down.

"You came all this way so we could talk, but you look tired. We can do this another time, if you like. Allow me to take you home," Scanlin offered.

"You know, I'm going to take you up on that offer. Thank you kindly."

Scanlin was right; I was completely done in. At the moment, I didn't have the energy or presence of mind to figure out even simple tasks, like how to get myself home.

As we headed toward the elevator, McAllister came up to us. A single sheet of paper fluttered in his hand.

"No dice. The text came from a burner phone," he said. "It originated from a bootlegged number that closely resembled Vic's number. The call was routed through a cell tower in the Annapolis area. I'm afraid there's not much to go on."

I thanked McAllister for trying. It was a disappointing dead-end—oops, that was in poor taste. Seriously, no pun intended. I'd have been more surprised if McAllister's inquiry had revealed something useful. Boris was not one to leave loose ends. Now he no longer had to worry about any threat that his girlfriend may have posed to him.

The image of that smug DA withholding witness protection from the two women came back to me in a rush, and it made me damn angry. We, all of us, should have done more to protect them.

At every turn, it seemed Boris was one step ahead of us. The ongoing and competing investigations had not produced useful results. Instead of putting him on the defensive, Boris was leading the charge and making all the right moves; he never put a foot wrong.

The idea of Boris as a strategic thinker would never have occurred to me. Boots was right; he was an expert at self-preservation, while he made the rest of us look like rank amateurs.

Scanlin held the elevator door for me, and then we descended to the lobby. We walked out the front entrance into the crisp autumn air. I breathed deeply; it helped clear my head, but only somewhat.

During the ride to my apartment, Scanlin pressed for more details regarding my conversation with Sabrina, but I had nothing more to offer.

"And she never named the source behind Boris's operation, the one calling the shots?"

"She was about to. She said I'd be pleased about what they found out, but I got distracted because I hadn't sent them the text message in the first place. I wondered how they came by that information."

"Damn! That would have been helpful."

"Sorry. I wasn't thinking."

"No, don't misunderstand. I wasn't blaming you. I was just hoping to get some insight into who is behind the smuggling racket and finally shut it down. That's all."

He was quick to reassure me. I suppose I was too quick to take offense in the first place, but it was a sensitive subject just now.

Scanlin followed the circular drive to the covered entrance of my apartment building. He came around to open the door for me and extended a helping hand. Yep, the last of the Southern gentlemen all right.

"No rush on this, but when you feel up to it, drop by the office and give me a formal statement. I'm coordinating with Maryland State Police on this and want to provide all possible assistance."

"I'll do that. Just give me a little time."

Back in my apartment, I headed straight for the bedroom and flopped down on the wide bed. I bounced poor Marlowe from his comfy spot on my pillow. He stretched and arched his back, and then came over and gave me a gentle nudge on the cheek. Marlowe was a cuddler, and he was just what I needed at the moment. He let me hold him tight while I cried my eyes out.

No matter your profession, you never intend to do harm. You only intend to help. But in that regard, I had failed miserably. Suddenly, I was awash in self-doubt as those old feelings from times past came back to me. I had questioned Goldberg's ability to run with the big boys, but just who the hell did I think I was? Had I become so smug and overconfident that I thought I could beat a street-smart thug like Boris at his own game?

The spirits of Sabrina Farkas and Katya Sevvin already haunted me; I couldn't get them out of my mind. They were so willing to help, so eager to put a stop to the evil that Boris and company continued to inflict on innocent young women. And now they were gone.

I should have let go of the case long before now, but no, I had to press on, just had to be the one who got Boris. And look what it cost.

My altruistic goal was to stop the sex trafficking; I wanted to save as many of those women as I could from a life of degradation and servitude. But in the process, two others lost their lives, and still the sex trafficking continued unabated. What had I accomplished?

Absolutely nothing.

I now understood how field commanders must agonize over the imminent loss of life in order to capture their objectives. How does one justify that loss in relation to the gain? What was the acceptable ratio of lives lost to lives saved? And how do you learn to live with those fateful decisions? I needed to know so I could accept and deal with the results of my earlier actions.

I don't know how long I lay in bed mourning Sabrina and Katya and wallowing in self-pity over my current predicament, but my big guy brought me back to reality. He pawed impatiently at my face to remind me it was dinnertime.

I rolled out of bed and realized it was well after dark. I heard my cell phone ring and ran to the living room to retrieve it from my purse.

"Hello, Victoria. I just heard the sad news about your two lady friends. I'm so sorry."

The warm voice of James Warren comforted me. In an instant, I was a bundle of raw nerves all over again. It took several minutes to compose myself before I could hold a rational conversation.

"So kind of you to call, Mr. Warren. It's been a hell of a day, I can tell you."

"Is there anything I can do for you? How are you holding up?"

"I'm okay for now; just having a rough time dealing with the fact that I put them in danger in the first place. How did you hear about it?"

"It's all over the news, my dear. When they mentioned the names of the two victims, I realized immediately they were the same two women you spoke of."

"Some help I was. They'd have been better off if I had never contacted them."

"Now, Victoria, don't blame yourself. Unfortunately, these things happen when evil men like Boris Zharkov get involved. I tried to warn you . . . Sorry, I don't mean to scold."

"No, you're right. I should have taken your advice and dropped the whole thing, but it's too late for that."

"What will you do now?"

"The DA said she'd have my head if I interfered again, so I'm staying away. Except that I have to see Lieutenant Scanlin one more time. He asked that I drop by tomorrow to provide a statement about the phone call from Sabrina. It's just a formality."

"I know you'll be fine once you've had time to process your emotions. May I suggest you take some time off for yourself? Go somewhere pleasant and forget all about this awful business. It would do you a world of good, I'm sure of it."

"I didn't listen to you the last time and look what happened. You know, that's a great idea. I think I will take a couple of weeks off to clear my head. Then I can get back to my normal routine. Hopefully by then, Boris and his gang are behind bars for good."

"That's the spirit. Get some rest and clear your mind of depressing thoughts. You'll call when you return so that I'll know you're all right?"

"I will, and thanks, Mr. Warren. You're so good to me. I appreciate your concern."

"Think nothing of it, my dear. I knew you'd be feeling low, and I wanted to check on your welfare. Good night, and we'll talk again soon."

I prepared Marlowe's bowl and got him settled for the evening. I leaned on the door of my refrigerator while I looked over the contents, but nothing looked appetizing. What I wanted was some company. The thought of staring at the four walls all night was out of the question. I grabbed my coat and purse and headed out the door to catch up with my old friend.

I hit the elevator button and waited. When the door opened, Boots Johnson practically bowled me over as he rushed into the hallway.

"Oh, sorry, Vic," he said as we disentangled ourselves. "How are you? I got here as soon as I could."

"I'm fine…for now. I was just on my way to the Grill. Want to join me?"

"Love to. When I heard what happened, I couldn't believe it at first. I'm glad you weren't involved. What happened exactly?"

We stood in the hallway as I repeated the story, which by now was not as painful as it had been at first. My head and my emotions had calmed down to a point where I could function once more, but just barely. As I related the series of events, Boots listened intently, not interrupting until I finished. I managed to convey the entire story without losing it again.

"We're going to get those bastards. Sabrina and Katya will not have died in vain—that's a promise," he said. I could feel the angry vibes coming from him. Something momentous was about to happen—I felt sure of it.

"I keep asking myself what I could have done differently. I should have executed on plan and gotten them out of town in spite of what that stupid DA said. I hold her responsible as well. I'm not shouldering the guilt all by myself."

"Lighten up on yourself, okay? I can sympathize because I know what you're going through. And I can assure you; today will live in your memory forever. Trust me; I speak from experience."

"I appreciate what you're saying, but for right now, I just want to be free of all conscious thought. I want to put it completely out of my mind. How do you shut down the internal noise?"

"C'mon, let's get out of here. You need to get this out of your system once and for all. Tell me," he said enigmatically, "have you ever swallowed a worm?"

We took a cab to the Old Market Grill. It was early enough to catch Sally still pouring drinks and keeping up a running chatter with the bar crowd. How they all loved that girl. I did too—but not like that! She was my good and loyal friend, the kind of friend like Sabrina and Katya had been to each other. Dear Lord, I hoped the two of us never ended up in similar trouble because I stupidly got myself into a jam, and poor Sally got caught up in it.

I really needed to let this go, but I didn't know how. At least, not at the moment. I hoped that old saying about how time heals all wounds was true. And sooner rather than later would be most welcome!

Boots commandeered two stools, and we parked ourselves at the bar. Sally came over to take our order and automatically placed two beverage napkins in front of us. Sally knew me well enough to studiously avoid the day's major topic, which was crucial if I was going to hold it together while in public.

"We'll have a bottle of your Clase Azul Reposado, if you please," Boots said with a flourish.

Sally gave him an incredulous look. With a grin, she went to the storage room to see if she had any in stock.

"What kind of trouble are you getting me into?" I asked, not sure of what was coming.

"You'll see."

Sally returned, carrying a highly decorative blue-and-white bottle. I'd never seen one like it before. Obviously, this was not your run-of-the-mill rail liquor.

As Sally cracked the label, Boots described how each bottle of this aged premium tequila remained untapped upwards to a year, making it a Reposado. In contrast to Anejo tequila, he explained, which is aged more than one, but less than three years. The bottle itself was a distinctive hand-painted work of art by artisans from a small village in Mexico. Already my education in liquor was broadening. This promised to be an interesting evening.

Boots poured two shots of the intense amber liquid, and we toasted one another. That first shot went down smoothly. It didn't have the pleasant burn you get with some other tequila. It was sweeter and had a robust smoky flavor than I wasn't expecting, but I found it quite satisfying.

The Clase Azul was to tequila what, let's say, a Jack Daniels Sinatra Select was to Tennessee whiskey. I could taste a hint of caramel and vanilla. With its unique flavor, this was the sipping variety of tequila as opposed to a blanco used in margaritas, mojitos, and other specialty drinks.

Sally placed a plate of shrimp cocktail on the bar for us to sample. It was the perfect complement to the tequila we were enjoying—and quite a bit of it, too, I might add.

"Before I forget, Pete and Melanie invited us over for dinner. Are you interested?"

"I, uh…I don't know exactly how to answer that."

"For crying out loud, Boots. There's no hidden agenda here; it's just dinner."

"I know. It's just that I don't normally…that is, it's been a while since I've done normal things like that. You know, couples stuff."

"What are you talking about 'normal'? You do eat dinner, don't you?"

"I didn't mean it like that. You know the kind of world I live in, mostly in the shadows. Polite company, it's not something that I'm used to."

"As I live and breathe. Don't tell me that Boots Johnson, agent extraordinaire, is shy about meeting some decent folks? I'll tell you what; I'll have them meet you at the door with guns drawn so you'll feel at home."

"Okay, smartass; I guess I asked for that one."

"So, I can tell them we're on for dinner? Afterward you can slink back into the shadows again, possibly never to be seen or heard from again. That is, until the next time I need a dinner date."

Boots inhaled deeply, then let it out slowly. "Sure, you're on. When and where?"

"Pick me up tomorrow night around seven. And just so you know, it's customary to bring a bottle of wine. I promise we'll ease you back into polite society gently," I said with a smile.

I was about to bust his chops some more, but thought better of it. It's curious the things you learn about people. Here's a guy comfortable in the company of murderers and thieves, a guy at home in the volatile world of illicit international arms deals. But then he gets all goofy over something simple like dinner for four.

Men—go figure. But, you must admit, it was kind of funny.

Boots poured a couple more shots, and we knocked them back together. To sort of seal the deal, I suppose.

Normally, I don't do shots anymore, especially not tequila. It always brought back embarrassing memories from my younger days. I believe the phrase "let me find my pants, and I'll go with you" figured prominently in one drinking episode I was still trying to live down. Just ask Pete Beckham; he loved telling that story about me.

I had vague recollections of my going-away party before leaving Germany, but I recalled it involved a lot of drinking and dancing. As it happened, my departure coincided with St. Patrick's Day, which only contributed to the massive quantities of liquor consumed that night.

We met at our local *gasthaus* the night before I was scheduled to fly home. Starting out, there were about twenty of us, and we were having a roaring good time. The German patrons had sort of gotten used to a bunch of GIs raising a little hell from time to time. Before the night was over, we had the whole place singing, dancing, and drinking together like old friends. You could say we were just doing our part to improve international relations. At least, that's what I've been telling people for years. But it sure was fun!

Despite the passage of time, I still remembered with absolute clarity the raging hangover the next day on the flight back to the States. Yeah, strong memories that stayed with me even after all these years. And here we were putting a serious dent in that bottle of Clase Azul.

Tequila and me—need I say more?

Between shots, Boots confided that Donker Dave had a line on a minor player in Boris's organization, Oscar Sabo. Boris used him for security detail and extra muscle. Just your average thug with a promising future.

Yeah, right. The guy was a real prince among thieves.

"Oscar Sabo, I saw him at the party in Annapolis. He bugged out when I tried to approach him. He didn't want to be interviewed. So when do we pick up that bad boy?" I asked as I downed another shot of tequila. I think I even giggled.

I was starting to get that "tequila tingle" in the pit of my stomach. I knew I was in trouble when the room shifted on its own. Sally quietly suggested that I should slow down, but I was having the most delightful time. Besides, this was quite possibly the best tequila I'd ever tasted. *No worries, mate*, as the Aussies are fond of saying. *I think I'd like to hang out with the Aussies for a while. Friendly folks, although I don't believe I actually know any personally.*

Whew! Where did all that come from? I gave my head a shake to clear the cobwebs.

Boots said, "What's this 'we' stuff? Donker and I will pick him up. We've got this covered. Besides, you should take it easy for a while."

Hold on. Did I hear Boots Johnson correctly?

"I hope you're not suggesting that I, as the recently traumatized 'little woman,' should sit this one out, are you?"

"What? What are you talking about?" Boots gave me a quizzical look.

"I'm perfectly capable . . ." My eyes became unfocused briefly. I gave my head another shake and continued. "I'm perfectly capable of taking care of myself."

"No one's questioning your capabilities. It's more of a legal matter. We can't have a material witness involved with the investigation, certainly not at this stage. The lines of responsibility can become blurred."

"Speaking of blurred," Sally said.

She leaned over and whispered to Boots, but I overheard her suggest he should take me home. Gimme a break; it was one little head shake. It didn't mean I was past the tipping point. What a bunch of party poopers.

"What's that?" Boots asked.

"What's what?"

"You said 'party poopers.' Were you referring to the two of us by any chance?" Boots gave me a big grin.

Was I suddenly being funny or something?

"Oops. Did I say that out loud?"

Sally reached across the bar and took away my shot glass and then retrieved what little remained of the Clase Azul.

"That's all for you, girl. You've been hitting the stuff pretty hard since you got here. Time to go home and sleep it off."

I protested, but Boots pulled me from the tall barstool and propelled me out the door. I was being kicked out of my favorite bar. Not for the first time, but you probably guessed as much. Hell, when it came to getting kicked out of bars, I could claim international experience in that department!

Thankfully, Boots was parked close by. On the ride home, I kept my eyes closed to keep my head from spinning; it would be too embarrassing if I got carsick.

We made it to my apartment without incident. Boots did the walking, and I leaned on him for support. Boots helped me to my bedroom and sat me down on the edge of the bed.

"I'll leave you to it," he said.

"Thanks for a lovely evening. It was nice, right up to the end, that is. I guess I had a little too much to drink." I felt the room tilt and rotate.

"Just a little," Boots said. "I'll call you tomorrow, and we'll catch up."

I stood up too quickly and almost lost my balance. Boots reached out to steady me and we stood close together. I had to look up to see his face clearly—or as clearly as I could see under the circumstances. You know what I mean.

"Too bad you have to leave," I heard myself saying.

We stood there holding onto each other for a long, uncertain moment. I'm sure he was wondering what was about to happen here. The question crossed my mind as well.

"I'll, uh…call you tomorrow, Vic," Boots said.

I may have been a teensy bit drunk, but I couldn't help noticing he got out of there in a hurry.

Nice going, strike-out queen, I thought. *You certainly scared him away. Now hit the sack and sleep it off. You've got work to do in the morning.*

Chapter Fourteen

Was it really after eleven o'clock already? Even before I was fully awake, the jackhammers drilling a hole through my head were already hard at work. No, wait a second; it was only the tequila talking…again. As hangovers go, it wasn't too bad—at least not so far, but I wasn't fully vertical yet either, so stand by.

The pounding in my head was not even close to some of the epic hangovers from my younger, wilder days. When would I ever learn that tequila was not my friend? I just wished someone would please tell Marlowe to stop twitching his tail so darn loudly.

I remembered how Sergeant Major Godfren used to run circles around us, young troops, back in the day. He'd often join us at the local *gasthaus* for a few beers at the end of the workday, where, more often than not, we all stayed until closing time. We eventually made it back to the barracks, and without fail, the next morning, the old gray-haired Sarge rolled us out of the sack at the crack of dawn for a five-mile run. No matter how much he drank the night before or how late he stayed out with us, it never seemed to affect the Sarge. I think he delighted in running our asses into the ground, and he had a good laugh whenever someone dropped out of formation to puke their brains out. We never figured out how he managed it, but he was one tough old bird, as he showed us time and again.

After a steamy shower, I felt shades better. Not great, mind you, but better. I should have eaten something more substantial besides the shrimp appetizer before diving into the tequila. The morning after was not the ideal time to contemplate bacon and eggs and whatnot; the very thought of it made me want to heave, but I kept it together.

Coffee, on the other hand, was different; coffee was medicinal. I downed a couple of restorative cups, which helped tremendously.

I sat at my dining table for the longest time, deep in thought, and sipped my third cup. My feet rested on the chair rails to keep off the icy floor. Even though my head was still foggy, yesterday's tragic events came back to me in a rush. The brief respite was over, and now it was time to face reality.

I called Scanlin to see when I could drop by for that brief chat he requested. The desk sergeant informed me Scanlin and McAllister were on assignment at the moment and not expected back until late afternoon. I left word for him to call when he returned.

I could sit around and mope all day over the tragedy, or I could get motivated and do something about it. *You're better when you're in motion*, I thought, and kicked myself into gear.

I wasn't contemplating revenge per se; however, to honor their memory, I wanted justice for Sabrina and Katya. Justice for two women who left it almost too late to do some good in this world, but they came through in the end. I was determined to do the same for them.

I turned on the news and caught a couple of follow-up reports about the bombing, but there was no additional information. If there had been, I'd have heard about it by now.

Before the day got away from me, I called Pete to confirm dinner that evening. He expressed surprise that Boots had accepted the invitation and said he was looking forward to meeting my new beau. I didn't want to get into it with him just then, but I knew Pete liked to tease. I warned him not to embarrass me in front of Boots.

What was I saying? I certainly didn't need any help from Pete on that score. I'd already done that all by myself, I thought to myself as images from the night before came back to me.

"I have nothing new to report, Vic. My guys tell me there was no evidence that even remotely linked Boris to the bombing."

"There's got to be a connection somewhere. We're just not looking in the right places, or talking to the right people."

"What I don't get is the text message purportedly coming from you. Someone had to know you three were in contact. It was clearly a setup."

"Why now? I mean, the Feds never approached them about testifying or had even issued the first indictment, so, technically, they posed no threat."

"What if Boris eliminated Sabrina simply because she had outlived her usefulness to him? And since the two of them were best friends, Katya got caught out as well.

Brutal, yes, but that seems to be his style. Do you think the bomb was meant to include you as well? That it blew up prematurely?"

"That's a thought, but I'd say no since I've been keeping my distance. I had no reason to meet with them."

"Then Boris is definitely cleaning house, and he's not above snuffing out his own girlfriend. That's one ruthless bastard!"

"Sabrina said she hadn't heard from Boris since the night they nearly killed Boots. He's been in hiding this entire time. So why does he need to do anything at all? It makes no sense. What's behind these continual outbursts of violence?"

"Maybe Boris is working on another big shipment. Have you noticed the circle of people who know about his business and how he operates keeps shrinking?"

"I really doubt that—about the new shipment, that is. He's still in hock for the last one that he lost. I'll ask Boots if he's heard anything. By the way, can you run a background check for me on a guy named Mike Carver? He runs the Dirty Whaler out on Riva Road in Annapolis. That's Boris's jumping-off point when he ships out. It's just a hunch, but I'm betting Carver was the shooter."

"This Carver guy is new to me. I'll see what I can dig up."

"Boots only got a brief look at the guy who shot him, but from his description, it sounded a lot like Mike Carver."

"I'm not sure when I can get down there."

"Then send one of your boys. All I really need is a picture of the guy. Say you're doing a story on local marinas and want to feature the Dirty Whaler. Most people love seeing themselves in print."

"Okay, I'll get on it. See you guys later tonight, and don't be late!" Pete hung up.

I tried the station once more and learned Scanlin was back in the office. I waited while they transferred my call to Scanlin's desk.

"I tried calling earlier. I wanted to stop by and give you my statement if you believe it's still necessary."

"As a matter of fact, I do. We traced all the calls Sabrina made and received yesterday. Just as you said, she only spoke to you the one time, just before the explosion. However, still no luck with the text message."

"Someone was smart to use a number similar to mine. That was a clever move."

"You know, it occurred to us that message might have been a test."

I was confused. "A test for what?"

"To see if Sabrina would respond to a text supposedly coming from you. That she did made it clear to whoever she'd been in contact with you all along."

"That's one way of looking at it, I suppose."

"It's just an idea. If true, it would reveal just how devious Boris could be. So, when are you coming over?"

"On my way. I need to get out of my apartment for a while anyway."

I grabbed my coat and purse and headed out the door. The sooner I got downtown, the sooner I could close one more chapter on this wretched affair. No matter the outcome, I still wanted them to pay for what they did to Sabrina and Katya, and to those poor girls. They turned them into sex-bots, and while I was at it, for every other evil thing they'd done.

Such was my anger and frustration, railing at things I had no control over and could never change. As the Bard said, "That way madness lies."

It was going on five o'clock by the time I left my apartment. I figured it would take about fifteen minutes to get to Scanlin's office. Once I gave my statement and resolved any outstanding details, I should be out of there, say, no later than six. Then get back home in time to meet Boots for dinner. No problem.

I cabbed it down to police headquarters and arrived on time per my estimation. I crossed the street and was about to run up the steps when a voice behind me called out.

"Miss Carella? May I have a word?"

I turned to find Marvin Bocci struggling to get out of a long, black car parked in the no-parking zone along the curb.

"If you could spare me a moment, this won't take long," he said. He breathed heavily as he slowly disengaged his enormous frame from behind the cramped steering wheel.

What was he doing here? And what could Marvin Bocci possibly want with me?

"Actually, I have an appointment with Lieutenant Scanlin. Can this wait?"

Something in his slow, ponderous movement should have warned me, but I didn't see it coming until too late. As he shuffled closer to me, his massive hands suddenly shot out with lightning speed and grabbed hold of both of my wrists with a powerful grip.

He twisted my arm behind my back, forcing me to bend forward, and propelled me toward the curb. In an instant, he shoved me into the car and pushed me across the seat.

I reached for the door handle, but Marvin jerked me around to face him.

"Just what the hell do you think you're doing? Take your hands off me!"

"Don't make me hurt you. If you scream, I promise it will be the last thing you ever do," he warned.

The intense look on his face made me hold my tongue. My mind calculated the myriad possibilities for escape, but I kept coming up with the same answer: I was trapped!

I couldn't get over the fact that the sonofabitch was actually kidnapping me right in front of police headquarters! How ballsy was that?

It was then that I noticed several strips of duct tape stuck to the dashboard. Marvin had anticipated our meeting and came prepared. With deft movements, he wrapped my wrists with the gray-colored tape. His crushing grip never let go for an instant. In less than thirty seconds, he totally controlled the situation, and I was now his prisoner.

"We're going for a little ride, you and me. We're going to settle a few things between us. If you're smart and tell me everything I want to know, you'll be free to go, but until then, don't give me any trouble, my girl, or you'll regret it."

I didn't know what to think. I needed to buy some time.

Marvin put the car in gear, and we sped away from the curb. He deftly maneuvered in and out of traffic, but each successive turn carried us farther away from headquarters as we headed toward the southeast part of the city.

As he drove, he held on to me the entire time, which preempted any sudden attempts to escape. In what felt like no time at all, we were among run-down, abandoned tenements and warehouses. I'd never been in this part of the city before. The street had a desolate, deserted feel.

The big Cadillac bounced over potholes and came to a stop in front of a dilapidated boarding house that appeared to be post-WWII era; the sun-faded walls were devoid of any paint.

Marvin Bocci dragged me from the driver's side of the car and hauled me up the concrete steps. He frog-marched me down a long hallway to the last room that I guessed he used as a hideout. He pushed me down on a squalid roll-out bed; the mattress was foul with stale sweat and extensive use—for what purposes, I didn't care to think about.

Marvin emptied my handbag on a small table in the center of the room and rummaged through the contents. With a smug grin on his face, he picked up the tiny Kel-Tec .32. With his giant-sized mitts, it was not a weapon he could easily manipulate. He tossed it carelessly on the bed next to me.

"Where's the other one?" Marvin said. He turned the bag inside out and ripped open the concealed pocket where I kept the Glock. He laid it on the table and then sat down heavily on the rattan chair.

"That's better," said the fat man. He clasped his hands across his wide girth and chuckled to himself. "It was almost too easy."

"What's that? What was too easy?" I said as I looked around at the decrepit room. It looked so filthy I doubted a homeless person down on their luck would find it the least bit hospitable.

"How do you think I knew where to pick you up tonight? I assumed you'd eventually contact your police friend, so I used him like a Judas goat and tapped his line. And you were so accommodating. Thanks for making it easy, Miss Carella."

"It was no bother at all," I snapped back. "You're such a loser. Haven't you figured it out yet? The police are on to Boris and the lot of you. You won't get away with this."

"We'll see about that. You've pissed off quite a few people, me in particular. And because of you, I have to abandon everything I've worked for, everything that matters to me," he said, his voice rising. "But before I leave here, dammit, I will have satisfaction!"

He slammed his hand down hard on the tabletop; it bowed inward like it was about to snap in two.

Using my teeth, I tore off the duct tape that bound my wrists. I rubbed them to restore circulation to my hands.

"So what is it you need to know? Why am I here?"

"Don't you get it? I'd have thought it obvious by now. There's nothing you can tell me I don't already know. That earlier bit was just my little ploy to get you to cooperate."

A sudden chill ran down my spine, but I continued to bluster my way through. "It doesn't matter. I'm still taking you down, along with Boris and the rest of them. You're too well-known; you'll get picked up wherever you run."

"Look around you. Look where you are. Is this your idea of taking me down? You've been a royal pain in the ass, lady, but not for much longer. That's a promise."

Before he could react, I scooped up the .32 from the bed and aimed it at his head, using a classic two-handed grip. I backed away until I felt the wall against my shoulders; I wanted as much distance between us as possible.

Marvin couldn't be bothered with my theatrics. He merely shook his head at the folly of my desperate move and calmly pulled on a pair of leather gloves.

"Nice try, Miss Carella, but you don't intimidate me. You see, I know all about your little decoy pistol. Your friend, the lieutenant, kindly documented that little street incident in your file. Sorry, my dear, but it's going to take a lot more than blanks to save you this time."

Marvin nonchalantly withdrew a stiletto from his jacket pocket. The glistening blade flicked open like the tongue of a steel viper. It was at least five inches long and razor sharp.

Indicating the Glock that was within easy reach, he said, "I'll tell you what. I'm going to leave your pistol here on the table. If you can get past me, you might have a chance."

He laughed out loud, clearly enjoying the game.

And then he came for me.

With his shoulders hunched forward, he moved with surprising grace and balance for such a heavyset man. I could tell he knew how to use the deadly weapon by the way he kept it low to come up under my rib cage and drive the blade into my heart.

And I'd be dead before I hit the floor.

Marvin maneuvered closer with a sort of shuffle step, and then lunged forward. The spear point came dangerously close to my torso. In quick succession, I fired twice, hitting him center mass.

The surprise that registered on his stupid face was almost comical. Marvin looked down at the spreading stain on his shirt.

"The gun… It was loaded," he stammered out.

With a guttural roar, he made one last great effort to reach me as the blade started its upward arc.

I double-tapped him again. He clawed at his throat as blood spurted between his fingers. He staggered and fell backward, taking the table with him, and thrashed about on the floor. I stood back to watch as he twisted and turned in agony.

Marvin raised his leg and repeatedly stomped the floor again and again while he wrapped both hands tightly around his own neck, as if by choking himself, he might stem the flow of blood. He made gurgling noises, coughed, and then exhaled one long sigh. Finally, the rattle deep in his throat stopped, and he lay still.

I sat down on the edge of the bed and breathed in deeply. My hands shook so violently I was a danger to myself, so I laid the gun down and tried to regain my composure. After a long while, it dawned on me that I should notify someone.

I searched for my cell phone among the debris and found it partially hidden under Marvin's outstretched arm. It was a childish notion, I know, but as I pulled the phone free, I kept a wary eye in case he suddenly came back to life and started all over again. Like one of those freaks in a horror movie that won't stay dead.

I dialed Scanlin's number, and for once, he answered on the first ring. He started out demanding to know why I hadn't showed, but I cut him off. He listened without further interruption as I described the situation. I could have bet money on it, but right on cue, he instructed me to stay put, as if I was about to run off somewhere.

Honestly, I ask you.

I waited outside on the steps to the boarding house. In almost no time at all, detectives and uniformed police converged on the old boarding house. In due course, they roped off the area, took photos, and gathered evidence. Basically, the whole rigmarole that goes into investigating a crime scene, except from my point of view, they rightly should call it a self-defense scene, but no one asked for my opinion.

What they asked, many times and in various forms, was how I got hijacked to this isolated spot, and why was the mayor's man lying dead on the floor.

Scanlin and McAllister didn't make things easy for me as they fired one question after another in quick succession to see if I gave different answers. This must be the secret technique they learned in cop school to determine whether I was lying to them.

I told them about the wiretap and how Marvin knew to wait for me outside police headquarters and then snatched me right off the street in record time. I ended with Marvin taking it for granted my little Kel-Tec was nothing but a decoy pistol, although it wasn't necessary, as the results were plain to see.

One thing was certain: the situation had reached critical mass if Boris was desperate enough to send Marvin Bocci to shut me down. Never mind that it was too late to cover his tracks now that I had exposed his organization. Even Marvin, their clean-up artist, couldn't stop the inevitable.

For once, the socially awkward McAllister didn't hold back. "Lately, it seems like every time we run into you, there's some big event or new development. Do you naturally attract violence, Miss Carella? Maybe we should put out a public service announcement to warn the citizenry of the imminent danger where you're concerned."

"You do that, and my attorney will deal with you."

"Your attorney…right!" McAllister said acidly. "No dirt will stick to you; he'll make sure of that. You've certainly got the right man for the job."

"What do you mean?"

"Don't play the innocent. You know the score."

"No, seriously. What do you mean by that comment? James Warren is the top man in his firm. I'm lucky to have him on my side."

Scanlin and McAllister exchanged looks; both had lopsided grins on their mugs. What were they hoping to achieve by throwing shade on James Warren?

"You want to tell me something I don't know?" I said as I looked from one to the other.

Scanlin spoke up. "It's the company you keep. How convenient that your former client's slick-ass attorney is now your mouthpiece, but hey, that's your business."

"What are you talking about?"

"Oh, come off it. You know damn well Mr. High-and-Mighty James Warren was Goldberg's attorney," McAllister said.

"That's no secret. I found that out as soon as I got back from Crisfield and checked on Goldberg's next of kin, but I was told there weren't any."

McAllister laid it on heavy. "No next of kin. Imagine that. So what happens to Goldberg's estate and all his holdings? What about his megabuck yacht? Who do you think is going to take over all that?"

"If they cannot locate any legitimate heirs, it reverts to the state. That's how intestate laws work."

"You can't be that naïve," Scanlin interjected. "Do you really think Warren's going to let his client's fortune go to waste? He's got Goldberg and that entire gang sewed up tight. And now he owns you as well."

Clearly, the subject of James Warren got Scanlin all worked up, but I was losing the thread of the argument. The look on my face must have confirmed my confusion.

"Try this on for size. We ran a background check, and it turns out your lawyer pal may have been Goldberg's attorney, but a couple of years before that he was also the attorney of record for Zharkov, Anatoly Sevvin, and the rest of that Russian gang. I'll bet you didn't know that, did you?"

"You mean…? No, that can't be right."

Scanlin's little bombshell just obliterated my mind.

"It's true, Miss Carella. Your precious James Warren represented Boris Zharkov and his gang when they ran into immigration problems with ICE. Boris was about to be deported until Warren intervened. We now believe Warren then took over Boris's operations and even expanded the business."

"But how did Goldberg come into all this?"

"Goldberg was already laundering money for some other clients. The Feds were about to bust him. While cleaning up that mess, Warren must have realized Goldberg could be useful to his new enterprise. So Warren introduced Goldberg to Zharkov, and as they say, the rest is history."

"I never ran a background check, but I should have. I just assumed…" I stammered. "Warren denied ever knowing Boris."

I struggled to comprehend the upshot of these revelations. The two of them seemed pretty confident of their facts. If true, then I'd been a complete fool. How blind could one person be?

"How long have you known Warren represented both Goldberg and Boris?" I asked.

"We only found out yesterday. After the car-bombing, we went back to square one and started a deep search on everyone's background. That's when we discovered the same law firm represented all of them at one time or another. What was especially interesting is they were all represented by the same attorney."

My mind was in turmoil. But if Scanlin was correct, then it explained a lot. And here I was being led around like a complete simpleton. James Warren, my generous benefactor and avuncular confidant, had played me well, and I had fallen under his charming spell.

Obviously, I was dealing with an expert at reading people, and although it hurt my pride to admit it, he had me figured out from the very beginning. Could I possibly have been more gullible? Warren had well and truly burned me. I'd never felt so utterly betrayed.

Here at last, I finally knew who was the driving force behind the smuggling organization, and he had been right under my nose the whole time! It all made sense now. Everything fell into place as I recounted the recent series of events in my mind.

Shortly after my initial encounter with Boris at his boatyard, Goldberg gets whacked, and soon after, I was nearly killed as well.

Following my lunch date with Warren, the gang suddenly moved up their departure plans for the arms shipment heading south.

After leaving the DA's office, I'm followed on the Metro and assaulted in broad daylight.

And after telling Warren that Scanlin still needed my statement, I get snatched from the streets and nearly killed by Marvin Bocci.

Every time I stuck my nose into Boris's operations or unburdened myself to Warren, the danger immediately escalated, which also corresponded with the targeted attacks on me.

Like he had done for me, Warren had bailed Boris and crew out of trouble. Not only were they indebted to him, but the next thing you know, they're all working for him.

And when they needed an expert at money laundering, Goldberg fit the bill nicely. He got himself so ensnared in their illicit activities he couldn't extricate himself.

It stood to reason it was Warren who gave the orders to do away with Sabrina and Katya; the master puppeteer at work. It made me wonder what James Warren had in store for me.

Warren was the consummate user and abuser; he exerted his control by playing each against the other. It was a sweet setup, but what he hadn't counted on—none of them, in fact—was how obstinate Goldberg could be. In my mind, that was the beginning of the gang's downfall. If only they had left Goldberg alone.

Then I appeared on the scene looking into Goldberg's missing yacht, and once again, fate handed James

Warren a golden opportunity, which he quickly seized upon. By hiring me, he could keep tabs on my investigation and would know whether I was close to exposing him.

Good old James Warren was there whenever I needed to bounce ideas off someone, the concerned and wise counsel to whom I confided everything. Warren had been well ahead of me at every turn, and I never suspected a thing.

I imagined how it must have frustrated Warren beyond endurance every time a hit on me failed. Well, too damn bad, and it was too late now. For his part in the smuggling ring, I was about to expose the great James Warren as a common run-of-the-mill crook.

I'd bet that, ultimately, his monumental ego would be his downfall. Exposure was tantamount to admitting a crushing defeat. I doubted Warren could handle the notoriety. And that made him every bit as dangerous as my old nemesis, Boris "the Bear" Zharkov.

I should have seen all of this coming. That I didn't was a searing humiliation for me, given all the telltale signs. Some detective, right?

There was Warren's conspicuous display of wealth with his Rolls-Royce, ten-thousand-dollar bespoke suits, five-star restaurants, and exclusive wines. The man was an addict, plain and simple. He was addicted to wealth, and he didn't even bother to hide it. Of course, I neglected to read the signs and assumed he derived his wealth through his successful law practice and an enormous inheritance. What was that old saying about never assume anything?

In retrospect, you're probably as surprised as I am that I'd lasted this long, considering how dangerously close I'd gotten to disrupting Warren's revenue stream.

After it was all said and done, this was going to make for a great what-not-to-do story at the next Detective's Convention. I could be their pin-up girl, the one with "sucker" stamped across my forehead.

It was almost too much to take in all at once. My head was spinning with these new revelations.

Suddenly, it dawned on me that I was supposed to be at a dinner party. I pulled out my cell phone and noted several missed calls from Boots and Pete. I wondered why my cell phone hadn't chirped at me until I noticed the silent button had become activated during all the commotion. I switched it to ring mode and dialed Boots.

His anxious voice immediately came over the line, loud and clear. "Vic, thank God you're okay! We're approaching your location now. Pete called around and found out what happened. We'll talk when I get there."

I ended the call and looked around for my weapons. One of the officers took notice and handed over my two *pistolas*. I stashed them in what was left of my ragged purse.

After he and McAllister finished taking my statement, Scanlin suggested I go to the emergency room for a checkup, but I nixed that idea. They went back inside to confer with the other investigators.

A minute later, Boots Johnson and Pete pulled up in front of the boardinghouse. At first, the officer on guard stopped them at the perimeter until Scanlin motioned to let them pass.

Boots got to me first and swept me up in his arms. He lifted me completely off the ground, and we held on to each other tightly for a moment before he set me down again. It was a totally unexpected but exhilarating moment, to say the least. Several exciting possibilities quickly passed through my mind; however, now was not the appropriate time or place.

Still…like, wow!

"When are you ever going to learn?" he scolded, but I could hear the intense relief in his voice. "Are you all right?"

"I'm fine. I'll be better once we get out of here."

Pete came over and gave me a big hug as well. Pete had a wild look on his face that told of the strain of the past couple of hours. If I thought Scanlin and McAllister had put me through the wringer, it was nothing compared to what Boots and Pete probably had in store for me later on once the excitement wore off.

Scanlin made his way over to our little huddle.

"Mr. Johnson, we meet again. Lieutenant Scanlin." The two men shook hands.

"Sure, I remember you, Lieutenant. Do you know Pete Beckham? Pete and I just met this evening as well."

"I know the name, and I've read several of his articles. Pleased to meet you."

"Same here, Lieutenant. I thought we were about to walk into another tragedy."

"Not a chance. I'm still trying to figure out how she did it, but it appears Miss Carella took care of business all by herself."

Everyone turned to look at me. I suddenly felt embarrassed by all the attention, but all things considered, I was grateful to still be alive.

"Some mess you've got here," Boots observed. It stood to reason the inevitable political fallout could be radioactive to certain careers if one wasn't careful.

"It's going to take quite a bit of explaining to the brass, but I think we'll manage. Although I don't envy the mayor; he's got a lot to answer for." He smiled at the thought of that happy diversion.

"I promise you, by tomorrow, the mayor will deny knowing anyone named Marvin Bocci. You wait and see," Pete said with a laugh.

"When things calm down, I'd like to compare notes with you," Scanlin said, addressing Boots. "We seem to have a running street battle on our hands, and it's got to stop."

"I'll clear it with my superiors and get back to you. What do you think the mayor's going to say about all this?" Boots indicated the body covered by a bloody sheet as the EMTs wheeled out the gurney.

"He'll make it political and quickly distance himself. Nothing says scandal like dead bodies with ties to the mayor's office."

We all watched as two medical attendants wrestled with the gurney. Marvin's massive weight made it almost impossible to negotiate the pitted asphalt of the abandoned lot. Four police officers came to the aid of the attendants. It took all six men to load Marvin's body into the back of the ambulance. After a brief struggle, they got the body loaded for that last long ride.

Boots escorted me to his car, and Pete crawled into the back. When we left, the police were still processing the crime scene. They'd be there until the wee hours of the morning.

Back at Pete's apartment, Melanie was standing in the doorway when we got off the elevator. She had a concerned look on her face, and she said out loud what I'm sure they all had been thinking. "You look like hell. What happened to you?"

We settled on sofas and chairs while Melanie poured the wine. I felt bad about ruining dinner. Melanie had set a beautiful table, complete with candles and fine crystal.

As we sipped our wine, I described my ordeal. I gave them the abbreviated version I'd given Scanlin. Pete nearly went nuts when I mentioned the role that James Warren played in all this. This was the stuff that launched literary careers. He reached for his laptop.

Pete said, "Don't feel too badly about it, Vic. Even I didn't know Warren and Goldberg were connected, much less the rest of their gang."

"I'm supposed to be the hotshot detective, but I let a big fish like Warren off the hook simply because he expressed a little concern for my welfare. What a fool I've been."

"No use crying over spilled milk. What's your next move?" Pete asked.

"You mean, provided I can stay alive another day?" I nodded in Boots's direction. "I need the kind of muscle only his agency can provide."

Boots piped up. "We're all over it. I've been trying to get you to stay put. Maybe now you'll take it easy and let us handle things."

"That close call was the last straw. When I realized Marvin Bocci never intended to let me leave there alive, I nearly panicked. I truly thought it was all over this time. Believe me, from here on out, it's all yours."

"At last! I told you all along to let the Feds handle this mess." Pete reached over and gave me a light rap on the head with his knuckles. "It took nearly getting killed to finally get through that thick skull of yours, but it's a start."

I drained my wine glass and declined Melanie's offer for a refill.

"I'm sorry I spoiled your dinner plans. I was really looking forward to a lovely evening. You'll let me make it up to you, won't you?"

Melanie was gracious about it. "It wasn't your fault, Vic. Don't give it another thought. We'll catch up some other time."

I set my glass on the coffee table. "If you all don't mind, I just want to go home and get some rest."

No one was about to argue with that. After hugs, handshakes, and goodbyes all around, Boots and I headed out the door. As we were leaving, Pete waved to us from the couch, but he was already on the phone to his editor while furiously pounding away on his laptop. Sensational scoops like this didn't come round often.

Melanie walked us to the door. I knew she was not being judgmental when she quietly urged me to take better care of myself, but we both knew that was a slim possibility. Still, I appreciated the sentiment.

Boots surrendered his jacket to me before we stepped into the cool nighttime air. As we cruised down M Street toward my apartment, I leaned back and let the seat cushions envelop me as I went over the terrifying events in my mind.

I had poked the Bear yet again, and he would continue to retaliate with every weapon at his disposal. I needed an edge, something to draw Boris from his hiding place. I couldn't continue to be the sacrificial lamb, not unless I was willing to accept the inevitable outcome. And there could be only one outcome at the rate things were going. It was him or me.

There was still much to do, and after tonight, the rats would jump ship all over town. I could not anticipate the depths to which James Warren and Boris would go to protect their worthless hides, but I was about to find out.

Boots unlocked the door and went in ahead of me. He made me stay near the entrance until he had checked the entire apartment. I thought it was a little over the top, but then after a moment's reflection, I appreciated the effort.

Word of Marvin's demise must surely have made the rounds by now. Certain ears were hoping to hear positive results from my brief encounter with Marvin and would be highly disappointed at the total reversal of the outcome. So, the extra precaution was welcome.

I wondered how James Warren was taking the news. My creative imagination conjured up images of James sitting in a luxurious penthouse, surrounded by fine art and beautiful antiques. However, for him, the trappings of wealth could not console him from the disastrous failures that befell him one after another. Surely his patience was near the breaking point. After all, how hard could it be to kill one chick? And why couldn't his inept goons finish the job once and for all?

It had to be tough to be James Warren right about now. He was used to having it all his own way. Well, not this time. They say money can't buy you happiness, but apparently it's no guarantee for success either. Just ask James.

My cell phone chirped at me. I fished it out of my purse to check the number.

Well, speak of the devil, and he will appear. I put it on speaker so Boots could listen in.

"You've got a lot of nerve calling. What do you want?"

The wizened voice that I'd come to admire cackled over the line. "I take it you finally know what's what. Well, it had to come to this sometime, my dear."

"Don't call me 'dear.' You tried to have me killed from the very beginning; only it didn't quite work out that way, did it?"

"I have to admit, I'm amazed at your continuous run of good luck, but that's all coming to an end real soon. That is, if I have anything to say about it, and I believe I do." He laughed again.

To hear it said out loud, it suddenly dawned on me that my streak of crummy luck had, in a manner of speaking, finally turned the corner. I had managed to stay alive in spite of James Warren's best efforts to put me down. I could appreciate things were finally looking up, but for how much longer?

"You're an evil man, Mr. Warren. Tell me, how do you square with your conscience the number of lives you've ruined?"

"Are you still crying over a bunch of whores? Spare me the violins, please. Whether one or a thousand, what do I care?"

"You can't be this callous. I hold you directly responsible for all the pain and suffering you've caused. We're talking about human beings here; people with dreams of the future, and families. But you used them like disposal objects."

"Oh, boo-hoo! They were merely a means to an end. I told you before I preferred a decadent lifestyle. Unfortunately, it takes a boatload of money to maintain the comfort that I've become accustomed to. I'm not worried, though; there are plenty more where they came from."

Completely stunned by what I was hearing, I turned to look at Boots. He merely shook his head in disbelief.

"I take great comfort knowing you can kiss all that goodbye, Mr. Warren. To hell with you and your pampered lifestyle," I retorted.

"And I had such high hopes for you, Victoria. You could have been a tremendous help to me. I would have made you rich, but I'm afraid your sophomoric beliefs in morality would never allow you to consider the alternatives."

"For a supposedly brilliant man, you're a sad disappointment. Not everyone is a heartless, money-grubbing bastard like you."

"What can I say? For one brief moment, I let my fondness for you cloud my judgment. At times, I can be such a sentimental old fool, but you must understand one thing: in the end, you cost me a lot of money. That is the unforgivable sin, my dear. For that reason alone, you'll be hearing from me again. It won't be long now, that's a promise."

With that, he hung up. I had no doubt he meant every word he said. I was not about to press my new-found luck and give him the satisfaction. Until the case wrapped up, my personal defense status would remain on high alert.

Boots gave me a lopsided grin. "So, your luck is changing for the better, is it? Maybe you should give the lottery a shot."

"Yeah, maybe I should at that."

My big guy, Marlowe, came out from the bedroom to greet us. He meandered over to Boots and rubbed against his pant legs, leaving traces of fur behind. That's my boy.

"Can I get you anything?" I offered.

"No, thanks. Considering everything that's happened, I'm going to suggest something that you may not like, but it's for your protection. I'm staying the night and sleeping here on the couch. So don't give me a hard time about it. Not after that run-in with Marvin, and now with James Warren sending his love."

"You won't hear any objections from me. Of course, you don't have to go to the trouble, but you're more than welcome to stay. I've got a spare bedroom available."

"Actually, I prefer to be here. I want to be close to the door, just in case. Until this case is over, you're still a target. I'm not leaving anything to chance at this stage. I'll relax when we have everyone in custody, but not until then."

"My knight in shining armor! All kidding aside, I truly appreciate it. Let me find you a pillow and a blanket and get you settled in." I went to the bedroom to retrieve the bedclothes.

I know what you're thinking, and you can clean up that dirty little mind of yours right now. Just because I've got Boots Johnson all alone in my apartment is no excuse to abandon all reason and give in to temptation. We shall conduct ourselves with dignity and restraint. After all, we are not slaves to our base instincts. Besides, I didn't have that much to drink tonight, unlike last night, when things almost got out of hand. And I'll thank you to kindly forget all about that near slipup as well. That was then, and this was now.

I returned to find that Boots had taken off his jacket and tie. The leather harness of his shoulder holster criss-crossed his broad back. I couldn't help noticing the well-pronounced V-cut of his physique. He shrugged out of the holster rig and set his weapon on the end table within easy reach.

He turned around and caught me staring at him. He turned on that killer smile of his and made me blush like a schoolgirl with a crush on the star quarterback. I could feel my cheeks flush hot pink. Sometimes I read too much into the simplest things. In case I didn't mention it before, I'm cursed with an overactive imagination.

I picked up Marlowe, and we headed for my bedroom so Boots could settle down for the rest of the evening. He was still grinning when I left.

As exhausted as I was, there was little chance of getting much sleep tonight, not while "visions of sugarplums danced in my head."

I'm sure you get the picture. I know I did.

CHAPTER FIFTEEN

The fallout over Marvin Bocci's demise was mostly a blur to me. When news broke that an assistant to the mayor had been killed, the news media erupted into chaos, lasting several days. So far, my name had not appeared in the press, and no one associated me with what happened at the deserted boardinghouse.

Pete's article, hastily submitted prior to his newspaper's nightly deadline, was on the streets first thing the next morning, and soon after the media circus began in earnest when the talking heads from all the cable news networks picked up on the breaking story that involved money laundering, arms deals, and of course, the sordid details surrounding sex trafficking.

The news media in all its forms badgered the mayor's office nonstop for details about his now-deceased assistant. For his part, the mayor was virtually nonexistent. He was not in his office, and no one would admit to knowing his whereabouts. As a result, the mayor's press corps were thrown to the wolves and devoured on a daily basis.

The mayor's office remained silent on the subject, which only fueled further speculation as the feeding frenzy intensified. Reporters attempted to interview anyone and everyone who would stand still for five seconds. The withering editorials accused the mayor of covering up for one of his political cronies, but he steadfastly refused to play the game of "what did he know, and when did he know it." The mayor was far too savvy to fall into that trap.

Finally, the newshounds grew tired of pursuing potential leads only to be told "no comment" time and again. They quickly pivoted to a new international crisis developing in France. All attention turned to that emerging situation, thus sparing the mayor further scrutiny and criticism.

At the start of all the excitement, the DA's office came under intense pressure as journalists demanded information. Kavanagh, bless her little self-serving heart, took full advantage of the free publicity as she test-piloted her case in the court of public opinion. She scheduled daily press briefings to announce the latest details of the investigations and impending trails.

At one point, someone leaked James Warren's name to the press, and he was publicly outed as the mastermind behind the illicit operations. Thereafter, the law office of Warren, Sifkin, and Moore quickly fell victim to the negative publicity. Almost immediately, the mass exodus began as scores of clients abandoned the firm owing to the notoriety.

Melanie called around midafternoon to invite me over for a spaghetti dinner, knowing that I was home alone. Pete was in his element as he described the flood of inside confidential information he had received following his explosive report. We finished our meal and were enjoying a nice Chianti Rufino when Scanlin called.

"Good news, Vic. James Warren has been arrested. We got a tip he was about to board a private jet bound for South America."

"That's fabulous. Congratulations," I said. Pete immediately started pestering me for details. I put Scanlin on speaker and had him repeat the news all over again for Pete's benefit.

"So what happens next?" I asked.

Scanlin said, "He's in custody at the moment and facing multiple racketeering charges. I had the pleasure of putting him in a cell myself. The Feds will pick him up in the morning."

"Not my old cell, was it?" I asked, being my usual smart-assed self.

"No, that's reserved especially for you," Scanlin shot back. "It turns out the owner of the jet is a personal friend of Warren's. Now that guy's in hot water for aiding and abetting a fugitive from justice. As they say, the hits keep on coming."

The domino effect was spreading far and wide, and many people only peripherally associated with the case were being swept up in the ongoing investigations. Some, I imagined, were being questioned for no better reason than they happened to be an acquaintance of James Warren. The madness continued to escalate to levels where rational thought and common sense had flown out the window.

"Thanks for the update, Lieutenant. I'll be in touch."

I ended the call and looked across at Pete. I could see his mind was working out how he could spin this new development in his next article.

"What do you think?" I asked.

"I believe James Warren's criminal empire just came tumbling down. And it's all thanks to you, Vic. Nice going."

I had to admit to a certain pride knowing the arms smuggling and sex-trafficking ring were now defunct. There was more to do, but things were quickly wrapping up.

I thanked them for a lovely meal and got out of there. It had been a hell of a week so far. Who could know what tomorrow might bring, but with a good night's sleep, I'd be ready to face any new challenges.

As it turned out, I was glad I got my beauty rest after all.

# # #

Bright and early next morning, and well before the news hit the wires, Boots called to report they had made several more arrests. I was still in that half-asleep, half-awake world where you're just not ready to open your eyes quite yet. I reluctantly answered the phone, dreading what might be waiting for me at the other end of the line, but was pleasantly surprised.

Boots was all cheery when he described how the Coast Guard had positively identified Anatoly Sevvin, Oscar Sabo, and Mike Carver and arrested them onboard Sevvin's yacht. All three fugitives were apprehended off the southern coast of Maryland as they attempted to escape. It pleased me to learn Chief Cloverman was being hailed as the hero of Crisfield for his quick thinking and proactive response.

Someone alerted the Coast Guard to a suspicious boat dodging in and out of small inlets and marinas, in general hugging the shoreline as they headed south.

Cloverman dispatched his crew to check it out. They boarded the craft and made the arrests without incident.

However, the most notorious gang member remained at large; an intense manhunt was still on for Boris "the Bear" Zharkov. Meanwhile, those already in custody would soon face charges at the federal courthouse downtown.

Boots instructed me to meet him at the DA's office tomorrow at noon. The case against Warren and the gang was in its final stages. Pending his arrest, they could try Boris *in absentia* for his crimes.

I spent the rest of the day puttering around my apartment. At one point, I scrubbed the kitchen counters and cabinets for something to do, but in general I just chilled out; a little down-time was called for after the last couple of days that I'd had. Marlowe was good company as always, and we kept each other entertained when we weren't napping or stuffing our faces.

The next day I arrived to find Kavanagh's office crowded with a dozen or more attorneys and law enforcement personnel. Everyone was getting in on the act.

Boots and Donker Dave occupied a corner of the office along with their director, Jerome Peters. All three turned to greet me as I approached.

"I was afraid we'd never see this day," I said as I observed the government lawyers busily organizing their case files and notes.

Director Peters said, "I'm pleased to see you're doing well, Miss Carella. I know you've been through absolute hell."

"Things turned out all right for some; not so good for others."

Indicating the frenzied activity around us, Peters said, "We're waiting for the DA's team to pull their case together. You'll be asked to provide a statement about your encounter with Marvin Bocci."

We appropriated chairs for ourselves and parked it while the lawyers wrangled over their paperwork. I overheard snatches of conversation as they formulated their strategy. They would present the case in a logical progression, detailing the long list of charges along with the supporting evidence to prove the government's case against each of the defendants.

At one point, Kavanagh looked up and gave me a nod. She came over to join us. "Miss Carella, thank you for coming in today. Sorry about the delay, but it will be a little longer before we're ready for your deposition."

Her conciliatory tone surprised me, considering how our initial meeting ended.

"No worries. I'll be here when you're ready for me."

"Allow me to say how sorry I am for what happened to Sabrina Farkas and Katya Sevvin. I never occurred to me the lengths to which Warren and Zharkov would go to protect their enterprise. I feel awful about what happened."

What could I say to that? She had been warned of the risks.

When I didn't respond, she continued, "There's no word on Zharkov, but I imagine he's left the country by now. If I were in his shoes, you wouldn't catch me hanging around."

"I suspect you're right," I said. "I just hope they track him down soon. He was the worst of the bunch."

Peters said, "My team alerted every law enforcement agency between here and San Paulo. If he shows his face, I'm confident he'll get picked up immediately."

Kavanagh went back to orchestrating her case. The four of us settled in for what promised to be a long afternoon while the attorneys continued to cross-check their case notes and evidence files.

When Kavanagh finally got around to taking our depositions, she wrung every last detail from Boots and me until she was satisfied her case was solid before letting us go.

By the time Boots escorted me from the federal courthouse, streetlights illuminated the city. We caught a cab back to my apartment and rode in silence, each too exhausted for conversation.

Although the case had not wrapped up to my total satisfaction, thankfully the Feds shutdown the human trafficking and gunrunning operations. Raids at several locations along the Chesapeake Bay resulted in liberating a handful of young women who were about to be transported to parts unknown. Their captors were arrested and thrown in jail. It was a small, but important, start. At least these women were safe and would soon rejoin their families. The search continued for others who had passed through Boris's hands. It would likely prove to be a long and tedious investigation.

While Marvin Bocci and Andre Adema did not survive the ordeal, I doubt anyone mourned their passing. Although several other lower-tiered gang members were still being hunted, my biggest concern was Boris Zharkov. Like Boots said, he was an expert at self-preservation, but only time would tell whether the law ever caught up with him.

My disappointment over Boris's escape was mollified, knowing that my erstwhile benefactor and betrayer, James Warren, was behind bars along with several of his henchmen. None of them would ever know another day of freedom, and that was good enough for me. You celebrated your successes where you found them.

We arrived back at my building and rode the elevator to my floor. That euphoric feeling that comes from knowing you've accomplished something worthwhile still glowed within us. That is, right until we walked through the door of my apartment.

At first glance, it looked like the aftermath of a typical frat party. Either my taste in décor was objectionable, or I had pissed off someone badly because the place was totally trashed.

Lamps were smashed and lampshades crushed underfoot, sofa cushions shredded, and the contents of my bookcases tossed across the living room floor. My wall-mounted television was torn from its mounting, the glass screen shattered. Boots looked at me in disbelief and then began sifting through the wreckage while I hurriedly searched for Marlowe.

I headed toward the bedroom to find my big guy. On the way, I got a glimpse of the kitchenette, which was a wreck as well, torn to pieces as if in a fury. Someone had ripped cabinet doors from their frames and destroyed every one of my place settings, cups, and saucers. The gutted seat cushions had the stuffing strewn across the floor among splintered picture frames, smashed crockery, and broken glass.

I started down the short hallway and then froze as Boris Zharkov edged soundlessly around the corner. He motioned for Boots to join us. Boris didn't have to say a word; the short-barreled pump shotgun he pointed in our direction did all the talking for him.

Boots righted what remained of a couple dining chairs, and we sat down obediently as Boris circled behind us. There was no telling how long Boris had waited for us, but he obviously was not at a loss for something to do.

"Make one move, and I'll blow your damn heads off," Boris said.

Yeah, as if the shotgun he stuck in my face wasn't convincing enough.

Ever the Boy Scout, Boris took a roll of paracord from his pocket and tied Boots to the chair. I saw Boots wince as the cords bit deeply into his biceps; the gunshot wound started to bleed again. In hardly any time at all, he had us both trussed up like Thanksgiving turkeys ready for basting.

"I'm surprised to see you. I heard you'd left the country," I said, stalling for time.

"Soon enough. You didn't leave me much choice. But that's okay, because you and I have some unfinished business to attend to," he said and leered at me.

"That's what the fat man said. He didn't make out so great."

I never knew when to shut up, but I couldn't help needling him, not at this stage. I was pissed that I had let my guard down; we both did.

With no proof to the contrary, we accepted the DA's assumption that Boris had fled the country, when in fact all he did was camp out in my apartment and waited for the opportunity to finish the job. And like a couple of suckers, we walked straight into his arms. Now Boris had the upper hand, and he would make us pay dearly.

I struggled to loosen the cords, but it was no use. I looked around for something that I could use to free myself. I did not intend to go down without a fight, but quite possibly this was fast shaping up as my great last stand and Boots's as well.

So, this is what it felt like to finally run out of road. To hit the brick wall. To reach the end of your rope. To…oh, hell, you know all the clichés as well as I do. Unless a miracle happened, this was all she wrote for the two of us. The realization that I was about to fail in my primary mission suddenly overwhelmed me. Strangely, however, the sick feeling in the pit of my stomach at the thought of failure was suddenly of lesser concern; it came secondary to the humiliation of having Boris watch as I puked my guts out down my shirt front. I managed to hold it together and denied Boris the Bastard the satisfaction of knowing he'd finally gotten to me. No matter. I was done, and we both knew it.

Still, I strained with all my might, hoping that my small hands might slip through the knots, but it was impossible. The cords were so tight I barely had any feeling left.

Boris came round to stand in front of us. His face was a cold-blooded, pitiless mask devoid of all humanity or compassion. In light of our predicament, I wanted to scream at the futility of it all.

He laid the shotgun on the counter, and without preamble, swung his massive fist in a tight arc that caught Boots on the side of his head, toppling him to the floor. With a powerful backhand, he sent me flying in the opposite direction. My split lip streamed blood as I lay facedown in the debris.

From my prone vantage point, I watched as Boots lashed out with both legs to crush Boris's knee. The Bear cried out and cursed like a stevedore as he went down hard. Again, Boots kicked his legs out straight and stomped Boris in the face, snapping his head back. The Bear was a tough old bastard though; he was dazed, but still conscious.

I didn't wait to see what happened next, although from the grunts and dull thudding sounds, I knew Boots was kicking the hell out of Boris. I had only a few moments at best. I scrabbled around on the floor for something I could use to cut myself free, but with both arms tied, I had limited mobility.

With a ponderous movement worthy of his namesake, the Bear shook his big head from side to side as he struggled to stand upright. He slowly regained his balance in spite of the wicked beating that left him wobbly. Now Boots was going to get an ass-whipping, and the Bear laid it on hard.

He grabbed Boots and tipped his chair upright and then started in on him. Boris clubbed Boots repeatedly with those massive tree-trunk arms of his, swinging fists as hard as Thor's hammer. Boris bent low at the waist to deliver a couple of savage body blows, then came back up top with several head shots. I knew Boots was taking a beating, and I worried about how badly Boris was hurting him, but there was nothing I could do to help him at the moment. I focused exclusively on the task at hand.

As I rocked and twisted across the littered floor, my hand closed on the remnants of a broken tumbler. The sharp curved edge sliced into my fingers, but I didn't care.

With my wrist bent at an awkward angle, I sawed at the strands of cord, working as fast as I could before Boris finished giving Boots a thrashing and then came for me.

The last cords finally let loose, and I hurried to free my other arm. I scrambled from the floor at the same time the Bear lurched forward.

Boris almost beat me to it, but he wasn't quite fast enough. I had that beautiful, precious shotgun in hand and pointed at his chest.

"Get back, you bastard, before I shoot you dead."

Boris shuffled back a couple of steps, but only nine or ten feet separated us. At that distance, I knew it was possible for him to quickly close the gap before I could properly react. I kept my eyes riveted on the monster standing only a few feet away.

"Are you all right?" I asked Boots.

"Hell, yeah. I am now. Cut me loose if you can, but *listen to me!* Do not hesitate to blow his ass away if he takes even one more step!" Boots advised. "Shoot him to the ground!"

I kept the shotgun pointed at Boris while I knelt beside Boots to untie the paracord, but I couldn't concentrate on what I was doing. I fumbled with the knots, but it was no use because I needed both hands.

I reached for the piece of glass that I used to free myself, but stopped short when Boris saw what I was after and made a move toward me. I stood up and leveled the shotgun at his gut and held it steady.

Slowly and deliberately, Boris said, "You're gonna die tonight. I am going to enjoy breaking your scrawny neck like I did that Goldberg bastard." He balled up his massive fists and simulated a strangling, twisting motion. A chill rippled down my spine.

By now, the Bear was nearly unrecognizable from the blood running down his cheeks, and his swollen eyes were almost welded shut where Boots stomped him and cut him up badly. Those cowboy shit-kickers sure came in handy for once.

Boris leaned to one side to relieve the stress on his shattered knee. He stood with his arms held away from his sides, poised like the great ape that he was.

Here before me stood a defiant and unyielding hulk of a warrior. He breathed deeply, taking in a lungful of air, and drew himself up for one final battle.

I could see what was coming, but believe me, there was nothing I could do to stop him. Ignoring the great black hole of the twelve-gauge, Boris lunged at me. His raised hands clawed for my throat.

I had no choice. Within the confines of the small apartment, the roar of the heavy charge instantly deafened me. The double-aught buckshot tore a savage hole in his chest, but the impact barely impeded the big man's forward motion.

I jacked another round into the chamber and hit him again. Blood splattered the wall behind him. He took one last step and dropped to the floor.

Boris Zharkov, or what was left of him, could no longer fill out his suit, much less the body bag he'd soon be wearing.

I racked the bolt to the rear to clear the weapon and, with sagging arms, let it fall from my hands. I found a kitchen knife among the debris and cut the cords that bound Boots. I helped him to his feet, and we stood close together, holding each other tightly. Although he didn't need me to steady him, I still had my arm wrapped around his waist as he leaned on my shoulder.

"Hello, you," he said, looking down at me, his face close to mine. "You're making quite a habit of this. I nearly lost you…again."

My ears were still ringing from the shotgun blast, but I didn't miss a beat. "And here's me thinking I've got you exactly where I want you."

"I'd only end up disappointing you." He looked into my eyes intently. He was about to say something but ended up brushing the hair from my face.

In the background, the wail of sirens cut short our sparkling repartee. From outside my second-story window, I heard tires skid on asphalt and car doors slam while Scanlin barked orders at the troops.

Time was running out.

"I can't stay," he said. "It's…the job."

"I know."

Boots gathered me in his arms and planted a long, warm kiss on my lips. It hurt like hell, but it sure was nice.

He stepped back and resettled his wreck of a jacket on those broad shoulders. With a wink, he disappeared down the back stairs. And right on cue, the cavalry arrived just in time to find the pool of goo that Boots Johnson had left behind…*Me* that is! What did you think?

Chapter Sixteen

It's been two weeks since I got mauled by the Bear. I know you'll forgive my terrible attempt at humor, but you have no idea how apropos. The purple and yellow bruises covering my body from the violent encounters I had with several trolls had mostly faded. And my split lip had almost healed completely, although some more of that Boots Johnson sugar would be nice.

Lately, I'd been wearing my general contractor hat as I monitored the restoration work on my apartment. So far, I was pleased with the progress the construction crew had made, but it was proving to be a long-term project. The destruction was so extensive that the walls and floors in all the rooms had to be refurbished. They practically gutted the place and started over.

I barely heard the knock at the front door over the hammering and whine of electric saws. When I answered, Sally breezed in carrying an enormous vase of flowers.

"Gee, flowers for me?" I said in my little girl voice.

"Actually, it was just an excuse to come over to see how the redecorating is coming along," Sally said, looking around. "What did you do, take it down to the studs?"

"Yep, pretty much. I'll say one thing for Boris. He was one thorough sonofabitch. I had to replace *every* single thing I owned, but it's coming together nicely."

"Not bad. Not bad at all," Sally said as she walked around checking out all the new furniture, lamps, and whatnot that continued to arrive daily.

I'd been hitting the online shops and home furnishing catalogs pretty hard lately. Since I was starting from scratch, I wanted to try something new and went with a fresh, modern look.

Sally laughed when I pointed toward Marlowe. He obviously approved of my choice in décor; he'd already appropriated one end of my new sofa for himself.

"How's the trial going? Any news? Any convictions yet?" Sally asked.

"Now that the media hype has settled down, things are back to their normal slow pace. James may be a clever attorney, but even he can't escape the inevitable. Not for what he's done."

"Good. The bastard deserves whatever he gets." Sally was still livid that my former benefactor attempted to have me killed on several occasions. And nearly succeeded!

"Don't laugh, but I may have to take back everything I said about Kavanagh. She cleared me of all involvement with the smuggling operations. And those little 'run-ins' I had with Boris and company? She agreed I acted in self-defense. I think she purposely left the records vague on the details, which is fine by me."

"So, how do you like your crow? Medium well?" Sally grinned at me. She knew I still didn't care much for the district attorney.

"Have you spoken to Boots?" Sally gave me a sly look, but I knew she was fishing.

"Not since he bugged out and left me to deal with Scanlin. He's back in his shadow world. He seems to prefer arms dealers and Caribbean pirates to something more local."

"Don't take it so hard, Vic. He travels in different circles than the rest of us."

She was right, of course. I was feeling miffed at being left behind. But really, how was this supposed to end? What was I even thinking? Guys like Boots don't settle down for picket fences, weekend barbeques, and shuttling kids to Little League. Can't say women like me do either, but you never know. Someday the odds will catch up with one of us, and then what? Let's face it; neither of us was destined for domestic bliss. I needed to accept it and move on.

I knew the noon hour had arrived because the construction crew filed out *en masse* for lunch. I reached into the refrigerator to retrieve a bottle of Pinot Grigio.

"Lunch is on me today," I said and handed Sally a glass.

"Is Scanlin still pestering you?"

"Not anymore. Not after Pete intervened."

"If you ask me, I think he's got a thing for you."

Sally referred to the many times Scanlin had called. There was always some "urgent business" he wanted to discuss with me. As far as I was concerned, the case was closed, but he was persistent, I'll give him that. I had to believe he was just kidding, but at one point, he hinted that if I didn't cooperate, my old jail cell was still available. I guess Pete tired of hearing me bitch about it, because after he made a couple of calls, Scanlin finally backed off.

Did I mention Pete knows everyone?

Scanlin must have thought I owed him one for coming to my rescue there at the end. Apparently, Customs tipped Metro police Boris hadn't left the country after all. Being quick on the uptake, Scanlin knew he was headed my way and rallied the troops.

By the time he arrived, it was all over, and Boots had slipped away rather than get tangled up with local law enforcement. I understood Scanlin's frustration, but I thought it rather rude that my Southern gentleman should take it out on me.

"Sorry to drink and dash on you, but I've gotta go to work. You stopping by later?"

"Yeah, I'll be there after the crew knocks off for the day. See you."

Sally placed her wine glass in the sink. With a wave, she left.

I went to inspect the bedrooms to see the progress the construction guys had made so far. They worked clean and fast, but it was still a big job. From the look of things, I guessed it would take another two weeks to rebuild my apartment.

I sat down at the desk in my kitchenette to sort through the morning mail. Nothing but junk mail and bills, although one item caught my eye. I almost threw it out, thinking it was merely an ad for a Caribbean travel agency. The colorful postcard sparked fond memories.

So tell me, what images come to mind when you think of the Caribbean islands?

For me, I still remembered the sun as it reflected off the shimmering water and the hot sand burning my feet as I ran across the beach to dive into the rolling surf.

Staring out at the ocean, I was always mesmerized by the blend of deep blues, sea greens, and stunning shades of turquoise. And whenever I snorkeled among the shallow reefs, scores of brightly colored fish and sea turtles surrounded me. They were so plentiful you could reach out and almost caress them.

I loved the beauty and the serenity of the Caribbean islands. There was no place on earth where I'd rather be.

So you can imagine my surprise and excitement when I realized I would soon return. The alluring postcard I held promised miles of pristine, sunny beaches. And the simple message scrawled on the back was my call to action: "Wish you were here."

Not that I was anxious or anything, but I had my bags packed and sitting next to the front door in thirty minutes. I even remembered my beach towel and skimpy swimsuit. How much more did I really need?

I called Sally at the Grill and told her to eat her heart out because I was headed south for a couple of weeks. She wished me luck, and said she'd keep an eye on my apartment. Next, I called Mrs. Shepherd. Without the slightest hesitation, she agreed to keep Marlowe for me.

And then I found myself looking out the window every five seconds for my taxi. I didn't want my hunky welcoming committee to have a change of heart before I got there.

No doubt you'll want to know whether things panned out between us, but I'll have to get back to you on that. Um, just in case, don't wait up.

THE END

This book is dedicated to my dear wife, Barbara,
whose love, encouragement, and support made it possible.

Especially warm thanks to Jean Smith, Nancy Adcock, and Averi Lassiter for the suggested improvements and your keen eye for detail in catching so many mistakes early on.

To the folks at eBookLaunch, please accept my heartfelt thanks for your meticulous work editing and formatting my book. To the folks at 100Covers and Andrewgraphics at SelfPubBookCovers, thank you for your collective creativity; your book cover images certainly captured the essence of the genre. And to Belinda at Blurbs by Bel, the back-cover description was spot on.

www.ingramcontent.com/pod-product-compliance
Lightning Source LLC
Chambersburg PA
CBHW021123190726
48288CB00008B/2464